OUR
NARROW
HIDING
PLACES

OUR NARROW HIDING PLACES

A Novel

KRISTOPHER JANSMA

ecco
An Imprint of HarperCollinsPublishers

HarperCollins books may be purchased for educational, business, or sales promotional use. For information, please email the Special Markets Department at SPsales@harpercollins.com.

Ecco® and HarperCollins® are trademarks of HarperCollins Publishers.

"Honestum Petimus Usque" © 1937 Albert Verwey, English translation © 2024 Klaas van der Hoek. Used by permission.

FIRST EDITION

Designed by Angie Boutin

Library of Congress Cataloging-in-Publication Data

Names: Jansma, Kristopher, author.
Title: Our narrow hiding places : a novel / Kristopher Jansma.
Description: First edition. | New York, NY : Ecco, 2024.
Identifiers: LCCN 2023045480 (print) | LCCN 2023045481 (ebook) | ISBN 9780063352896 (hardback) | ISBN 9780063352902 (trade paperback) | ISBN 9780063352919 (ebook)
Subjects: LCSH: World War, 1939-1945—Netherlands. | Netherlands—History—German occupation, 1940-1945. | LCGFT: Historical fiction. | Novels.
Classification: LCC PS3610.A5873 O97 2024 (print) | LCC PS3610.A5873 (ebook) | DDC 813/.6—dc23/eng/20231011
LC record available at https://lccn.loc.gov/2023045480
LC ebook record available at https://lccn.loc.gov/2023045481

24 25 26 27 28 LBC 5 4 3 2 1

For Leah

Do you not suffer? The world has declined.
It no longer rolls melodiously from God's hand.
Beautiful peoples turned into hordes,
The human mind raised into madness.
The firmly founded bond of all together
Bursts at the seams and there is no law.
There is no more shame and no decency.
No fixed road where everyone puts their feet.

—*Albert Verwey, "Honestum Petimus Usque," trans. Klaas van der Hoek*

The world must surely have collapsed at least once in the lifetime of
every individual, yet strangely enough it still exists.

—*from* The Letters and Diaries of Etty Hillesum, 1941–1943, *murdered at Auschwitz*

The Dutch famine of 1944–1945, popularly known in the Netherlands
as the "Hunger Winter" [. . .] took place in the urbanized western
Netherlands during the final months of the German occupation when
the Allies had already liberated the Southern part of the country.
After November of 1944, official daily rations [. . .] dropped below
an already meager 750 calories per capita, decreasing to less than 370
calories just before the German surrender in May 1945.

—The Hunger Winter: Fighting Famine in the Occupied Netherlands, 1944–1945, *by*
Ingrid de Zwarte (2020)

OUR
NARROW
HIDING
PLACES

THE NAAKTGEBORENS

~

In the days when the rivers and streams of the Low Countries often flooded with seawater, we eels flourished near a small village known as Dorp. It was a peaceful place, and a happy life was lived there as well by a fisherman known as Wilhelmus, until the day a pair of emissaries arrived on horseback to proclaim that the former Kingdom of Holland was now part of the French empire. Henceforth, Wilhelmus and the others in Dorp would be subjects of his mightiness, General Napoleon Bonaparte, who had taken command of the seaports, dissolved the Dutch army, and decreed that each citizen must choose a last name by the new year.

Of course we eels were unconcerned. We had lived in those drowsy creeks long before Napoleon, even before the Romans had built their fortifications there, ever since it was all free land.

But Wilhelmus was sincerely upset by the demands. To his surprise, his neighbors were swift to begin choosing their new identifiers. A fellow fisherman, Johan, rushed to claim Van der Beek, or "from the brook," fearing Wilhelmus might adopt it first.

A neighbor to the south, Pieter, somberly declared that he would become Pieter Thijssen, "son of Thijs," in honor of his dear late father.

"And will your children be Pieterssen?" Wilhelmus asked.

"No," Pieter replied, "still Thijssen."

"Thijssen forever?" Wilhelmus cried. "Can't anyone see this is madness?"

None did. In short order, they all selected names: Hendrik, the town clerk, became Hendrik Klerk, and the widow Anki, a fine seamstress, became Anki Naaister—and so on.

In the end, only Wilhelmus refused. His neighbors muttered their concerns to one another. Why was he being so stubborn? What would happen to him? Imagine, going to prison over something as absurd as a name! Much to his annoyance, people began to call him Wilhelmus Van der Aal, meaning "of the eel," in the hopes that he would come around to it.

Of course, we eels would have had no objection to him taking our name in this way. No more than the brooks could have cared about Johan's claims, or the thread spooled in Anki's baskets could mind hers. What humans do with their brief lives has little effect on those of us who know in our feathered bones that we will outlast their affairs.

But we did wonder what would become of this obstinate man. You see, we had developed an abiding respect for each other, hunter and hunted; always he would lovingly release the elvers, our young, and we admired his exquisite, hand-carved traps. Not a bad way to go! we joked. Better than getting snatched by an osprey or gobbled up by a raccoon. Dignity is essential to eels—as it was, we saw then, to Wilhelmus.

When the new year arrived, the emissaries of Emperor Bonaparte returned to Dorp in their fine blue woolen coats, their red collars embroidered with gold. The Frenchmen came to the village square and diligently recorded the names presented by each head of household.

At last, they came to Wilhelmus. When he informed them that he would not choose a name, he was promptly arrested. For his disobedience, Wilhelmus was sentenced to a year's imprisonment. The emperor's men said that if he still refused to pick a name upon his release, he would be assigned one of their choosing.

"Van der Aal is a fine name," they said. "When people hear it, they'll think of your eels, and come to buy more and more."

His eels! We admit, we did coil briefly at the audacity of those words.

Still our friend refused. "They buy enough! Besides, I'm the only Wilhelmus in my village."

"Yes, but you are one of a hundred Wilhelmuses now in our empire. We must know which is which and who is who."

"But why?" he asked. "I can think of nothing good coming of it."

The jailers ignored him. "Don't you want your children to know where they come from?"

"How should they be stuck with my name forever? Think of it! They'll never be free."

But Wilhelmus saw now that he was already not free. And that his future children would not be, either. They'd be subjects of this empire or the next one or the one after that. And beyond was history itself, burdening and constraining them, always. He saw the past and the future stretching away, twinned horrors, time immemorial, time inescapable.

Wilhelmus swore. "No. I will not choose!"

He faced his year in confinement nobly, patiently, and with the dignity that we had come to expect from him. Still, we eels assumed Wilhelmus would be assigned to us in the end. Even he was prepared to finally become Van der Aal. But his jailers had another punishment in mind.

After his sentence ended, they declared their prisoner would henceforth bear the name Wilhelmus Naaktgeboren, which meant "born naked," a mark of shame that must now pass on to his children and theirs.

In disgrace, Wilhelmus returned to the little village of Dorp. And many there did say it served him right, though already a few were feeling regretful over their chosen names, beginning to realize what Wilhelmus had seen right away. That they would be stuck with what they'd selected for their whole lives. Even worse, so would their descendants be—forever.

Quietly, Wilhelmus returned to his fishing boat, and to carving his traps. But we could tell that his spirit had been broken. The care he'd once taken with his work had slipped away. History had come down on him. Indeed, his very soul seemed to have been extracted from him, leaving a hollowed man to go through the motions of daily life without joy or anger or sorrow or any true feeling at all. Deep inside the four chambers of our venous hearts, we mourned the loss of his once-noble spirit.

By now our passing appreciation for this obstinate man had become a kind of entanglement. For refusing to be "of" us and not taking us as his name, he now suffered. Name a man anything you like, we thought, but what is he without a soul?

Truly, we were not alone in feeling for his loss. Soon a young woman fell in love with Wilhelmus, and his dead eyes again began to brighten. Gusta, a great beauty, was eager to discard de Witt, the name that her father, a silver-haired peddler, had chosen.

Spring arrived, and at the Tulip Festival, Wilhelmus asked her to marry him, begging forgiveness for his stubbornness and for the fact that Gusta would have to take on his humiliation if she agreed to be his bride.

But no, she said, with pride would she become the first person in Holland, perhaps in all of history, to take the name of Naaktgeboren by choice.

And when, one year later, she gave birth to a healthy baby boy, they named him Robrecht Naaktgeboren. As Wilhelmus held the child and considered its bare, slimy, beautiful form, he saw that his jailers had done him a favor after all. Of all the names in all the tongues in all the world, what could be more perfect? Naaktgeboren. Born naked.

And we, the eels, watched from our narrow hiding places, pausing then in our forever wriggling as Wilhelmus kissed his son's forehead and soothed him until he slept.

—V.S.

SLIPS AND FALLS

~

With dusk approaching on her eightieth birthday, Mieke Geborn slipped and fell. One moment she'd been hurrying along the unpaved edge of Sand Dollar Street, in the little Jersey Shore town she had called home for fifty years, and the next she was wincing up at the gray-pink sky. Sharp pain seized her leg and her head throbbed. The squat hardcover she'd been carrying had tumbled into the wild grasses to her left. She rolled this way and that but could not see anyone around. The peaceful neighborhood was still mostly empty vacation homes in March. All she could do was yell for help, as she tried and failed to get up again.

Earlier that afternoon, Mieke's friends had taken her out for a birthday lunch at El Legado, a Spanish restaurant up in Manasquan where they had live music. The group had eaten, danced a little, and finally sung karaoke: "Bésame Mucho" and "Por Tí Me Casaré." Then, to Mieke's embarrassment, the others had ordered her an enormous slice of soft, rich chocolate cake. The waiters cheered, "Feliz cumpleaños!" and she'd blown out the flame from atop the sole twisted blue candle. It was all much too much, and afterwards, Mieke had driven home stuffed and exhausted.

In her own living room again, she'd turned on the news without thought and placed her leftover paella on the counter. She'd begun absentmindedly adjusting the edge of the large Persian rug, which kept flipping up, and then ran her finger to check for dust on the framed paintings on the far wall. Only then had she remembered that during dinner, she'd promised her neighbor Shoshana that she'd stop over before she went to bed.

Her neighbor had been wanting to show Mieke this Dutch book she'd found, *Verhalen uit de Lage Landen*, or *Tales from the Low Countries*. When the two women had first met, years ago, Shoshana had been a professor at the local community college, specializing in Holocaust literature. Mieke had been a middle-aged student, earning her associate's degree in communications, trying her best to keep busy after the recent passing of her husband, Rob, from leukemia. Shoshana had enjoyed hearing Mieke's youthful memories of Holland during the war, and the two became close friends. After her retirement, Shoshana had moved into a house just down the street from Mieke. Now they visited each other a few times a week.

For years, Shoshana had been trying to help Mieke track down any information about her husband's father, Professor Willem Naaktgeboren, who had disappeared in the fall of 1944 and was presumed to have died in a concentration camp in southern Holland. At the birthday dinner, Shoshana had told Mieke about this Dutch book she'd been sent to review. It had been in print briefly before in the 1960s, but, thought to be a somewhat fantastical work of fiction written by a prisoner there, the book had been overlooked by historians. Only recently had it been reprinted by a small academic press in Leiden, billed as being of anthropological interest, mainly to folklorists. Some ambitious publicist at the press had sent it to Shoshana along with any other scholars they could find who had written about the camp before.

Now Shoshana thought it might have an interesting lead: the first tale in the book was titled "De Naaktgeboreen," which Shoshana knew had once been Mieke's last name.

"'The Naaktgeborens.' Yes," Mieke said. By now Shoshana

had heard the story many times. It had been Mieke's name only briefly, after she had married Rob and before it was truncated in 1955 when she and Rob had immigrated through Chicago.

Rob had been pleased for a new name to mark their start as Americans. But Mieke had winced as the pen had scratched across the page, moving like a scalpel, severing the past. This was what it meant to come to a New World—the old one had to be carved away. In Illinois they were starting fresh; the past could be forgotten. Nothing terrible had ever happened to the Geborns.

"Whoever wrote this book could have heard the story from my uncle," Mieke had suggested to Shoshana earlier, at dinner. "What was the name of the author?"

But her friend hadn't been able to remember.

"It's all in Dutch. I'll need your help translating!"

And so, curious, Mieke had decided not to stay home after dinner and get to sleep, but to hurry up the street to retrieve the book. She'd imagined it would not take more than a few minutes, but of course Shoshana had made a pot of silver tip tea and begun rambling about an NPR segment on climate change. All the way out in the Pacific, off the coast of Seattle, there was an extratropical cyclone moving inland, bringing intense and lashing rain.

How could people not see what was going on? How could people not understand the certain doom approaching?

"Isn't that how it is in Seattle most of the time?" Mieke had asked.

But truly, it hadn't been this specific weather system that Shoshana had been concerned about, so much as the inevitable future, rife with mega-storms and wildfires, where powerful unnatural phenomena moved in from all sides, constantly rending everything everywhere into dust. Heat waves and ice storms and tornadoes and earthquakes. Anger and fear, leading to political upheaval, leading to mass migrations, leading to more anger and fear, and on and on—Shoshana had gotten quite worked up. It had taken an hour for Mieke to calm her.

Mieke didn't say so, but privately she did not understand it. Shoshana had no children. She was eighty-two years old. Why did she care to what degree Celsius the planet would warm by 2050? Fine if Mieke did—her grandson, Will, would still be alive then, presumably. And he and his wife, Teru, had been trying for kids. It was Mieke's as-yet-unborn great-grandchildren who would inherit a parboiled world after she and Shoshana were both long forgotten.

And yet Mieke knew this was not fair. That her friend had every right to care about the condition of the world without her.

That she was just grumpy it had taken so long to ease her friend's mind. Such that it had been getting dark when Mieke had embarked for home, and then—she'd remembered the leftover paella, still sitting out on the counter, slowly spoiling. She'd begun hurrying.

And so she'd slipped. And so she'd fallen.

NOW MIEKE WAS lying in the grass beside the road, gravel in her hair, calling for someone, anyone, to help her up. Her house was not far, but whichever way she squirmed, she could not get more than an inch or two before she was paralyzed in pain again. Shoshana's house was just a few hundred yards the other way, but Mieke knew she was already in the shower and would then immediately fall asleep while watching the news at maximum volume.

Feeling a drip forming above her left eye, Mieke wiped it with her sleeve. An alarming red stain slid into the fabric. Her cell phone was in her purse back at the house. She'd neglected to take it with her, and it was off anyway. Always off unless she was using it. She didn't like to use her minutes, even though her grandson, Will, kept telling her that there weren't *minutes* anymore, that she could keep it on all the time, and it wouldn't cost any extra. But to Mieke this still felt wasteful. She was unlike others in this way; she'd long since made her peace with that.

Her hand felt something to her left, a few inches from her ear. It was an exploded mayonnaise packet, quite possibly the very thing she'd slipped on. People could be astonishingly thoughtless. At home she kept all her extras, and the Dunkin' Donuts sugar packets, and the crinkly salt and pepper things from the deli, and the extra chopsticks, even though she always told Hunan Dynasty not to send two sets. It was not so crazy, she told herself. People did much stranger things. Like toss mayonnaise packets out on the road, for example.

As Mieke tried to sit up, she was seized by a shooting pain in her right leg. Broken hip—she was sure of it. That's just what had happened to Shoshana on the steps at Sunny Pines Retirement Village, where they'd once gone together to do tai chi. She'd never been the same. Everybody knew hips were the beginning of the end.

At last Mieke saw the corner of her friend's book through the grass just a few feet away. It had a deep red cover and the title stamped in flaking gold. A stylish eel coiled in the center. Mieke stretched out her arm and batted at the book's corner. With her fingertips she inched it closer. Finally she gripped the spine and pulled it tight to her body. For a long time, she clutched the book as if it were a life preserver. Her eyes would not focus on the words, but even in the blur, she felt their Dutchness and this warmed her.

How long had it been since she'd read a book in her own language? Decades, surely. What a shame! She called out and waited. Again she cursed the food going to waste on the counter.

Every second, spoiling.

She pressed her bloodied sleeve to her head and hoped it wasn't getting worse.

With one finger, she lightly caressed the cover of the book. She caught the faint smell of the pages. The author's name on the cover was Vraagteken Schrijver, and when Mieke had first seen it, she'd assumed this must be a joke.

"*Schrijver* means 'author,'" she'd explained. "Although lots of Dutch people have names coming from whatever their ancestors did. Like here you have Miller or Cooper or Smith."

"And what about Vraag . . . tek . . . en?"

"That's the funny part. *Vraagteken* means a question mark."

"You mean like a mystery?"

"No. No. An actual question mark. Like the punctuation."

Between them in the air she'd drawn a hook and a line down, with a jab for a dot at the bottom.

"How strange!" was all Shoshana had had to say about that.

NOW. ABOVE. THE universe bloomed busily to lilac and then descended into a deep, bruised purple. Black forms of birds moved across Mieke's field of vision as she listened for cars coming. She was far enough off the road; she was pretty sure they wouldn't hit her. Fear radiated through her body. What if she was out there all night? Had the bleeding stopped? She couldn't tell if she was lightheaded from knocking her head on the road, or just from the shock and the pain.

Would she die there? She might, yes, if no one came. Or if they came but didn't see her. Or if they saw her but didn't stop. She went back and forth when it came to the subject of human decency. Often it seemed to her that it was nowhere anymore. Mayonnaise-flingers, all of them! But then she'd think back on her childhood, and how, during the war, she'd found that human decency did exist, often where and when one least expected to find it. With all the damage that life did to everyone, it was remarkable, when you thought about it.

Vraagteken.

Questions, all questions. Her last moments would be nothing but questions, now or later.

Breathing heavily, Mieke listened for the sounds of the shoreline: birds calling out, waves rolling back and coming forth, grasses rattling lightly against one another. The same steady rhythm that persisted behind her day and night.

The sky darkened further and there came whispering noises, all around her head.

High voices, soft voices. And then—a little burst of light. It was too early in the year for fireflies. These were whiter, anyway; they might have almost been snowflakes, but no—they were *glowing*, as brightly as distant stars, but moving, and closer.

Swiftly a memory came back. Mieke had seen these lights

before, on the other side of this same ocean, during a different end of the world. Seventy-three years ago. In the final phase of the war, she'd been eight years old, lying on a bed made from tattered clothes, trying to stay warm in her family's apartment in the Hague. Den Haag. By then, five bare, cold rooms with almost no glass left in the windows. Waiting for the sound of another rocket firing on the beaches. Waiting for one to fall back and crash through her roof. Dying, stomach empty, mind scattered, skin taut against her ribs. Eyes fixed on the jagged cracks in the ceiling, losing focus.

That's when these same small white lights came all around, flickering in and out. Otherworldly, moving in spirals and then shooting off like sparks. Slipping through the gaps between the gauzy curtains that hung between their realm and hers. And then it had been as if those curtains themselves had been pulled away by some unseen stagehand, allowing the most magnificent and piercing light to pour in from all around, a light unbraiding itself into colors that had never been named. Hues that rang out in a symphony—glorious and filling—warming Mieke like the summer sun, heralding itself after months of absence.

"Ben ik op het strand?" she'd said, back then, or so they told her. *Am I at the beach?*

Now, seventy-three years and 3,600 miles later, she *was* at the beach. Tucked away in the dunes amidst the grasses, beneath the night birds, in the ever-long roar of the waves. And these same lights flickering all around. Pushing through, just as before.

It was the same this time as it had been then, and all the decades between seemed to fold together. And there was one more thing the same, then to now, which had been the same every moment since.

She was hungry.

NEEFJE

~

Mieke rides her bicycle through the dunes on a quiet March morning. It is 1941. She is with Rob and his father, Professor Naaktgeboren. The hilly path ahead is slick with overnight rain and the sun is coming up, warm and white behind the orange rooftops. On one long gable, a magnificent goose squats beside the chimney. Feathers white, mottled in crimson and chocolate. The bird croaks angrily, warding off a few rock pigeons that are getting too close for comfort. Mieke sucks in some of the cool air and releases a warbling cry of her own, mimicking the goose so expertly that it twists suddenly her way, concerned some new front has opened in its war for the rooftop. It scrambles and nearly falls, then rights itself again.

As the goose settles, Mieke takes in the fresh silence of the world. The way the creaking of her bicycle wheels radiates into the emptiness. Out in the darkened north, the sea hangs back. And deep within the thin green dune grasses are the insects that will, in just two months, surround everything in immense summer clouds, but are for now larval, hidden.

Mieke's eyes follow the distant line of Scheveningen's seawall all the way to its vanishing point at the horizon. "God made the world," her father often says, "but the Dutch made their own country." Without these barriers, everything around her would be underwater. In the story, Hans Brinker sees a dike leaking and plugs the hole with his finger. Her father has told her that in reality they're built ten feet thick and engineered to withstand even the worst storms to ever strike the shores. But Mieke is aware that every day things happen that have never happened before.

Like Rob and the Naaktgeborens coming to stay with them. Like the great V of black planes that had passed over her father's bakery, and which had started the war. Back then, just a baby, Mieke had thought they were a flock of enormous birds. Now she knows they were German bombers heading for the city where the Naaktgeborens had lived before. Rotterdam. She tries to imagine it—their little house near the bustling port, down the road from the boys' school where Professor Naaktgeboren had taught Latin. She's never seen these places, and now, she never will. She imagines it all like stacks of burnt logs that remain in the oven at the bakery toward the end of the day. Wood collapsed to blackness, only a shell flecked with white ash and orange embers. Seething and alive, still hot. Never to be touched except with the long dark poker, and then when she does nudge one, it sends sparks up into the air, flickering like the stinging wings of fairies.

Not that she believes in fairies.

That's Rob, who does. Rob, who sits quietly for hours at a time, looking at the pictures in his storybooks, reciting the tales to himself—she hates that he can read and she can't, but their fathers have told the stories so many times that by now she has memorized them. Still, Mieke doesn't care for such nonsense. Why, after she's explained to Rob that the stories aren't real, does he insist on coasting behind, eying the green and blond fringe grasses? Looking for fairies.

The three of them pass through little valleys in the sand, cut with long paths of stone. Closer to the shoreline, the Germans are building great stone bunkers in case the Allies should attempt a landing there in the Hague. But just now, all is quiet. Professor Naaktgeboren leads them on the back trails, farther west, toward the woods that surround the grand Ockenburgh estate. The professor smokes from a dark brown pipe that lends a sweet smell to the air. The legs of his checkered pants rub against each other and make a faint *zwishhh* with each step. Mieke hurries past him, wondering, does everyone in Rotterdam dress like this, or is it just Latin teachers? The chestnut trees are budding now, reaching high above the silver lindens. A slice of blue-black sky runs upside down along the river's surface, reflecting white clouds and leafy shade. Woods all across the eastern side, and then to the right, a field of beige and amber: tall stalks of grain; circling hawks, brown and white, a beady eye of golden glass that trains on them, uninterested. Fishermen in reds and yellows and blues, resting on a green-hulled boat. Mieke spots two white-capped swimmers and imagines the bracing cold of the water against their pale bodies. Professor Naaktgeboren points the way into the woods with the stem of his brierwood pipe and looks at his son—but Rob is lost. Gazing into the brush for something that isn't there.

Mieke's own father is at the bakery, Brood van Menke, like he is every morning. He and Rob's father have known each other since childhood. They grew up together in the last war, and still call each other "brother." And they all call Rob her cousin, *neefje,* but this isn't true. Still, they are close—so close that Mieke's baby brother, also named Rob, is now called Broodje, Little Bread—because otherwise no one ever knows which boy is being summoned—and Rob has a tiny crybaby sister, Truus, who wails all night most times.

"Mieke!" the professor calls up to her. "Slow down. You're too far ahead."

Steaming, Mieke brakes her bicycle and waits, for *hours* it seems, until Rob at last catches up. Free again, she exaggerates her slowness, like a clown pretending to pedal, hoping to humiliate Rob—but he doesn't notice, and a moment later she's forgotten and zoomed off ahead.

THE NAAKTGEBORENS HAD come to stay one week after the day of the black birds in the sky: the professor, Tante Sintje, Rob, and tiny baby Truus. Back then, Mieke had not known that she lived in a country, or what a war even was. Now she understands, a little: there is a queen, exiled in London, whose face is still on the shiny guilders her father collects. Much of the rest remains foreign to Mieke—even the idea of "foreign" is foreign to her. Germany, America. England. Colored shapes in her uncle's atlas. They may as well be fairylands. To her there is only home, these dunes, the bakery. All other places are Elsewhere.

Still, Mieke knows that surrendering to the Germans the day after the bombing of Rotterdam is either a disgrace, as Professor Naaktgeboren sometimes thunders, or a sad practicality, as her father shouts back. If they hadn't signed the accords, the Germans would have bombed them next, and *then* what?

Mieke takes this side only because it is her father's side. Because these birds had flown right over her head, only to destroy her "cousin's" home instead. Because that's just what happened, and Rob came to stay with her, and that is all.

THROUGH THE DUNES they ride: Mieke and Rob, with Professor Naaktgeboren walking behind them, smoking his pipe, carrying a light metal bucket and a small satchel filled with waxed lines and sharp hooks and lead weights. For Mieke's birthday, he has promised to teach her how to catch eels, which she's been begging him to do for months.

"Eels are mysterious creatures," he has explained. "They live in the water, but can cross the land among the grasses, completely hidden. You can find an eel in a pond or a puddle that has no tributaries at all—often miles from any other body of water. In ancient times, people believed they appeared by magic."

But Mieke does not believe in magic. This is partly why she wants to see an eel so badly. To look it in its beady eyes and *know* that it is merely flesh and bone and slime and gook. After they catch one, the professor has promised he'll teach her how to clean it and cook it, too. All night she's thought about that and hasn't slept.

Vaguely, Mieke is aware that her parents never cease fearing for her. Sees how they have sought to tame her—for her own good, they say. But promises of Droste chocolates for good behavior fall just as short as threats of punishments for bad. Other girls her age are capable of sitting quietly at the table, doing as they are told in the shops, and obeying the rules—at least in front of others. But Mieke cannot.

Cannot sit still. Cannot help touching each item on every shelf. She runs headlong into the streets. At school, her focus doesn't just drift—it careens left to right, top to bottom, near to far.

It took a long time for her hair to grow out as a baby, but now that it has, her sandy brown mane is wild and tangled all the time. She cannot be still long enough for her parents to put it into the braids all the other girls wear, or even to brush it smooth.

And yet there are moments of perfect stillness. They puzzle her. They puzzle her parents more. Her gaze moves to some invisible point in the distance, as if receiving some radio signal no one else can hear. Her mind goes blank. These moments never last long and are shattered by any attempt at hair-brushing whatsoever, but they give Mieke a vague hope that, within her, something civilizable does exist.

In the meantime, it is hopeless; they are all resigned. Worried. What kind of life is there for a girl of such inveterate recklessness? She hears them arguing when she is supposed to be asleep. Her father loves her, she has no doubt. Unspeakably strongly. That's why he fears it all so much, he tells her. These are not times for girls like her.

PROFESSOR NAAKTGEBOREN'S FIRST name is Willem; he grew up in Den Haag, where his own father had owned a popular toy shop, Magisch Speelgoed, Magical Toys, filled with little marvels carved from wood. Mieke's father was his best friend even then, and has told her many times about dolls so lifelike you'd think they might get up and move around on their own. Little jack-in-the-boxes with wooden gears and cranks, and cars with wheels that spun, and cuckoo clocks that burst into song every hour—a hundred all at once. Jigsaws with a thousand pieces, none the same shape. There'd been no place in the whole town that any child would rather be, Mieke's father recalled.

Adults came to the shop as well, to purchase ten-shelf curio cabinets and ornate writing desks with roll tops or wings that folded out on brass hinges. Quite often the things that Willem's father made might have some secret function—a hidden compartment, a false bottom. He was known for his discretion and took many orders from officials with things they needed kept private.

His true specialty, however, had been inlaid woodwork, halfway between a puzzle and a painting, with thousands of tiny pieces of different woods in different shades: amber, ochre, blond, cherry, and dark walnut, all fitting together seamlessly to create scenes of majestic Alps and proud fortresses along the Rhine. His work had been so accomplished that he soon earned a commission by the rich American Carnegies to install a mural in the ceiling of the new Peace Palace, on display for the ambassadors and envoys of the world to see.

Rather than taking up the family trade, Willem had become a scholar—teaching Latin at a nearby boys' academy. Not long after the Naaktgeborens came to stay with Mieke's family, he began filling their living room with books: Voltaire, *Het Kapitaal*, slim volumes of poems by Albert Verwey. He's down at Janssen's bookshop twice a week. Mieke's father tells her that Willem once even wrote books of his own, and Mieke is dying to know what they were about, but her father just laughs *oh oh oh!* and says they were not for *kinderen*. Supposedly they were all destroyed in the bombing. When the Naaktgeborens arrived, all they carried with them was the single black trunk, carved with courtly Japanese scenes by his father many years before—the only thing that had survived the fire, miraculously with neither singe nor scratch.

ONE YEAR AGO, the day of the dark birds in the sky, Mieke was with her father. Herself a bird in the night, but a tiny one, rushing along the streets of Den Haag on the handlebars of his bicycle. Gusts of wind, frosty and brackish, pushing against her, sent by the North Sea. Her hair blowing back into her father's breath. The bakery was only a few minutes' ride from the apartment, and from the back of the shop where they left the bicycle, you could see all the way out to the blond strip of sand and the churning dark cauldron of the sea, lit faintly by the quarter moon. The waves were invisible at that hour, but she could hear them rolling in and out, as her father kneaded the dough in perfect time, back and forth, along the wide oak countertop. Keeping the windows open allowed the oven steam to flow out and the salt air to roll in. This cut the sourness of the dough that otherwise punched at her nose.

Her father sang in French as his strong fingers pressed the surface. Mieke was learning to care for the sticky, sour goo that they kept in the storeroom vat. The surface speckled with air bubbles meant that this beige glop was *breathing*, a universe of dark stars. Each morning it required feeding. Fresh stone-ground flour. Mieke churned it with a paddle until her arms ached.

The sourness stayed on her father all day. It lived in the thin shirt sleeves pressing against his swollen arms. It lingered in the bristles of his mustache and among the blades of his dark beard. But the sourness was the secret, he told her—the reason his loaves lasted a whole week, unlike the squashed, sad Dutch breads sold elsewhere. It was why the painters came to him. They stopped at the bakery on their way to the dunes, before first light.

Old men, young men. "Meneer Menke," they called, *"een brood behagen?"*

And her father told them to call him Ambrosius and sold them each a single gigantic, fresh loaf. They'd eat perhaps a quarter of it through the day; the rest would keep all the way to the week's end. These artists earned nearly nothing on their seascapes, her father explained—and so he earned little from feeding them on their way. But they were his patrons; he was theirs. He served them and so served their art. It was a blessing to be there with such men. Early risers like him, needing to be at the dunes already with easels spread, en plein air, with the wind in their sideburns and the sand getting into their paints, which had to be mixed before the dawn began: a holy conflagration, different every time. Purples, oranges, pinks, blues. Frantically they adjusted their pigments to answer whichever hues arrived on the horizon.

At the bakery, the men talked excitedly of Ruisdael and of Van de Velde. Mieke did not understand. Why would they go to paint the same dunes if these others had painted them so perfectly already? And when anyone in Den Haag could simply look out the window anytime they liked? But her father worked hard to impress and satisfy these penniless men in their patchy suits, crumbs in their long beards.

On the day of the dark birds, Mieke had been helping herself to a week-old loaf that they had not sold—it was still rich and wonderful, especially toasted near the oven's fire. She'd listened to the crackle of the wood, the singing of her father, the roaring of the oven, the crashing of the waves. It was some time before she'd noticed that other sound. Something new.

One of the painters, Mr. Akkeringa, had stopped on the road before the bakery. His easel had fallen to the ground. His head was tipped up and his hair blew back in the wind like a white waterfall. She followed his gaze into the clouds, where she first saw them, too. She'd never seen an airplane before. She'd certainly never seen a squadron of German bombers rising out of the sea. She did not know where they were going, or that they held a firestorm in their bellies, or that it would not fall on her today. In Rotterdam, thirty kilometers away, a thousand people would die in eight minutes, but none of this was certain still in that instant.

What did her father know, there, then?

All he said to her was "It is starting."

NOW THEY JUST wait for it to end. The war, the occupation. Mieke can barely remember a time before these things. Because of the "capitulation," they've been spared for the most part. Paris is half destroyed, the rest of France run roughshod with German tanks and guns. But in Holland, the swift surrender after Rotterdam has meant that life goes on almost normally. Her mother spends hours organizing newspaper coupons, but the vegetable bins are usually still full. Mieke attends school, her father bakes his bread. They all get by. It's just that there are always questions. Why can they no longer go into the Meijmans' butcher shop on the corner, where the German soldiers linger, buying their wursts and bacon? Why does Professor Naaktgeboren need to keep the volume low when he listens to the Radio Oranje broadcasts coming from London? Why do all the grown-ups now need a *persoonsbewijs* card with their picture on it, and why, when she asks if she can have one of her own when she turns fifteen, do they say they pray she'll never need one? (And who do they pray it to, anyway?) And what happened to the Meiers, the family of six on the first floor, who have not been there in months—and how does this connect with the signs she sees everywhere, and that Rob tells her say, VOOR JODEN VERBODEN.

What does it mean, to be forbidden?

"LIFE IS FULL of questions, child," Professor Naaktgeboren tells her as they come at last to the streams west of town, Rob still trailing behind. "And precious few answers."

Soon the professor shows them where the salty water comes in from the ocean and begins to mix with fresh water and become brackish in their flow inland. They trudge into marshy terrain, swatting away gigantic mosquitos, listening to the ululations of unseen frogs. Rob keeps his eyes trained for strange patterns in the sediment along the riverbanks, for odd markings in the tree bark. He gathers evidence, constantly. The deeper they journey into the unpopulated woods, the surer he is of moving into magical territory, of hearing whispers in the wind and lights glinting messages in the dewdrops.

Schoonheid onthult ons, the fairies say, in the story of Fostedína and her Golden Helmet.

Beauty reveals us.

Mieke tugs Rob along, holding his hand, already grubby, as he keeps slipping and falling. His father marches on, possessed, until at last they arrive at a spot he approves of.

Professor Naaktgeboren holds up a pair of wooden spikes that he whittled the day before. "Take these and drive them down into the earth. Push them in deep, high up on the bank so that they don't slip."

Mieke hastily complies, jamming the spikes in with her soft palms. Her uncle moves over with a rock to pound them down a few more times, until they are firm in their purchase. Then he begins to unwind long pieces of fishing line from the roll in his satchel, thin as sewing thread, but so strong it cuts into her fingers if she pulls too tight.

"Loop one end around the spike so that it knots," he says. Then he ties a small lead weight to the other end of the line, which keeps it from floating on the surface. Rob finds bugs and worms, ample in the riverbank, and his father ties their still-wriggling bodies a few inches above the sinkers.

Satisfied, the professor tosses the lines into the rushing waters; these meet the surface with a plop and glide downstream, becoming taut. It is her turn next. Six lines in all, they cast, and then he shows Mieke and Rob how to crouch between two of the lines and pinch them with their fingers.

"When you get a bite, you'll feel the vibrations change."

Mieke pinches and waits. For what feels like an hour. She stares at the water, hoping for motion, but seeing nothing at all, the river is so thick with dark grasses.

Then . . . a sudden rippling on the line in her left hand. "*Ooooop!*" she cries out in excitement as Rob's father hurries over to see what she has.

And she has something. A very strong and angry something.

Steadily he pulls the line in, gently at first, and then with increasing force, making long smooth motions, hand over hand. Mieke stares and stares at the water and—

A huge, writhing black form, long and snaking, breaks into the sunlight from the protection of the river below. It cuts the air violently as the professor calmly tugs it closer. Mieke cannot breathe.

It is so awful, so incredible. A monster from a fairy tale, but real, whipping about in thin air. Rob drops his own lines, cries, and tries to scramble clear, slipping on the wet ground, panicking to think he might fall into the water—now that he knows what else is in there.

An eel. She's seen them at the market, but far smaller than this leviathan, and always dead already, more greenish brown than this one, still cloaked in the wetness of the river.

Mieke recoils at the sight of its beaded eyes—spherical, black, like the ball on the end of a straight pin. As the eel drags onto the bank of the river, it flips end to end, swirling up into a knot and then flying loose like a living ribbon. Rob's father grabs it with his free hand and immediately Mieke sees the gray slime the creature leaves everywhere, which will stink for hours even after it has been washed off.

The massive eel curls itself around the man's thin forearm, orbiting like a dark comet until at last Naaktgeboren flings it down into the bucket, which has been filled with river water.

There, finally, the beast goes utterly still, as if it has spontaneously died, but Mieke knows it must be alive. And she feels, deep down, a revulsion for it, a horror at having ever unknowingly swum alongside it. The way it rippled and thrashed will remain on her mind the whole way home. After another hour without a second catch, Rob's father declares the day done.

"This one will be more than enough for all of us anyway."

Eagerly they walk to the bicycles and then ride back through the dunes, the bucket clanking from time to time as Rob's father sets it down to change his grip. Mieke is now the one trailing behind so that she can keep an eye on the bucket. What is she worried about? That the eel will leap to freedom, she guesses, or simply disappear.

She can barely breathe, thinking about it in there, swirling around in the murky water.

When they finally get home, she follows silently as Professor Naaktgeboren sets the pail down on the paving stones in the yard.

He finds a hammer and a piece of wood in the shed and leaves these close by. He tries to give the long nail to his son, but Rob refuses to take it from him.

Instead, he turns, offering it to Mieke. "When I say, you hand it to me."

He rolls up one sleeve without speaking and then slides it into the bucket, groping around in the brown water for the beast inside.

There is nothing.

She cannot believe it. How? It has gotten away. It's impossible.

And then it's all happening again. The eel has reappeared as if by magic. It has the professor, or he has the eel. There is a hurricane of sadistic action, the thick black band of eel flesh wrapping itself wildly around the man's forearm. But the professor calmly grips its giant head between his thumb and middle finger and presses it onto the plank of wood. With his free hand, he lifts the hammer and then looks at Mieke.

He grunts as the grotesque thing thrashes about, going absolutely upright, defying gravity.

Mieke hurries over with the long carpenter's nail. He waits for her to hand it to him, but instead, following an instinct, she places the tip above the eel's cold black eye.

You're not magic, she tells it. Even if she isn't sure she believes that anymore.

Then with one heavy smack of the hammer, Rob's father drives the nail through.

The thing continues to curl and writhe about, but now there is no escape. Professor Naaktgeboren, having both hands free at last, takes his knife and slices—deep—all around the neck of the beast. With his fingers he yanks its skin free like he is stripping a casing off a gargantuan sausage.

Even after all this, it moves. Even as a mass of sinew and blood, it fights for life.

The frenzy finally ceases only as the professor begins slicing away its thin organs, one by one. When the monster has been completely cleaned, he chops it into half a dozen pieces, each a few inches long, and carries them into the kitchen. There, Tante Sintje will dredge them in a bowl of flour and fry them in her great black cast-iron cocotte.

That night at supper, Mieke eats her segment wordlessly, in awe. With each warm bite she thinks how all that lithe dark power is inside her now.

THE NEXT DAY, Mieke and Rob go out after school, back toward the woods. While their mothers play in the grass with Broodje and Truus, the older children scamper off. There are ruins deeper in: a line of old stone pillars, crumbled and well covered in thick green moss and vines. Rob says they are from centuries ago, when the Roman empire stretched all the way to Velsen, but Mieke isn't sure that can be real. Rob claims he's seen fairies nearby, tiny buoyant embers of colored light that waft around the vines and along the stone paths. No bigger than a gnat, they move so slowly that you cannot see them unless you are perfectly still.

"This is where they cross over," Rob breathes, "from Luilekkerland."

Mieke knows this is all from the stories her father reads at night. Luilekkerland, where houses are made of barley cakes and sugar and the streets are paved with pastries and everything in every shop costs nothing at all.

"Aren't you going to tell me it's stupid?" Rob asks.

Mieke doesn't believe in any of it, but for reasons she can't explain she doesn't feel like telling him it's all nonsense. Not today, anyway. She's still thinking about the eel. The thwack of the hammer against the nail she'd been holding. All that life, gone away. All the slime and viscera. How can it have become that tender and sweet, fatty-tasting thing?

"Let's climb." She points to one of the nearby trees.

Rob is too scared, no surprise, so Mieke goes it alone. And even though the bark eats at her fingers, she gets up to the third limb, which she's never managed to do before. She sits straddle-legged, surveying her lands, a queen, an empress.

"What do you see?" he shouts up.

In truth, there's nothing much to see, just more of the same tangled green forest. There is a line of dark clouds way off to the west. She feels a rumble of thunder, without hearing it. She hears her mother singing to the littler ones, not far off. But she waits, watching, still. Listening to the birds sing warnings in the branches. A yellow one darts out from the cover of one tree and into another. There's a red one higher up. A brownish shape, too, that warbles madly. She misses her father suddenly and wonders if they can ride back past the bakery where he's been working since the very start of the day. Even though the painters don't come by quite as often as before.

No one has seen Mr. Akkeringa in three months. It is like this all over. In her class at school, Ina and Siny, the twins, have not been there all year.

And where are the Meiers? She asks herself this question once a day, to keep it fresh.

"I'm going to be a painter when I grow up," she shouts to Rob.

"I'll teach you how to draw!"

"I don't need you to *teach* me."

Rob looks around anxiously. "You'll scare them away."

He means the fairies, and she thinks about telling him he's such a baby she can't even believe it, but she doesn't. Instead, she climbs back down the tree and studies him. He's breathing hard, even though he hasn't moved from the spot he's been in for ten minutes or more.

"What? You think they're here?" she asks.

She looks around, pretending. It doesn't make any difference anyway, and he's more than happy to tell her how, in the olden days, the fairies lived in the forests undisturbed. How they joined her pagan ancestors in the war against the Romans. How when their forebears had been subjugated into the empire, the fairies had retreated to their own kingdom, apart from mankind. In times to come, the stories said, when the Dutch people finally returned to a free life in the forests, then the fairies would come live among them once more.

"What?" her father liked to tease Rob, "you want to give up the grocer's? The butcher shop? Nice shoes, clean water? This city? These roads? And what about electricity, and the coal stoves that keep you warm at night? All the fairies will say, 'You fools! You had it all! What happened?'"

Mieke's cousin, who is really not her cousin, settles down with his sketchbook, not to *teach* her how to draw, but to show her how he does it.

Though Rob still has baby chubbiness all over, his hands move quickly enough to snatch ladybugs from the air. When he wraps those fingers around a pencil, he can summon all the spectacular creatures from the legends that his father reads: Sleipnir, the horse who could ride through fire and water at the speed of lightning; Spin Head, the spider, who wove the first linen from the blue flax stalk; the majestic wild aurochs with their enormous horns; the King of the Dwarves and the Moss Maiden of the trees. No other hands are as deft or as swift. No other hands can make what Rob's make.

Quickly he reaches up and grasps something she can't see. He opens his palm carefully, studies its emptiness, and resumes his search.

"Trying to catch a fairy?" she whispers.

"You can't *catch* one. But if you make a house, sometimes they'll go in and poke around."

"Show me."

Rob wastes no time gathering up little sticks and leaves and dried flowers and the needles of evergreens. Finally he shows her how he leans them against one another, patiently making little connected spaces.

"Here's the bedroom," he explains, laying down the softest fibers of stretched bark he can find. "And here's where we eat."

Soon they are rushing about, finding leaves and pebbles and bits of bark, gathering materials. Rob sets a silver leaf table with golden flower petals, laying each out like a place setting, his fingers sliding delicately in and out of the makeshift rooms so expertly, Mieke thinks, while hers stumble and thud against everything.

Before long, she's frustrated and tired of breaking everything, and she wants to smash the whole structure, but she stops herself.

Rob is there, but not there. Somewhere else, in his mind.

"Here's where we sit by the fire at night," he says. "And here's where Papa reads."

Slowly he re-creates the rooms of the house that burned to the ground when the bombs fell. She's amazed he can even remember. He works and works, so long that the sun starts going down and Mieke hears their mothers calling.

Rob gazes down in sadness and pleasure at his creation. He pulls a cluster of rank-sweet onion grass from the ground and curls the long green chives around his finger until they form a kind of ring. This, as a finishing touch, he places in the center of the fairy house. He tells Mieke, "Tomorrow we'll see if they've been here."

"How?"

"They'll leave a special dust," he explains. "It sort of sparkles."

"Okay," she says.

And they go.

AFTER DINNER, MIEKE and Rob rest on their beds in what had once been her own room. Thin cries come through the wall; Truus is refusing to feed. For some reason Truus will drink only from Mieke's mother, and so when Broodje is barely half fed, Mieke's mother must surrender the rest of her milk to Broodje's cousin, who is not his cousin. And Tante Sintje limply sulks about and sometimes sobs quietly as she looks through her magazines, and now Mieke's mother needs to console her, too.

"Sintje," she whispers, her features pitying in a way Mieke already resents, "you must relax. The baby cannot latch when you're so upset. It says so right there in the article."

"Cora! How can I relax?" Rob's mother hisses back, cheeks red with fury even at the best of times. "Should I write to the editors at *Libelle* and ask their advice? *Dear sirs: My husband's school has been reduced to matchsticks by the Krauts and I'm homeless. What position do I put my fingers into for optimal pressure?*"

"You're not *homeless*."

"Yes. Yes, I am. I had a home and now I don't."

It isn't getting better. Mieke has figured that out by now. There are shouted conversations, followed by whispers, followed by more shouting. She sees Sintje with her Bible, praying. She speaks of taking Rob to church more. But the professor calls religion "myth and fantasy," and they begin screaming at each other. Sometimes Mieke thinks this is simply the way adults are. After all, she and Rob will cry over nothing whatsoever. Skinned knee, bumped elbow. Night terror, thunderstorm. Broken toy, a shattered cup. Why not them?

But then Mieke does know.

That night, with the taste of the eel still silky in her mouth, her father tells them the story of the Boar with the Golden Bristles. It is one of Rob's favorites, in which Fro and the fairies create Gullin, the great tusked pig, to serve as Fro's steed and Fro goes riding all through the forests. Men in ancient times knew only how to hunt and fish and eat things made from the honey and the acorns the women collected. But when people saw the huge rows of earth torn up by the fire-boar, they realized the power that resided in the tilled soil, and so created the first plowshares to work the land themselves. Birds flew from far-off worlds to drop seeds into the long rows the men had created. And so came the first stalks of wheat, and the children of the forest tore the heads apart to find hundreds of seeds that could be chewed as well as planted. They roasted them in the fire, pounded them with stones, took the mush, and baked the first-ever loaves of bread.

"By and by," her father proclaims, ending the story as always, "the wild boars were all hunted, and today there are no more in the woods here. But the Boar with the Golden Bristles was painted on the shields of the men who protected these lands and can still be found on our feast tables each Yuletide as Mother Night passes and we sing carols of Christmas and Sinterklaas."

Just then a horrendous violent snorting erupts from the closet—and Rob and Mieke both leap out of bed in fear. In that instant, Mieke is certain that Gullin, the great boar himself, is in there. That Fro and the fairies have sent him to get her for so brazenly climbing their tree.

But when her father opens the closet, Mieke sees Professor Naaktgeboren inside.

After another fight with Tante Sintje, he'd gone across the hall to their neighbor, Mr. DeVries, to borrow some gin. The professor had gone into the closet to drink it in peace. He'd woken up at the end of the story in a delirious state and thrown up all over his checkered pants. Now he moans like nothing she's ever heard before. Worse than when Truus or Broodje wake in the night, needing to be changed or fed—but closer to that than anything else.

The smell of rot and juniper stings at her nostrils. It takes her father a few minutes to get his friend off the floor and help him out of the room. Mieke's mother comes in soon with a bucket of hot water and a fistful of rags to clean his sickness. When she leaves, Mieke can see the red streaks of tears on her cheeks. She does not say good night. Mieke gets up to turn off the lights herself. The smell lingers, putrid and heavy and hot in the air. Worse than onion grass. Worse than the slime of the eel. Worse than the foulness that hangs in the air after German soldiers walk by in the street. It is the smell of dead things in the grass in the forest, covered in flies and maggots. Things that Rob has made her poke with sticks to be sure they were all the way dead, and which were.

IN THE MORNING, Mieke and Rob go to breakfast and find Professor Naaktgeboren cranking the coffee in the great wooden grinder. Mieke waits for Rob to ask his father why he'd been hiding in their closet, but he does not. Instead, her *neefje* stares down at the paper in his sketchbook, moving his pencil around in widening circles, making the great hollows of the snout of the Boar with the Golden Bristles darker and darker.

Mieke sits still, watching. Her father has already gone to the bakery. Her mother urges her to eat her toast. Dutifully Mieke lifts the brown square to her mouth and chews slowly. She tastes the salty air from the window and the sourness of the sticky glop in the vats. She imagines the universe of dark stars.

"Will you put my hair in a braid today?" she asks abruptly.

Her mother tries not to pause so long that Mieke notices, but she does. Mieke has stunned her mother, and this in and of itself is more satisfying than her usual refusal.

"Just one. In the middle."

After they finish breakfast, she and Rob go downstairs, passing the door to the Meiers' apartment, and climb onto their bicycles. They hurry past the little gardens of purple lilacs and magenta tulips. The soldiers are gathered by the Meijmans' butcher shop and one waves at her, but she does not wave back. He stands with his hand on the butt of his rifle, upside down at his side. He turns to his friends and says something in German, and they all laugh. In a moment she is icy all over.

Mieke and Rob ride on. Out into the dunes again. Rob is still looking out at the grasses. She glares off at the seawalls, daring them to crack. Later she and Rob will go into the woods to see if the little house he left there has been covered in dust. And it won't be, but he'll try, or she hopes he will. Now as she pedals, Mieke feels the pull, all around her head, of her hair wound tight into the braid dangling gently behind her neck. Dark and long, and powerful.

A SKY, OR VOID

~

Alas! We imagine you have never heard a story told by eels. Ordinarily we take pains to remain apart, living in the bottomlands and moving secretly through crevices. We slide unseen over the open lands, consuming lazy worms and sometimes unsuspecting frogs—yes, it's true. We have four nostrils and a second heart at the ends of our tail fins. We breathe through our skin. We can be almost anywhere, can see almost anything. If we choose, we can go weeks or even months without the slightest motion. Some of us will live through entire centuries, end to end, and pass between realms quite freely. And so, you see, we have gathered up such marvelous stories, witnessed from the shadows and creeks and crevices, throughout the ages.

If you were ever to sit by the bank of a muddy river on a quiet night, you would be serenaded by a hundred earthly instruments: birds and crickets and bats and the wind in the leaves and the tallest grasses. In all that noise you would never perceive our whispering, our slurping, and our chirping, but we are there, undetected.

It is only due to a strange set of circumstances that these stories are transmitted to you now, and through an odd vessel. We communicate with a human being who himself hides behind the initials V.S. He is a descendant of that naked-born family that captivated our anguilliform collective so many generations ago.

Thanks to him, we may at last invite you into our bed, into our swarm. Like a consortium of octopuses or a murder of crows, a group of us is sometimes referred to as a fry of eels—but this we do not enjoy: it evokes sizzling oil, cast-iron pans, the crisping of our flesh.

In the islands of the South Pacific, we are known as the igat and are considered to be sacred beings. Certain lakes where we teem are off limits for any fishing, in fear that a giant eel known by the locals as Abaia will wreak havoc on the villages there, creating powerful waves with the lashing of its tail and summoning winds and rains so intense that the waters of the lake will rise and flood the land, drowning everyone in a rage.

Fantasies, of course, we assure you. We are harmless. Very harmless.

Of all the myths and stories, around the many oceans and inland waters, we are most partial to how our kind are known on the island of Japan: *utsubo*, just a shade off from *utsuho*, meaning a sky, or void.

Humbly, we request therefore that you think of us in this manner during these tales. That is to say that we are an absence, touching everything.

—V.S.

BLOOD ON THE BRAIN

~

The day after her fall, Mieke was released from the hospital with five stitches on her right eyebrow and a mostly clean CT scan. She'd had blood on the brain, they'd told her. Concerning, but eventually it had cleared up. No fractures to her hip, and her ankle had only been twisted. Already she could walk on it, just more slowly than before. A nurse had brought Mieke down in the elevator and sent her home in a cab—its driver, bent over the wheel, whispering to himself as they went along. It had been raining, just lightly, but still not the sort of weather she wanted to be out in. When at last they arrived on Sand Dollar Street, Mieke handed the man his fare, plus a tip for his trouble, and said, "I hope that you can get home soon." But the man had just stuffed the bills into his shirt pocket and pulled away, not even waiting to see if she made it inside safely.

Now Mieke sat at her kitchen table, watching the waters gently rolling outside in the bay. The smell of the abandoned paella still lingered, though she'd reluctantly thrown it in the trash can outside. To mask the smell, she inhaled close to the bouquet of purple hyacinths she'd brought back from the hospital and then ran her finger along one thick green stem, making the heavy blooms bob above. Each flower was made of a hundred tinier flowers, which coalesced into one dense cone streaked with blue and lilac and violet. At least she had these, and their scent was beginning to fill the kitchen. At least her hip had not been broken. And though she had been stuck out on the road for an hour, at least Giancarlo had come by in his truck. He was a local handyman, Cuban, who also did landscaping. That night he had been finishing a power-washing job over at the Jacobsons' house when he'd heard her yelling. After cleaning the blood from her face with his neckerchief, Giancarlo had driven her to the hospital and stayed with her until she was settled in a room for the night. Then in the morning he'd come by with the hyacinths. Beautiful, and not from the gift shop in the lobby—she'd checked.

"Can I call someone for you?" he'd asked. "Your husband? Your children?"

"No," she'd said, without explaining her husband had been dead nearly thirty years, and that her son had disappeared not long after that.

She did tell him that her grandson, Will, lived about two hours away, up in Manhattan, but he was very busy. He was a doctor, the head partner in a successful medical practice. Proudly she'd taken his wedding photo out of her wallet to show Giancarlo.

And he'd smiled, duly impressed, and then said, "Asian," of Will's wife, Teru, a literacy aide at a public middle school in Red Hook.

"They met in Germany while he was there doing research. But she grew up right in East Rutherford," Mieke said, taking the photo back. "Just an hour from here. Isn't that funny?"

Giancarlo seemed to think little about any of this. But for a while he sat with her, watching the TV, which he'd changed to Fox News. Not her favorite, but it didn't seem right to scold him about politics when he was taking time to sit with a stranger whose eye socket had been cracked and her ankle sprained.

"Crime is so terrible now," Giancarlo said. "When I saw you out there, lying in the road, I thought you had been mugged."

"I just slipped," Mieke said, trying to hear the report—which had switched to foreign affairs. A war, somewhere else. Soldiers, tanks, buildings all bombed out. Concrete, baked black from bomb heat. An ash-stained man carrying a child in a pink pom-pom hat. The child looking back at their home, a fire rising inside it. Her father gazing hard, away.

"It's not safe to walk around at night anymore," Giancarlo said desperately, gazing out the hospital window, as if the dangers lurked there, even now.

Mieke was about to say that she felt perfectly safe, thank you very much. That unless Giancarlo wanted to lock up the litter-bugs, the only criminals in her seaside town were the occasional drunk drivers, and that was mostly just the summer people.

"Your grandson lives in New York City?" he said. "Up there is the worst."

"When they have children, I think they'll move," Mieke said graciously.

Giancarlo shook his head, as if there was no place her hypo-thetical great-grandchildren could ever move from the ruin the world was becoming. He reminded Mieke suddenly of Shoshana. In her mind, the next generation would be swallowed by rising seas. In his, slaughtered by phantom thugs. Was Mieke crazy for thinking they were both just watching the news too much?

She had seen devastation: flooded farmlands, streets overrun with soldiers. Neighbors turned into petty thieves by hunger.

And it was true, things had turned bad quickly back then. Very quickly indeed.

NOW, HOME AT last and all alone, Mieke thought about how kind Giancarlo had been. How nice, not to be in the hospital now. On the Weather Channel they were talking about the storm that Shoshana had mentioned the day before, which was tracking through British Columbia and toward the northwestern states. An Alberta clipper, the weatherman called it, like one of those old three-masted wooden ships. With a cool swipe of his hand, the forecaster had drawn a line across the continent, showing how the storm would move across the Great Lakes, pick up cold air, and become a snowy nor'easter that could possibly, eventually reach the East Coast.

"Oh, *please*," Mieke said out loud. Such a fuss! Why was everyone expecting the worst all the time? A little rain, all the way off in Vancouver, and they acted like it was the end of the world.

Immediately she felt a pang of hunger, and though she told herself it was just the memory of hunger, she still had to get up and eat two slices of bread straight from the package. She'd never had her father's knack for baking her own. And when she sometimes splurged on a round loaf of sourdough from the bakery counter, it never tasted anything close to his, either.

She brought her coffee into her living room and sat down on the purple couch. Beneath the television was the large chest from the apartment on Laan van Meerdervoort, the one Professor Naaktgeboren's father had carved from dark wood—petrified cedar, in fact, so perhaps it was more stone than wood. This, too, had a deep familiar smell. She studied its elaborate Far East scenes: bowed cherry blossoms, majestic ships on choppy seas. Great snaking dragons exhaling plumes of smoke. Huddled men in regal robes, their hair pulled up majestically, conferring eternally about secret things.

Mieke stared at the chest for a long time, as if the figures on the side might spring to life. Meanwhile, her mind turned unbidden to those freezing months in 1944 and 1945. The Hunger Winter, they called it now, or De Hongerwinter. Months that, as they happened, she'd promised herself to never think about again, should she somehow survive. But since her fall the other night, these old memories had been flooding back. Maybe it was the blood on the brain. Maybe she was just tired. She wished she weren't so alone. Through all the horrors of the war, her family had been in one place, together.

To keep from slipping back into those old memories again,

she picked up the book from Shoshana and opened it. She was just beginning to turn to the first pages when a knock came at the front door.

WILL GEBORN STOOD waiting on the landing of his oma's house with Teru, lifting a wide umbrella over both their heads with his left hand—the other was bound up in a cumbersome white cast. Three days ago, at work, he'd gotten frustrated about something and punched a wall—or really, a doorframe, which had turned out to be worse than punching a wall—resulting in a scaphoid fracture, a dislocation of the middle finger joint, and a tear of the ligament on his thumb. The injury would take six weeks to fully heal.

Teru carried a brown ShopRite bag containing a pair of lobsters they'd bought on the way down. Inside, the lethargic crustaceans collided occasionally with the walls of their paper prison. In another bag she had the fixings for a salad for herself. She was avoiding shellfish. Soft cheeses. Uncooked deli meat. Sushi. Etcetera, etcetera. Just in case. Her period was only a few days late. If she was pregnant, it would be the third time in eighteen months. They hadn't made it past the first trimester yet.

"I love that your grandmother's place is the only one with grass," Teru observed.

It was true. All the neighbors had long ago replaced their lawns with plain marble rocks that needed no care during the months they lived elsewhere. Landscapers came once in the spring to hose them down with a weed killer, and that was it. Unlike the vinyl-sided, plastic-railinged monstrosities on either side, Will's oma's house looked exactly as it had when he had come there as a boy to visit. The same dark wooden shingles, the same old split-rail fence, and even the same impeccably well-pruned flower garden in the front.

Over the rustling of the lobsters, Will heard his oma slowly making her way down the stairs to the lower level. He noticed Teru was shifting uncomfortably between the paper bags.

"Feeling okay?" he asked.

"Just a couple of cramps."

"Good cramps or . . . ?" Will asked, looking at the door.

She shrugged. Will could not reach it, but in his coat pocket he had stashed one little rectangular purple box—a pregnancy test he'd picked up at lunch from the Duane Reade near his office. He'd gotten the one in the purple box, which was supposed to be the lucky kind.

Or at least the blue one they'd used last time had been the unlucky kind?

But he had not shown her. Not yet.

He wasn't sure why she had not checked herself, maybe it was too soon, maybe she just didn't want to get her hopes up. Prying was not recommended. But if she suddenly decided she was ready to know, then Will would be ready. Obviously it was on her mind.

"What if it's just not meant to be?" she mumbled.

"What if *what's* not meant to be?"

But he knew. Teru had been arguing on the phone with her mother most of the drive down, and in Japanese about half of the time—never a good sign.

His grandmother was almost at the door. Will tried his best to answer Teru's real question. "There's no such thing as 'meant to be,' I don't think. There's just—it works out. Or it doesn't. There's we keep trying, and there's—"

The door was opening. What he wanted to end on, but hadn't, was, "and there's Osaka."

But she knew how the sentence ended. She was the one who had, months ago, quietly applied for the ten-week fellowship program to study at the International School there. She'd told Will only after getting accepted. Now her bags were packed, in the trunk of the car, and she had a car service scheduled to take her to Newark in the morning.

AT LAST WILL'S oma opened the door. He felt her breathing, labored, as he hugged her. She filled and deflated each second like an immense, soft balloon.

"We need to get you into a place without all these stairs," he declared as she embraced him.

"Your hand!" she exclaimed.

"It'll be fine in a few weeks. Just got in the way of a door-frame."

She sighed as if these things just happened all the time. "Oh, it's good to *see* you both," his grandmother said. "What a wonderful surprise! But you shouldn't have been driving in this mess."

Will looked up at the sputtering rain, about to say that this was nothing—that the parkway had been as busy as ever. But then he'd seen the cut on her eyebrow, noticed the limp as she moved back into the house to let him come in from the cold.

Teru hugged Mieke quickly and then presented the shifting brown paper bag.

"We gotcha some lobstahs," Teru said, trying to sound like she was from New England.

"Oh!" she cried out. "I love that. You're so funny, dear."

Will leaned between them to examine Oma's stitches, as if he might personally redo them. "Tell me what happened?"

"Oh, I just fell," she said. "It's nothing."

He could see she was embarrassed and guessed she was hiding more, but he did not push.

"Teru has an early flight in the morning and you're closer to Newark," Will said, as if this explained everything.

"We thought we'd stay the night," Teru said. "Just to make sure everything's okay."

Mieke nodded. "Of course you can. That would be lovely."

INSIDE, WILL URGED his grandmother to sit on the couch and rest a little while he worked on the dinner. Teru sat on the couch while Mieke used a golden letter opener to slice loose a few birthday cards that had come while she was in the hospital. Then they put her bouquet of hyacinths into a vase with some water, and placed them on the cedar chest, stunning in the moonlight.

"Last week, on the History Channel," his grandmother was

saying to Teru, "I saw the most interesting documentary about Hiroshima."

"Oma—" Will called.

But Teru was already saying, "Oh! Was it the one with the guy who collected August 7, 1945, newspapers from all over the world?"

"Yes! It is this Albanian gentleman," his grandmother explained to Will, "who has them framed, hanging all over his house. Hundreds of them! Some are worth a lot of money, apparently."

"I'll bet," he said.

"On eBay I saw one selling for like fifty bucks and I *almost* bid," Teru said.

Will pinched his mouth closed and tried to smile. "Only fifty?"

He turned to look outside, where things were clearing up. A bright, beaming circle had at last emerged through the dissipating net of rain clouds. Teru's grandfather had been alive then, just a child, on some farmland somewhere near Osaka, the day the bomb dropped, hundreds of miles away. He talked about it all the time—it seemed like anything could remind him. And lately Teru had begun fixating on it as well. Will didn't understand it. Why were people so macabre? So intent on living in the past, spending their precious days looking backward, instead of forward?

"In the back office, I might still have one from the Amsterdam paper. *Het Parool*."

Teru eagerly followed his grandmother off to go hunt for it while Will returned to the stove.

Quickly the water came to a boil in the great black cast-iron cocotte. Will had always been fascinated with cooking. He loved studying all the best techniques and ingredients. Understanding the globular proteins in simple eggs and how and why the amino acids folded and curled differently at certain temperatures. It was a science, and yet also an art. Following precise instructions yielded something rich, nourishing, and transcendent. He and Teru had met, in fact, at a cooking class in Düsseldorf, and fallen in love while making seafood, of all things.

In preparing lobster, most went wrong by using too much water. All that was needed was an inch, and half a tablespoon of salt—

because the lobsters were truly being steamed, not boiled. Will flipped the scrambling creatures into the pot, an awkward job with just one hand, and slammed the lid down before they could escape. As he waited for the sound of the water to return to its former bubbling, he bid a silent adieu to the creatures, half muttering a little prayer, *May God rest your lobstery souls*—though he did not believe in God or souls, either. Certainly not when it came to marine animals, anyway.

Will next pulled out a smaller pot to set up a double boiler for drawing the butter, a precise process in which the two kinds of solids could be separated by density as the water evaporated, leaving behind a transparent, incredible pure yellow butterfat.

Then with some difficulty he uncorked the bottle of cold white wine and poured a glass just as Teru and Oma returned from their search, empty-handed, talking of more boxes upstairs, to be searched later.

"She's going to notice I'm not drinking," Teru said through tightened lips.

"We only brought two lobsters. I think the jig is up."

"Could have *all* had salad . . ."

But no, the tradition was long-standing, since Will had been a boy, visiting the house in the summertime: his oma had always gone to the wharf and picked out lobsters for lunch. It had begun before he could fully remember, age five, back when the whole family had been over together to celebrate some good news—a birthday, maybe. His father's had been in June, and this would have been before he'd run out on them.

In any case, they'd all been sitting out there on the deck, at the long table together, watching the sunlight play over the water. On a whim, Oma had picked up an extra lobster for Will. "Worst case," she never failed to say in the retelling, "I could always make a lobster roll the next day." But young Will had seen the giant red creatures coming out onto the wide plates and demanded to try one. And then to everyone's amazement, he had dutifully begun to disassemble the creature with his metal crackers and needle-thin fork, watching the grown-ups carefully to see how they were handling it and then mimicking in his own fashion, small hands be damned. For a full hour he'd sat there, napkin tucked into his shirt, methodically dismantling every square millimeter of lobster, consuming every thread of the sweet soft meat from inside each slender leg. He'd continued calmly prodding and poking the carapace on into the second hour.

Oma repeated the story then to Will and Teru, in the same ways as always, with an air of reverence, as if it were a miracle that she had witnessed.

"We all said then he'd become a famous surgeon."

Will knew she'd go there. This was how the story always concluded. He'd been told the story now so many times that he could think of it only as an event recalled by others, imagined by him as they recounted what had happened.

"Thank *God* I didn't end up being a surgeon," he said. "They try and tell you in med school, but no one listens."

Instead of being shackled to some underfunded hospital in who knows where like his former classmates, Will was a GP on the Upper East Side of Manhattan, a partner at a practice with a pediatrician, Dr. Talia Mizrahi. Theirs was what was called a whole family approach. She attended to the children and he, the parents. Not only did this make for a convenient one-stop experience, but it helped identify connections in behavioral and environmental factors that might otherwise be missed. It was a more common practice in Germany, but there was a growing demand for it in the States now. He liked the work; he really did.

Will poured himself a third glass of wine, the first and second having been consumed in quick succession. They all sat down to eat. His grandmother asked how his mother was doing, and dutifully he filled her in—though to be honest he had little idea what she was up to these days. She'd remarried, not long after he'd left for college, and gone off with a man named Kevin who did contract work for the Air Force. They moved around a lot, and Will could not for the life of him remember if they were in San Diego or San Jose . . . Moffett Airfield, which one was that in?

Teru said, "San Jose," as Will noticed that his grandmother was not paying attention anyway. She seemed to be distracted, far away. Was it the effect of the head injury, or just of being eighty years old with failing hearing aids? It was hard, seeing her all banged up, moving slowly, getting winded so easily. He thought sometimes that he stayed away so much because, as long as he did, she remained fifty or so in his mind, the age she was when he was a boy, eating lobsters on the deck in the summertime.

There was just one thing that Will remembered, for real, about the lobster incident—and he was sure that it wasn't something he'd imagined, because it was never a part of the story when his mother or his grandmother retold it. Only Will seemed to remember it happening.

At the end of the meal, as Will had leaned back at last from the table to the applause of the others—his father had stood up and lifted one of the crimson carcasses into the air. With intent curiosity, he'd gazed long and hard into its dead beady eyes.

"They don't have a *brain*," Will's father had said, as if this were a tragedy.

"Robbie, sit down. What are you talking about?" Will's mother had said.

"It's true. They don't have a brain. They're like *bugs*—sailors used to call them that in the olden days. Called them bugs! Don't have a brain."

"What do they have then?" young Will had asked.

"They've just got a kind of a *nervous* system," his father said, his lock on the dead eyes unbroken. "That's why they don't feel any pain when you cook them."

Will had asked his mother about it once and she'd just said he'd always had an active imagination. That she had certainly not grabbed the lobster carcass from his father and thrown it to the ground and stormed off.

No, never. Absolutely absurd.

THEN WILL LOOKED up from his lobster at his grandmother, as if the years since then had only just now passed at once. The moon was nearly full and sharply white behind her in the window. Did she remember it? And if he asked, would she tell the truth? And if she did, what would be the next question? And then the next? He'd watched her after he and Teru had first arrived, crossing over to the big carved wooden trunk beneath the television and setting down the framed photo of his father she kept there among the other family portraits. He'd seen it hundreds of times, of course—teenage Dad in bell-bottoms and a paisley shirt. Why did she bother to hide it? Was it just out of habit? Or was it a way to signal that she did not want to discuss her absent son?

All his life, Will had been told that his father had just left. Nothing so unusual. It happened all the time. Men were inherently unreliable, his mother had told him. It was genetic. Hardwired, deep in the lizard brain. Men are selfish. Men are careless. Men cannot be trusted. Still. Will. You must never behave that way. Will. You must do better. Don't be a deadbeat, a wanderer; never break a fragile heart. And young Will had assured his mother that he never would.

And exactly as he'd promised, he had *not* become those things. Instead, he'd fallen in love with a woman who kept one foot out the door at all times.

And yet. He'd never really believed the story he'd been told about his father.

It had never really added up in his mind.

He had been ten when his father left, but he remembered his father truly loving him, truly loving his mother—remembered his father crying, even, once, just at the idea of losing her. And then he'd just disappeared.

Though no one else liked to talk about it, Will remembered his father had sometimes behaved a little strangely, and not just that day with the lobster. Never violently, never awfully. Just *strangely*.

Will hadn't thought much of it then, because what did grown-ups ever do that made much sense to an eight-year-old? But by now these things had begun to make sense to Will. Now that he'd done rotations in clinical psychology and dug through the DSM criteria and read up on bipolar disorder. Now that he'd seen patients in the throes of psychotic episodes.

Medical records from back in the days of paper charts could be hard to come by today, but he'd gotten ahold of one at least: *Robert Geborn Jr., admitted to the Brookhaven Home in western Pennsylvania, following a nervous breakdown, September 1993.*

He wasn't supposed to know. He'd never told anyone that he did.

"HAVE I EVER told you about catching eels when I was a girl? In Holland?"

Will realized that his grandmother was looking at him, and that no one had spoken in a minute or two. Teru shook her head. "Eels, like—?"

She made a wavy, wiggly motion with her forearm.

"Yes," Oma said confidently. "I used to go to this stream in the woods. And Rob would try to catch fairies while his father and I fished."

Will didn't remember much about his grandfather, his opa, who'd died of leukemia when he was only six years old. He'd been an engineer for Colgate-Palmolive and had sported a mustache as thick as a push broom.

"Fairies? Like what, Tinker Bell?" Teru asked.

His oma either didn't hear her or ignored her, Will wasn't sure.

Then as he chewed his lobster and Teru pushed around her half-eaten salad, Will's grandmother began telling them how she'd seen the bombers fly over her father's bakery and how his grandfather's family had come to stay with them. She kept referring to Will's grandfather as her *neefje,* so Will asked her what that meant and she said, "Like a cousin," and Teru stopped her again to make sure. "But not *really* a cousin, though, right?"

"No, no," Mieke assured her. "Our fathers were like brothers."

"But not *actually* brothers."

"No, no."

Eventually, when she came to the part about the eels, Will was impressed.

"He flayed an *eel*?"

"He did. I flayed another once. *Two*, actually," she said, although oddly without pride, almost blankly.

She got up then and began to clear their plates and place everything into the sink. Teru went to make some tea, and Will tipped the last of the wine from the bottle, feeling his vision blur pleasantly, enough that the carved figures on the side of the cedar chest seemed to move.

Will walked outside, wanting to feel the cool post-rain air on his face. He stood there a moment and listened to the gentle lapping of the waves against the dock.

HE WAS FULL, his cares and worries far away. It was hard for him to say why he loved it at his grandmother's house so much. It was more than just good memories, more than just the beauty of the water outside and the peace and quiet compared to the city. It felt like home, was all he could think. He loved the beautiful paintings she had collected over the years, now hanging densely on the walls. Loved the lush Persian rug and the warm crimson of the heavy curtains. Yes, it was odd for a beach house, but it made you think that it was the other houses that were odd. Pretend houses, owned by pretend people, who'd never know the peace of this windswept world off-season. The pleasant exchange of headlights and taillights on the causeway a few miles out, on the far side of the bay. The way it seemed to hold back the whole ocean.

Teru stepped out to join him on the back deck and they looked out at the long, empty dock. Moonlight gleamed white off its wet planks and continued in a long line over the dark waters, almost as if you could walk along it and keep right on going until you arrived at the moon itself.

"Did she ever have a boat?"

"My opa did."

"What was it called?"

"I don't remember."

"What had happened to it?"

"She must have sold it after he died."

He curled her into his arms. Felt her cheek, warm, against his neck.

"What would you name a boat if you had one?" she asked.

"You want to get a boat?"

"No. I just like the names. You could call it *Yachtzee*, or, like, *Schooner or Later*."

Will almost answered, "*I* could, or *we* could?" but thought better of it. Instead, he nudged her a little and said, "Super classy."

She nudged him back in protest and he started to move off, but she held him close.

"Pick a real name, then," she said.

And suddenly he knew they weren't talking about boats anymore.

"Yui," Will said, almost whispering.

"That's my grandmother's name."

"I know. I like it."

"It means 'elegant cloth,'" she said after a minute.

"I know it does."

"I'm coming back," she said, kissing him. "You know that, right?"

And he said that he knew and tried to believe it.

THEY CAME BACK inside to find Mieke yawning. Will and Teru urged her to get to bed, to sleep well. They'd find everything in the guest room on their own. In the morning Will would take her out to Costco to help her restock the refrigerator, and her grandson would cook some things to freeze so she wouldn't need to worry about going out. She said good night, thinking of this, and went into her room to try and sleep. She listened to the sounds of Teru washing the dishes, the two of them talking happily, being young and wonderful.

Mieke tried to read a little from Shoshana's book then and was delighted to find the tale of the Naaktgeboren name told almost exactly as it had been told to her as a girl by the professor—

only for some reason being relayed now by *eels*, of all things. She was positive that this Vraagteken Schrijver person must have known her uncle. It was the first real break in the mystery they'd found, after years of searching for anything at all. In the morning, she promised herself, she'd sit down and begin doing a real translation for Shoshana. If she wrote out a few pages a day, she could have it all done by the start of the summer. But first, she'd rest. Dream.

SOMETIME LATER, IN the middle of the night, when she got up to use the bathroom, Mieke noticed one of the lamps was still on out in the living room. She peered through the doorway, since she was just in her nightgown, and saw Will was standing shirtless near the closed guest bathroom door, speaking softly to Teru on the other side.

"I love you," he was whispering sadly. Desperately. "I love you. I love you."

Mieke began to go back to bed, but she was worried, so she stayed. She felt sick. She knew she should not listen, but she didn't know how to leave.

"Are you all right?"

Another pause.

"I'm so sorry, sweetie."

Another pause.

"Okay. Take your time. Good night. I love you."

IN THE MORNING the house was quiet. Mieke got out of her bed. She went out and saw the guest room was empty, the bed perfectly made, and no sign of her grandson or Teru, though their car was still in the driveway. She went into the bathroom; everything appeared the same as before except for a lingering smell of disinfectant spray in the air. Gently she opened the little trash can and saw a few tissues darkly streaked with mascara, balled up with the thin blue wrapper of a panty liner—not hers, certainly. It had to belong to Teru, which could only mean that she wasn't pregnant after all. Was that what it had all been about? Poor dears.

Just then Mieke heard something moving behind her, and turned, scared, to see Will sitting up on the couch, eyes pinched against the light. Mieke noted an emptied bottle of wine on the table—a whole new one, she realized.

"Teru left for the airport?" Mieke asked.

Will nodded slowly, trying to reconstruct the shattered memories of the previous night. Looking hazily out the window at the water, at the long dock there protruding off into it.

"Yeah," he said flatly, closing his eyes before lying back again.

DOLLE DINSDAG

~

*A*ufmachen! Aufmachen!"

    Mieke hears the banging coming down the street. Are there soldiers outside? She wakes up still reaching through grassy waters, trying to grip the arms of a drowning boy. It is a dream she has been having a lot lately. Each time, it feels so real—his slippery hands. It is always the same boy, but she does not recognize him from the neighborhood. Whoever he is, he is sitting on the bottom of a lake or a deep river of some kind, his legs crossed there in the green and waving weeds. Not thrashing or anything. Just looking around peacefully. She always wakes up right when she is about to plunge down into the cold clear water to save him. And though it is only a dream, she still feels as if he's waiting for her, running out of breath, beginning to go limp.

    It doesn't matter. He's gone and the apartment is full of noises now. Bedsheets being thrown off, bedsprings creaking, grown-ups muttering to one another. *What do they want?*

    "Aufmachen! Aufmachen!"

    Rob is still sound asleep in his own bed on the opposite wall, farther from the window. It has been three long years now that they've shared a room. It is 1944, and she's bigger now, but she can still climb up the side of his dresser, her bare feet cramping against the wooden knobs. She knocks a few of his books from the top. Rob arranges them all so neatly, it drives her mad. In alphabetical order, just like his father. It doesn't matter now. If she squats down next to the As and balances carefully, she can lean her head over to the window and look outside.

Many times, there are no Nazis around at all. Then they emerge in droves. Busy busy, always. Marching along Laan van Meerdervoort in formation, sometimes three and sometimes thirty, up to nothing and everything all the time. In the soles of their boots are iron nails that ring out with each stomp and stride. By September, she's become used to them coming and going, bellowing and barking. Approaching people in the street with random demands, or else thumping on the neighboring doors at all hours—

But this time they are at her door.

"Aufmachen! Aufmachen!"

Mieke holds her breath so that the steam won't cloud the glass. From the third floor, the angle is such that she can see only a quartet of gray-green hats hovering directly over the polished black toes of eight boots. One has a mustache prickling out from in between.

"Rob," she whispers over her shoulder. "Come look."

She's surprised he hasn't come already. Normally he's at her side every second. At night now, he reads to her from his little library. Not fairy tales anymore but real books, currently *The Memoirs of Sherlock Holmes*, and together they puzzle over each mystery—"The Adventure of Silver Blaze," "The Adventure of the Crooked Man," "The Adventure of the Resident Patient"— attempting to solve them before Sherlock does, but they never can. This is how she falls asleep, with Rob curled up next to her, instead of going over to his own bed.

"Rob!" she tries again. "Move it!"

He doesn't get up, even if he is clearly awake. She can see his body shift on the mattress.

No matter how Mieke arranges herself on the dresser, she cannot see much else. Who are the Nazis looking for? The Meiers, on the first floor, are still gone. Her father says they're probably lying low, out in the countryside somewhere where it is easier to blend in and they don't need to go around wearing the limp yellow Stars of David that say Jood in the center.

Then she hears the soldiers calling out a name.

"Naaktgeboren! Naaktgeboren!"

With a clattering of pans, Mieke hears her father rushing out of the kitchen, stumbling through the front door to answer the call.

Last month, the Germans closed Brood van Menke, the bakery—she has no idea why. Now her father works out of their tiny apartment kitchen, preparing the morning's loaves. He can't even get half his usual orders filled with only one small oven.

The last time she and Rob rode past on their bicycles, the bakery was all boarded up, a sign with red lettering saying the building was restricted. Her father won't tell her anything, aside from "It's only temporary, *mijn liefje*."

It seems to Mieke like there is never time to solve one mystery before another arises, if not two or three more. What did the Germans do with all the horses they confiscated last year? And then it was milk cans. Typewriters. Silverware. Then buses. Then radios. All their guilder coins, replaced with bluish paper money. Why? Mieke is left, increasingly, in a world of answerless questions, multiplying rapidly. Like: what is her mother whispering to Rob's mother as the Germans rap a fourth time at the door, even harder now, growing irritated?

In the Sherlock Holmes stories, there's always a clever solution at the end, deduced in startling fashion by the Great Detective. But there are never answers to the mysteries Mieke is trying to solve.

She hears her father arrive at the front door, apologizing that he's been working. She sees him show the men his hands, still covered in flour and tacky bits of dough.

"*Is meneer Naaktgeboren thuis?*" one of the Germans inquires, in ragged Dutch.

"*Nein, nein,*" her father answers somberly. "*Nee, nee. Hij ging vanmorgen naar buiten.*"

Rob still has not come over to join her at the window.

"Hey, dummy. They're asking about your father," she hisses. "Where'd he go so early?"

Why doesn't Rob even shrug or shake his head? Why does he stay still as a corpse, except for his breathing getting heavier? Somewhere, Mieke hears Sintje trying to soothe Truus, who still cries for half her waking life, even though now she is not really a baby anymore. Broodje is near silent, all the time, refusing to learn to speak, as if to balance out his cousin.

Mieke has trouble hearing the rest of the conversation downstairs before, abruptly, it is over. The soldiers have turned away and are now heading out toward Appelstraat. One of them gestures to the Meijmans' butcher shop. The others follow him inside. They'll sometimes stand around in there all morning, chatting with Mr. and Mrs. Meijman, who run the shop and who give the soldiers thick slices of ham for free.

"*Landverraders*," her father sometimes mutters under his breath when he walks by the butcher shop. *Traitors*. Does this have anything to do with why they've closed the bakery?

She doesn't know. Doesn't know what they know or how they could know it.

MIEKE'S FATHER COMES back up the four flights to their apartment, and she moves over into the bathroom, where she can hear through the swan-papered wall to her parents' bedroom. She's gotten good at being quiet now—when she wants to, she moves like a shadow.

Her father says something to her mother. Mieke can't quite make it out. Maybe *"Bedroefd, mijn liefje."* Sorry, my darling.

Her mother whispers back, "I hope you didn't lie to them."

"I swear, I have no idea where he is," her father assures her—this Mieke can hear clearly. "His boots were already gone when I got up. I'm sure he's just gone walking somewhere."

"What do they want with him?"

"Cora. If I knew, I'd tell you."

Then, from the other room, Tante Sintje shouts in frustration as Truus resumes wailing. And Mieke's mother hurries away to see if she can help.

It is quiet for a moment and then she hears her father call. "Brush your teeth, my little spy!"

Maybe she moves less like a shadow than she thinks.

MIEKE DOES BRUSH her teeth and then combs her hair. She can braid it herself now, if sloppily. At last she hears Rob coming down the hallway. He moves sullenly, with his big brown eyes cast toward the carved Japanese chest. It is made from Jindai Sugi, Mieke recalls the lecturing. Japanese cedar, preserved in a marsh bed, already a thousand years old when it was expertly carved by Rob's grandfather. Dark and rich in iron, the trunk is nearly black. Mieke loves to sit and study it with her fingertips, the slender shapes of the crowned cranes in the pond, the trunks of the hundred-year maples, branches jagging like thunder across a sky, so real she can almost hear them crackle. On top she caresses the butter-soft dimples of cherry blossom petals. In each scene there are men in elaborate patterned robes and women, their faces painted and their hair bound up in opulent strings of precious stones.

"My father's hiding," Rob says flatly.

Onderduiken, people whisper now. Disappeared.

"I'm sure he'll be back by lunch," Mieke says, less worried about where he is than the fact that the Germans have come for him. "It can't be too serious, or they'd have forced their way in."

Rob is unconvinced, but she pushes him on toward the kitchen.

"Come on," she says. "Let's eat before Broodje gets it all."

LATER, AT SCHOOL, Mieke is still thinking about the German soldiers. Mr. Wendelgelst reads to them from the same boring book about a little blue frog who does nothing interesting. *De kikker kan zitten*. He points to the picture of the frog, sitting on a rock. In the next picture the frog is sleeping. *De kikker kan slapen*. It is all so silly. Mieke tells herself that if Mr. Wendelgelst ever reads them a story where something actually happens, she'll be able to read the words. It just takes a lot of concentration to make the letters stop wiggling around. How do the other kids manage it so quickly? In the meantime, she has Rob to read to her. When he holds the book and points to the letters, they become still. When he sits there on the bed next to her, it is all so clear.

Mieke studies the girls in the row ahead of her. Marjo Mulder sits up so straightly, writes her letters so perfectly, gets praised every ten minutes for something or another. At recess, Marjo plays with Jacoba Kormaan from down the hall, who has the most beautiful purple coat. English cut, from London. Her father is a banker.

Once Mieke had been playing by herself behind some shrubs, and she'd heard them making fun of her plain yellow dress.

"Do you see how long it is? I heard it used to be her mother's."

Tante Sintje had sewn it, she wanted to say. From a pattern in *Libelle*, just for Mieke.

And then Jacoba had said of her hair, "It's so thick and black. Like a gypsy's!"

"More like a Jew's!" Marjo had shot back.

Mieke hates them. *Hates* them. It feels so good to roll this word around in her mind. Hate hate hate hate hate. She wishes she *was* a gypsy sometimes. Then she could go and live in the woods and travel all around and learn hexes that she could put on Marjo and Jacoba. She still doesn't believe in fairies, of course. But there are kinds of magic she wishes were real.

Through the abrasions on the school window, Mieke watches people sitting out in the park across the street. They drape over the folding chairs and benches. Sometimes they chew on a sandwich or drink some coffee. Every so often one of them brings something interesting: a dog, a chessboard, a violin. And then all the isolated slouched forms rise and gather. The stretched shadows of the trees are lost in the clouds of dust they soon kick up. As beige air swirls around, they all chase the dog or involve themselves in the chess game or stomp their feet to the music. But usually they just sit alone, squinting at a newspaper or tossing crumbs to the birds. It is barely less boring than Mr. Wendelgelst reading about the blue frog. So mysterious to Mieke why these grown-ups, free as they pleased, mostly chose to just sit there doing nothing. Once she saw a few of them turn to one another and discuss something in one of the newspapers. Mostly they seem afraid of one another.

Has it always been this way? Was it different before the Germans came? Were people happier? Busier?

Her father and Professor Naaktgeboren make it sound as if it all used to be different. They keep promising things will be *normal* again. Whatever that means.

"THE PECULIAR DISAPPEARANCE of Professor Naaktgeboren." Mieke reviews the evidence. What was the last thing she'd heard him and her father arguing about? The night before, she recalls, while she and Rob were reading in the bedroom—

"Rockets!" Professor Naaktgeboren had been shouting. "Big enough to hit London!"

"It's not *possible*, I'm telling you."

Once they think that she and Rob are all sleeping soundly, their fathers listen to Radio Oranje together. Professor Naaktgeboren has built a little device out of wood and wires, *de raam-antenne*, a kite-shaped cross that filters out the jamming signals. A few small adjustments with a tiny screwdriver and—*Ba ba ba bum!* The first four notes that begin each broadcast are from the opening to Beethoven's Fifth Symphony, Rob's father has explained to her. And *five* in Latin is the letter V, which he claims stands for "victory." She loves all this coded cleverness. Sometimes when they are out walking, her father will whistle these notes quietly to see if others will whistle back. And her mother and Tanta Sintje wear a ten-cent dubbeltje as a brooch because it has Queen Wilhelmina's face on it, a gesture of devotion to the exiled royals. And a neighbor will call out, "*O zo!*" which means, "So there!" and this is also a code for *Oranje zal overwinnen*: Orange will triumph.

All these small, secret ways to tell if someone can be trusted.

But what if the *landverraders* find out what they are? Professor Naaktgeboren hides copies of *Trouw*, the underground newspaper, between the pages of his books about Saint Augustine and the life of Napoleon. And inside of the hollowed-out copy of *Oorlog en vrede*, the biggest, fattest book they have, by Leo Tolstoy, he and her father hide their radio. *War and Peace*.

They don't think she knows these things, but she does.

Most nights they'll sit together near the hearth and listen for encouragements from the Dutch prime minister, hiding out over in England. Because Kijkduin is so close to the British shoreline, just a hundred miles across the channel, it is possible to pick up the pirate signals if the weather is right. And they can catch snippets, too, of resistance channels. Rumors, chatter, about where troops are or were, and what's fallen in France, and where the front lines are. The messages come in even more cryptic fashion: "The pear is ripe!" a low voice had said the night before Naaktgeboren's disappearance. "I repeat. The pear is ripe." And her father had clapped his hands. Then they'd fallen into silence as the broadcaster had continued. "Louis needs to see the pastor. Jan, it is time to trim your mustache." There had been a long argument about this. Did it mean the Allies were advancing? Or being delayed? Since June, it has been a source of constant speculation. Once the Allies push through France, they'll come to liberate Belgium and Holland next. Then they'll be right up on the German border at last—unless they are beaten back again.

And this, Rob's father has been insisting, is why the Germans are building these new rockets. He's been hearing about it from his friends who have eyes in the factories out East.

"V2, they call them. Vergeltungswaffen. 'Vengeance weapon.' Can you believe it? Vengeance for *what*? Who started this goddamn war, please remind me?"

"In *Trouw* the other day they said the Allies bombarded Düsseldorf for seven weeks straight, *day and night*."

"Well, what did the Germans expect! When they've turned most of France into a circle of hell?"

"I'm only answering your question, Willem."

"These rockets, *broer*, they're the size of oak trees. Going three times farther than before!"

German planes are crossing to England each night. The same dark shapes that Mieke sees through her window return the following morning in the light of dawn. They're back, bellies emptied of bombs, having dropped them down all over London and the countryside. Rob's father studies the shapes of all the planes; he has a book to identify them, which is also hidden, inside of the Dostoevsky. *Misdaad en straf. Crime and Punishment.*

That was the other thing he'd been yelling about—already drunk, getting drunker.

"These are the ones from today: Curtiss P-40 Warhawk. Northrop P-61 Black Widow. *American* planes. Only ten German bombers, total, for three days now."

"This is bad news?"

"No, but this is why they'll try something else. You must go see what they're building out in the dunes. It's the reason they all frog-marched across Holland in the first place. From here they can take a clear shot with these new rockets. They'll go all the way across and hit Brighton and Eastbourne. Canterbury and Dover. And even farther, to London."

"You're mad," her father had said. Going that far, any missile would be pushed off target by the North Sea winds. Even a tiny fraction of a degree means a miss of dozens of miles on the other end. And it would need tons of fuel, weighing it down even more. "It's impossible!"

"Go to the dunes! Go see for yourself."

Mieke had gone to bed at that point. It was nothing new. All they'd done the last few months was fight over things like this. Squabble over the radio, moving little colored buttons around on their rolled-up maps like it was some sort of board game.

Oranje zal overwinnen: Orange will triumph. *O zo!* So there.

THAT NIGHT BEFORE dinner, Mieke's mother asks why her face is covered in soot, even though she already knows the answer.

This has been, for weeks now, Mieke's after-school occupation: she waits until her mother is folding laundry or washing dishes, and then sneaks into the living room, pulls back the metal screen in front of the hearth, and quietly opens the grate at the bottom. She puts her fingers over the hole and feels for heat—but since it is September, it is just the usual cool air rising. Then Mieke gets her whole face over the duct, training her ear against the breeze, which carries with it the words of Mr. and Mrs. Müeller from 3A, the apartment directly beneath them.

Before dinner, Mieke was there to hear a little exchange between them, but in German, so there are bits she isn't sure about.

"Have you seen my . . ." Mrs. Müeller said, and then "*strümpfe*," which Mieke doesn't know. "I washed them yesterday and left them hanging right there on the *ofenrohr*."

German and Dutch words aren't so different, Mieke has figured out. Over the past year she's been picking up bits and pieces. Eventually, Rob's father had been saying, they'll all be forced to learn it. The Krauts are never going away, he says. Another reason Mieke isn't very persuaded by Mr. Wendelgelst and his little blue frog and reading in Dutch. If her uncle is right, won't she need to learn a whole other language soon, anyway?

In any case, Mr. Müeller responded. "Why would I have seen them?"

"Maybe *katze* took them somewhere. *Katze katze?* Where are you, *katze katze?*"

And Mieke heard Mrs. Müeller leave the room. Her husband waited a moment and then left, too, and Mieke had heard the call to come for dinner.

HER MOTHER ASKS her to please go wash up. Her father eyes her as she comes to the sink.

"My little spy," he teases. "You want to join the *verzet*, yeah?"

The resistance. How does someone join? Or is it the sort of thing where you just start doing it?

"They're *Germans*," she insists, speaking of the Müellers.

"Germans who left their home the moment that little rat face took over," her father reminds her. "Believe me, they are the kindest people in this whole building. Besides you, I mean."

"And you," she counters.

"Oh no. Not me. I'm terribly villainous, you see."

Her father twists his thin mustache and urges her back to the table, where they all eat in quiet. Roast parsnips and sugar beets. Mieke hates sugar beets.

Professor Naaktgeboren is still not there, has not been home all day. And no one says why.

THERE ARE EIGHT families in the building, including theirs. On the left side of the building, there are the Von Fliets on the ground floor and the Janssens above them. The Müellers live on the third floor, with the Menkes and the Naaktgeborens at the very top. Across the hall, on the right side of the building, is Mr. DeVries, who lives alone, and beneath him are the unpleasant Smits, who are always having dinner with the Meijmans. Mr. Smit is flabby-faced and small-mouthed, like a weasel. His hair is thin and yet he combs it over as if no one can see he is bald. Mieke's father says the Smits are *medewerkers*, collaborators—that she and Rob are never to speak to them beyond what's simply polite. Though Mieke would be happy to shove Mr. Smit down the stairs undetected, she does think his son Werner is nice—he is older, almost grown himself, and bikes around town after school delivering flowers from their shop, always smiling. Mieke likes to pass him on the narrow stairs. He smells, always, of something sweet. Roses, she thinks. "Hey, chatterbox," he teases her, because when he is around, she can never come up with anything to say. His mother, Mrs. Smit, is so beautiful, her blond hair always pinned up in big swirls, like Fostedína the golden goddess from Rob's fairy-tale book. Mieke hates that she could be married to such a vile person, hates to think they are in cahoots with the Germans.

Below the *medewerkers*, then, on the second floor, are the Vissers and their twin teenage girls, and then finally, on the ground floor, the Meiers—windows dark, door locked. Mieke checks it each day as she goes by on her way to school. A quick rattle, just to be sure, and then she's off.

The windows on the north side are easy to see from the right angle off the main road, not that anyone ever does much of interest. Even the Smits are mostly boring. The only neighbor she cannot easily inspect this way is old Mr. DeVries, across the hall, who keeps his heavy maroon curtains drawn, even in the summer. But her curiosity has led her to an interesting work-around.

A small space above their apartment stretches all the way across the building. The way up to it is a square cutaway in the hallway ceiling between their own apartment and Mr. DeVries's. With the tip of the fireplace poker, Mieke can nudge the hatch aside, standing on her tiptoes. A pull cord comes down, attached to a folding ladder that can then be eased out. She's been practicing and has almost mastered this process. She can get up almost silently in under thirty seconds. Once she pulls the ladder back up and slides the hatch in place, no one has the faintest idea where she is.

Inside, the attic is dark and stuffy. Jammed with extra belongings and old maintenance materials: spools of copper wire and spare light fixtures and rolls of dark tarp. She and Rob have turned it into their own private hideout, and while they've been rummaging around, she's discovered a hole in the insulation where she can peer down through a vent and into Mr. DeVries's apartment. Finally she has some access to a sliver of his living room, and she is surprised to see that it is lavishly decorated, with a fancy Persian rug and fine Indonesian carvings everywhere and a great crystal decanter on the sideboard. She's heard how much he enjoys listening to opera records, but now she can see his phonograph, its brilliantly polished brass, on a fine marble table that must have cost a hundred guilders.

Mieke has been wondering about him. Why he lives alone, and how he has gotten so much money. He reminds her of Moriarty in *Sherlock Holmes*, resplendent in all his finery—she imagines his treasures as the ill-gotten spoils of all his evil schemes.

"He could be a railroad tycoon or a robber baron," Rob suggests.

"Why would anyone who was that rich live in our dumb

apartment building? And why does he dress all ordinary when he goes into town?"

DeVries is hiding something, she is sure of it. Something he doesn't want anyone to know.

THE FOLLOWING DAY on their return from school, they find Mr. Smit outside. He is sweating, his combed-over hair swept back awkwardly, as he touches up the paint on the front steps, but when Mieke and Rob walk up, he sets his brush down and pulls out a new green pack of Eckstein No. 5 cigarettes. The same kind she sees the German soldiers smoking all the time. He slips the pack away in his pocket and lights one of the thin white paper rolls.

"Heil Hitler," he greets them. Mieke winces, hearing those words and looks away. Smit and his family were the first in the neighborhood to join the fascist party, the NSB. Nationaal-Socialistische Beweging. Rob also does not return the greeting, and for a moment Smit stares at them waiting. Slowly he redrapes his fallen hair, but it still looks terrible.

"Robert, is it? Yes?" he asks.

Rob nods, still unwilling to look the man in his beady eyes.

"Werner told me he's seen you coming out of the bookshop."

He gestures to the Janssens' apartment behind them, the couple who own the store and who have continually supplied Rob with children's novels and storybooks this year. *Miep en henny. The Swiss Family Robinson. Alice's Adventures in Wonderland. The Wind in the Willows.*

"How is it you two always have extra money for books?" Smit asks.

"He does chores for the Vissers," Mieke snaps. "We both do."

Smit hums a little as he inhales his cigarette, and she regrets having said anything.

"I haven't seen your father around the building in a few days, Rob," Smit says casually. "He had asked me about putting in some hyacinths. How can I reach him?"

Now Mieke almost breaks into laughter. Did Smit think he

was an SS officer or something? He must think they're both idiots. Rob doesn't answer him, and Smit, finished with the cigarette, flicks it away into the street before picking up his paintbrush again. The children begin to pass him, thinking he's finished, but then he reconsiders.

"Kinderen, kinderen," he says, casting his brush out toward the direction of the dunes. "Let me tell you something that I gather your parents have not."

Mieke pauses, sure she doesn't trust him, but also always intrigued by the idea that someone might know more than she does about anything. It's clear her parents are hiding things.

"We Dutch, we're fine sailors, yes? The best in all of Europe. Look in your history book. It was Holland who ruled the oceans, opened trade with the Orient and the Arabs and the African tribes, a century before the English or the Spanish ever built a galleon. We must take pride in that."

Mieke rolls her eyes. "So why do you say, 'Heil Hitler,' then?"

Smit is not upset by her impudence. In fact, he's delighted she's asked.

"Because! The Dutch and the Germans have the same blood. They are the good soldiers, and we, the good sailors. They've only come here to protect us from these invaders. These aliens, these *Allies* would have taken us over long ago. They act like the Germans are here enslaving us, but anyone can see that's not the case. Look around you, *kinderen*. Yes, there is order, there must be order, but we have our liberties. We have our way of life. I am grateful to Hitler for that, and so should you be."

Mieke wants to grab the bucket of varnish and hurl it at his head. To kick him in the shins and slam her schoolbook into his narrow jaw. But she restrains herself, taking Rob by the hand and dragging him inside, past the foul smell of the resin. All night she'll smell it, rising up through her window, haunting her dreams.

"AUFMACHEN, AUFMACHEN!"

The next morning the knocking at the door wakes Mieke

again, but this time the soldiers do not stay to chat with her father when he comes downstairs. They push inside, waving papers around so rapidly that no one could possibly read them. Mieke gathers the papers don't matter anyway. These men can do what they want, with papers or without them. They come up the stairs, their pounding footsteps echoing louder and louder, the iron nails leaving marks in the wood, and then they bust into the living room and begin rushing around, calling for "Herr Naaktgeboren? Herr Naaktgeboren?" Though Mieke is terrified by their presence—their pistols shifting around on their hips in gleaming leather holsters—she can't help but bite back a smirk. They sound like Mrs. Müeller calling for her cat, as if Rob's father might coolly stretch out from behind the stove at the sound of his name.

But it is no game. What about the copies of *Trouw*? What about the hidden radio? The filter jammer? Her eyes flick to the bookshelf, searching for the Tolstoy and the Dostoevsky. They are gone, she notices. Her father has guessed that this would happen and has already found some hidden place for them. Gone, too, are the dubbeltjes on her mother and Tante Sintje's scarves. *Ba ba ba bum*, Mieke mouths hatefully as the soldiers follow her father into the kitchen, where he has been baking for hours now. She turns to Rob and flashes him the sign of a V with her fingers. He waves at her to cut it out. But they aren't going to hurt a girl, she thinks.

"I have not seen Professor Naaktgeboren since we last spoke. I have no idea where he is."

"And his wife? His children?" the captain asks.

Her father points to Sintje, to Rob and Truus.

The captain's big ears come up round at the top, jutting up over the rim of his hat, dark blue wool with gold embroidery.

"What sort of scuttling cockroach abandons his family?" the captain asks his underling, lips curled cruelly.

"Sir, I don't know, Captain Schneider, sir."

Mieke studies the soldier who answers, whose eyes are rimmed with a pair of owlish glasses. He keeps eying the sobbing Truus. When the captain is not looking, the soldier sticks out his tongue and crosses his eyes in a funny face, to try and amuse the child. It does not work.

Rob gazes sullenly from the doorway to their room. The third soldier turns, bored, quietly inspecting the nail still jutting out of the stained wooden block, where Naaktgeboren flayed the eel last summer. Then Captain Schneider barks some new orders and the men fan out, beginning their hunt through the bedrooms, pushing clothes around in the closets and shouting threats in German at Rob's mother.

Mieke goes on watching. They are not expecting to find Rob's father, she realizes. This is now a punishment for making them look. They're letting them know they can come in anytime, do this anytime. To make them afraid.

Soon the men waltz into Mieke and Rob's room, overturning the mattress and looking in the closet (which smells faintly of vomit, after all this time). One of the soldiers takes care to stomp his ugly muddy boot right on the sheets. And then he kicks her Sherlock Holmes book with his boot's steel toe and sends it into the wall. Rob remains still, all through the raid, except for one moment—when Captain Schneider throws open the dark cedar chest.

"Don't!" Rob calls.

And because he's said this, Schneider is extra rough with it. Slamming the lid, heaving it against the wall. Trying to lift it so he can be sure there's no trapdoor underneath, but even with two men, it is too heavy. It is amazing the trunk does not break, considering how violently he treats it. But the trunk bears not a single chip or scratch when Mieke examines it later. And there are just sweaters and old clothes inside. She's checked a hundred times.

IT IS ALL finished in a few minutes. The soldiers leave, their footsteps receding down the staircase past the doors of each neighbor. The horrendous Mr. Smit stands in his doorway and salutes them as they pass. The toad. When all is over, the mothers begin picking everything up and talking softly amongst themselves, while Mieke's father helps the children find something to eat.

"Will they come back?" Mieke asks.

She can see that his fists are balled, his knees are shaking.

"You can bet on it," he says finally.

And then her father pauses, releases his hands, and reaches out for Rob's shoulder. "Time for school, you two. It's going to be okay. I'm sure we can clear this all up once he's back."

Rob looks up through watery eyes. Smiling, oddly. "They'll never find him," he whispers.

"How do you know?" Mieke asks, but Rob won't answer.

MIEKE IS BACK at her desk at school the following Tuesday, staring out of the window and thinking about the *Sherlock Holmes* mystery that Rob had read, finishing the night before. Holmes and Moriarty had been struggling at the edge of Reichenbach Falls when both men had fallen into the flume and gone down to their deaths.

"Is that the *end*?" Mieke asked as Rob read out the final lines.

She'd let out a cry of anguish so loud that her father had burst in to see what was going on.

"He's dead!" Mieke had wailed.

"*Who's* dead?" her father had asked, clearly panicked.

"Sherlock Holmes," Rob explained dully, showing him the book. "In the book."

The look of quick relief on her father's face soon turned to annoyance.

"Go to bed," her father had scolded. "No more."

Mieke had felt like such a fool. To care so much about a man who'd never even been alive in the first place. In the end, wasn't it all as stupid as believing in fairies and gypsy hexes and Gullin the Boar? But that night, as Mieke had lay there, Rob had turned to comfort her.

"There are three more Sherlock Holmes books over at Janssen's," he whispered. "So he can't be dead, can he?"

Mieke had sat straight up, almost forgetting to be quiet—

certainly forgetting she'd resolved to never be sucked in by some dumb book ever again.

"Let's go tomorrow," she announces. "Right after school."

SITTING THERE NOW, waiting for the end of the day to come, she's barely able to think at all. Mr. Wendelgelst is talking about adding and subtracting, which she understands better than reading. On her desk she digs her fingers into the wood. Holmes must be hiding out, tricking Moriarty. And Rob's father, too—he must be somewhere. And they'd find him very soon.

That's when she hears a roaring outside. A distant swell, and at first she does not know if the roaring is human. If they are sounds of fear or joy or of something else. It grows and grows and is soon so loud that Mr. Wendelgelst sets down the little nub of chalk he's been writing with, midway through a sum, and moves cautiously to the window. He pushes it open with one trembling finger. Mieke sees how scared he is, and then, slowly, the terror melts away. He mutters something under his breath. Tears come to the corners of his eyes like beads of dew.

"It's over," he gasps. "*Kinderen*, it's over!"

Mieke is the very first of her classmates to leap up from her own desk and move to the window he's opened so she can see what is going on. The others aren't far behind. Outside, the park is filled with people. Grown-ups from all over, pouring in from everywhere! Mr. Koot, from the gas station, in his oily coveralls, racing to embrace Dr. Mees, who was just having lunch at the corner shop and still has a soup-stained napkin tucked into the neck of his nice white shirt. There is a chortle at Mrs. Seyss, whose husband digs graves at the cemetery—she's bolted out of the house in her apron and has only flowery bloomers underneath. And what on earth is Mr. Veening doing? A seventy-year-old city councilman, running up and down with two pots, clanging them together like a toddler! It is not exactly a parade. There's no marching or moving in any one direction. All is chaos. Wildness. One honking car horn multiplies and spreads, soon echoed and answered by the horns of all the other cars until it sounds like every car in Holland must be honking. A woman Mieke doesn't recognize rushes by, waving a white tablecloth in the air, prancing like a woodland deer. Absolute jubilation! Mieke has never seen adults act this way before, like her classmates rushing out for recess. And the woman is soon joined by another man, waving the royal orange flag, the one that used to flap up on the pole outside the post office. It catches her by surprise. And then the sunlight turns orange, passing through the fabric, and it tints everyone beneath it. Ten people now are hoisting the flag, higher and higher. Two men trip and fall over, then roll happily in the dust together. Jan Snoek, from the frame shop, is kissing a woman on both cheeks; two old ladies grip each other like they will float away if they don't. There—Mr. DeVries, from across the hall, down on his knees, kissing the paving stones.

Suddenly Mieke is seized by a desire to see the Smits or the Meijmans, down at the butcher shop. Are they the ones looking scared now? Will they be the ones on the run tomorrow?

"Go home, everyone," Mr. Wendelgelst says, his chin trembling. He's weak, suddenly, and has to sit. All the other children begin to rush away. They throw papers and books up into the air, yelling and cheering. Mieke wants to go, too, but she pauses and stays next to Mr. Wendelgelst.

Her teacher is shaking, so Mieke reaches over to ask if he's all right.

"They've retaken Antwerp," he sobs. "The prime minister was on the radio this morning welcoming the Allies to Dutch soil. Oh, God, I thought I'd dreamed it . . ."

Outside, a news report echoes into the streets. Mieke hears those notes from Beethoven's Fifth Symphony, loudly. And then comes the voice of the Radio Oranje host:

Breda, across the border, is about to be liberated. Maastrict is a sea of orange. The Germans are beginning to flee along the Maliebaan. Allied forces are on the move, coming north, and could reach the Hague in only days. Queen Wilhelmina

would soon return from London to retake her place in the
Koninklijk Paleis . . .

Mieke can't find Rob anywhere. She races home as fast as she
can. She can't wait to see her father's happiness, unlocked again.
Now the bakery can be reopened, and Professor Naaktgeboren
will come back. As she runs, she looks for any sign of them—
swarms of Germans in their green jackets, rushing out to break
up the celebration. Or Smit! She wants to see him choking on his
own tongue somewhere, fearful of the troops marching up. There!
Next to Town Hall, a crowd of people are watching as scrambling,
besuited NSB party members rush from the building in terror.
Her father will tell her that night he'd been at the train station
to see for himself: a long line of *landverraders*, hoping to get safe
passage to Germany. One man carrying his typewriter, another
pushing an ornate chest of drawers, trying to get the porters to
check them as luggage. Mieke watches the cars line up, heading
east with bags strapped to the roof. Rob comes home and joins
her. She forgets to ask where he's been. He spots one with an iron
stove sticking out of the trunk. Mieke screams with joy, pointing
so her *neefje* will look: two dozen Kübelwagens moving off. One
with an empty chicken coop lashed to the back. She stands there
and crows in their direction. So marvelous to see that for all the
nonsense about dying for their cause, the Nazis were cowards in
the end.

NIGHT FALLS QUIETLY. Where are the Allies? Some nervousness
settles in. After dinner, her father switches stations on the radio,
hunting for updates about the advance into Breda. But there is
nothing. Outside, the celebrations have all fallen to silence. No
one knows what to expect next. "There should be more news by
now," he keeps saying desperately.

Then comes an angry broadcast warning from the SS, and
even after he lowers the volume, Mieke can make it out from the
darkness of her bed.

*The population must maintain order. It is strictly forbidden
to flee areas that are threatened by the enemy. All orders
from the military commanders must be strictly adhered to
and without question. Any resistance to the occupation forces
will be suppressed with force of weaponry. Any attempt to
fraternize with the enemy or to hinder the German Reich and
its allies in any form will be dealt with harshly; perpetrators
will be shot.*

She falls asleep thinking of those guns in gleaming holsters.
Mustaches being trimmed. Ripe pears in the hands of grinning
pastors. Green hats that swoop around freely like flying saucers.
Japanese courtiers, bowing and dancing beneath the cherry blossoms, with the peak of Mount Fuji there behind them, kissing
the clouds. And then the eel, dark and long, comes up her body
and around her neck, tightening slowly. There, through a sheen of
clear-green water, she can see the boy at the bottom sitting cross-
legged. She reaches in to save him, and—

WAKES UP TO a new day, to a bright sun, and to the sound of more
arguing in the kitchen. Mieke rushes in to check on her father and
finds him sitting there, speaking patiently to the same three German soldiers as before. They're standing in a little circle, hands
on chair backs. Boots tracking mud on the floor. The one with the
glasses is eating one of the fresh loaves of bread as the captain once
again presses for news about Herr Naaktgeboren.

"Naaktgeboren is a suspect in the bombing of the Amsterdam
civil registry office and the destruction of important population
files. This man is wanted by the Third Reich to answer for crimes
of espionage. I assure you we will find him, Meneer Menke."

ON THE LONG walk to school that day, the streets are quiet. There
are Nazis out on the same patrols as before. More Kübelwagens
lined up outside of Meijmans', draped in swastikas. There are no

orange flags at all. Mieke won't see another one for months, and then they will be brought out only to cover the bodies of the dead.

DOLLE DINSDAG. CRAZY Tuesday. Mad Tuesday. That's what they are calling it by the following week. Breda had not been freed after all, it turned out. News spread of the failure of something called Operation Market Garden and the retreat of the Allied forces back across the Rhine.

Now it is all like it never happened. Mr. Wendelgelst reads, as before, from the boring blue frog book. Does math with his chalk. There's no trace of the joy Mieke had seen that day. And outside, the other men sit there in the park with their chess games and their newspapers, quiet and stiff. The mess from the celebration has by now been swept away and put in the bin. The Germans are back at the corner, frequenting the Meijmans' butcher shop like before. And Smit glowers in the hallway worse than ever.

No one, no one, will tell Mieke what's going on.

And Professor Naaktgeboren is still nowhere to be found.

"WHAT'S A POPULATION file?" she asks her father as he works in the kitchen. She helps him roll out the sourdough, and it feels good to stretch and pound at it with her clenched fists. She has imagined her father would get upset about her question, but instead he nearly giggles.

"Last year," he whispers, "ten men dressed in police uniforms broke into the registry office in Amsterdam, where the Germans keep the files on all of us. Where we live. What we do for work. How old we are. Who is a Jew and who isn't. Hundreds and thousands of records used to identify us, to check against our identity cards. These ten men overpowered the guards, jabbed them in the neck with a sedative, and plopped them down in the zoo across the street."

Mieke giggles at this.

"Then they set fire to the records building and destroyed all those population files inside."

"Was Professor Naaktgeboren there?" she asks, wide-eyed. "Was he one of the men?"

Now her father becomes quite serious. "You must never ask. And never repeat that story to anyone. They execute—you know what this word means?"

Mieke nods. She does.

"They *execute*—" he repeats, and then he seems to reconsider the end to his own sentence. "Whomever they please."

ROB DISAPPEARS NEXT. Mieke wakes up on Saturday and cannot find him anywhere. At first she thinks he must have gone without her to search the dunes or climb in the ruins. Which they haven't done in months. Is he sneaking out to visit with his father somewhere? There's something he isn't telling her. Some reason he isn't more upset. If her father vanished, she'd be furious.

An hour later, she at last finds Rob. He's crawled into the Japanese chest in the hallway and closed it on himself. When she opens it, she can see he's been crying. It's a wonder he can even breathe in there—in fact she isn't at all sure how.

"What are you doing?" she demands, but he won't answer. Eventually she finds him something to wipe his nose.

"Let's go to Janssen's," she says, remembering, suddenly—their plan from before Crazy Tuesday. "For the book. Sherlock Holmes."

Rob doesn't respond until she literally jabs him in the side. Only then does he reluctantly uncurl himself and come out of the trunk.

"I don't feel good."

She smacks her hands together like Mr. Wendelgelst does when they're not listening.

"Let's go already. And on the way, we'll go past my dad's bakery."

"Why?" Rob said. "It's all closed up."

She can't explain why she needs to see it, so badly, just now. *Go to the dunes*, her uncle had said. *Go see for yourself.*

In her mind she turns another word around and around. *Espionage*. Professor Naaktgeboren, a real-life spy? And what about Tante Sintje?

She wishes she could tell Rob that his father wasn't a scuttling cockroach. But she's promised, so she doesn't. If she is to be a good spy, like her uncle, she must learn to keep secrets—even from family.

They keep enough from her, anyway.

She and Rob speed off through the streets, north toward the dunes. The avenues have been blocked off with low stockades. Wooden X's, wound in barbed wire, as if they expect the American tanks to come rolling through any moment. Mieke fixes her eyes on the horizon. She suddenly needs to see the bakery, the little square of it there, nestled into the rest of the skyline. Of course she won't see the glow of the fires inside the windows. But if she can go back, stand right where she stood when it all started. If she looks up, this time instead of black birds advancing on Rotterdam, will it be Allied planes coming to save them all?

But she cannot find the bakery. It is not there.

They pedal faster, getting closer.

When they finally reach the area, she sees that it isn't only the bakery that's gone. The entire area has been razed to the ground. And it goes on, a thousand yards to the east and to the west. It wasn't as clear from farther away, but now she sees the bare molars of the foundation stones, still there in the ground, like the footprints of the ruins out in the woods. But there the stones are smoothed over, moss-covered by the centuries. Here the cement is all sharp to the touch, the wounds fresh. It takes a minute to even find the place where the bakery should be. All that remains is the black pit of the basement, covered haphazardly with a few loose planks of wood.

"How did this happen?" she demands to Rob, to no one.

But what she wants to know is how could her father not have told her.

Rob carefully nudges some of the wood aside and stares down inside. It is all dark, but she can soon make out the shapes of the clay vats, all still there—too heavy to be pulled out, she guesses. Two have been smashed. She can smell it vaguely, the stale flatness of dough that has expired. But the third vat is still intact.

"Lower me down," she commands.

He shakes his head. "You'll get stuck."

"I won't. You'll pull me out."

Rob reluctantly does as she asks, and after a good deal of grunting and dangling, Mieke's feet touch the cool, bare earth at the bottom. She lets go of Rob's hands and moves to open the hatch on the side of the third vat, in vague hope that the glop inside might still be alive—but the tangy sour smell she's been hoping to find is long gone. What remains is sharp, acidic, all wrong. Still, she holds her breath so she can see inside. It is very dark, but she can see that all those little constellations of air bubbles are no longer peppered through like before. The stuff inside has separated, a thin layer of greenish oil on top of a wide, dense pancake beneath.

It is dead. It has been left for dead.

How has her father let this happen?

That's when the ground starts shaking all around her, and the wooden planks above her start to rattle and shift. One teeters and falls, inches from her head. Mieke is screaming, and then hands are on hers. Rob is there, hanging down, yanking her up.

"Bomb!" he yells.

Only there's no explosion. At first she does not know what to make of it. A warm wave of air passes by her and forces her eyes shut. When she opens them only a second later, she is lost in a cloud of white and gray. Dust stings like a sandstorm. A distant rumble is consolidating into the hiss and roar of a firecracker, and through the haze around her she sees a brilliant column of light rising. It is pure magic at first. There's a piece of her heart that seizes on the stories Rob used to read her about the fairies returning from Luilekkerland.

The light goes from white to green to gray, and gradually she begins to recognize a shape at the top: a gleaming silver nose cone, a rigid center length. And then it is moving too fast to take in as more than a blur, growing smaller as it goes higher and higher past the clouds and into the sky, leaving behind nothing but a great snake of yellow smoke.

And then another eruption, not much farther away, and a second burst of light follows the first into the skies.

Her fear is all in the surprise of it. She doesn't understand yet what these are or where they're pointed. That these are the rockets her father had said were impossible. That in only a few minutes they may well crash down onto Kensington Gardens and Piccadilly Circus and even 221B Baker Street—Mieke knows Sherlock Holmes doesn't really live there, but she thinks it might be a real place anyway. *Someone* lives there.

And after the initial violence of the sounds fades away, she has a moment to consider how beautiful they are, rising and rising into the pure blue sky.

Mieke ventures through the dust clouds toward the source of the noise. Rob comes after her but can't keep up. At the edge of the dunes there are more wooden stockades, strung with more barbed wire, with signs she can't read but she's sure are warning her to keep out. She slips easily between the barriers and won't notice until later that she's gotten a half-dozen cuts along her calves and forearms. The soldiers ignore her; they're all rushing over to look as well.

There are long fat tire marks on the pathway. She follows these farther and farther, gagging through the terrible stench of burned rubber and—she can't be sure—potatoes? She comes upon a place where the sand has all simply melted away. In wide rivers it has flowed out, then cooled instantly and hardened to glass, as if the Boar with the Golden Bristles has plowed his way along the sand, flames dancing off his cloven feet. She can't get close enough to see inside the hole, though she tries, but it is so hot that she has to turn back.

OTHER PEOPLE ARE starting to gather around by the time she returns, back past the barbed wire. She finds Rob waiting for her. He asks her what she saw, but she's speechless. Both are so thickly dusted that they look like they've spent a month in the fireplace. He takes her hand, and they walk slowly back to their bicycles and walk them all the way home, pushing against a steady tide of people going the other way, to see what's happened. In the coming months this will all be a regular occurrence. The vengeance weapons have arrived. V2. Great cylinders, the size of whole buildings, chained onto the trucks out in the pure white sand. She thinks about what her father said, about Düsseldorf reduced to rubble. About France, circling hell. It is happening to the East and to the West, too. That's what a war *is*, she thinks. And now the missiles go north and the only hope is rescue from the south. Until then, she is in the center of it all. She will see six more launches that day before nightfall. Each one, Death departing.

"I NEED TO show you something," Rob whispers when they return to the apartment. The grown-ups are all crowded in the front room, leaning out the windows, gazing out toward the dunes— and so is everyone else up and down the street. Waiting to see if another rocket goes off, not knowing that they will be going off now, every hour, every day, until the war ends. Really ends.

Rob beckons Mieke into the hallway. "Can you keep a secret? I'll show you where my father is."

So she was right. He has known, all along.

Rob squats down next to the dark cedar trunk and begins to tell her how it had happened, early that morning, long before the sun rose.

That day before the Germans came, someone else had come to the building asking for Rob's father. He'd heard his father going down to the door to the apartment. Rob had climbed up on the dresser to look out, just as Mieke had taught him. The man had whispered so softly that Rob had barely made it out. "Naaktge-boren?"

"Yes," he'd heard his father answer. "Can I help you, Officer?"

It was someone in the Dutch police force. "Look at my badge. The name. Do you see?"

"Officer Naaktgeboren," his father's voice whispered back.

"Yes," the man said. "I was reading over my list, and I saw your name. I don't have time to warn everyone. I only chose you because of the name."

"Chose me for what?"

"There will be a raid in a few minutes. The soldiers are gathering in the square. They will come to the door. We only just got the lists."

Rob waited for his father to reply, to thank the man, but there was no answer. Only the sound of rushing movement through the hall. His father flew past like an arrow. Outside, the shadow of the other Naaktgeboren, moving off toward the square. There was a squeaking then, in the hallway, and Rob saw his father's shoulders and the back of his head. He'd lowered himself inside the chest. With tender fingers, he'd kept the lid from slamming shut and waking everyone. Then he paused, turned, and looked at his son through the opening.

Was his father really hiding inside? How could he fit? Rob was sure he must be dreaming.

"Go back to bed," his father said, eyes soft. "When they ask, you say you don't know where I am. Promise."

Rob promised, but then stepped forward quickly as his father disappeared. He touched the cedar chest, and he simply ceased to be there anymore.

It wasn't possible. But he wasn't dreaming, either.

When Rob opened the chest again, there was just the usual jumble of old blankets and papers and other things from Rotterdam inside. He rifled around for a minute but could not find anything unusual at all. He shut the lid quietly.

That's when he noticed the motion in the wood. In the carving. The Japanese men and women were moving about, dancing, impossibly, their bodies shifting in a silent dance around the court floor, while the emperor gazed on from his throne to one side. And there, just there, in a shadow behind the mighty one's chair, Rob saw his father, dressed as he had been a moment before, about to slip away. His father turned, all made of wood now, an inch tall, and carved now, like the others. His father's little brown eyes locked onto his. He lifted a hand to wave and then ducked away, gone.

AS ROB FINISHES telling Mieke the story, she is not sure what to say. He's lit up, excited. Happily, he sinks down next to the Japanese chest and points to the carvings on the side.

"Look here," he breathes. "See him? Promise you won't tell."

Mieke studies the faces of all the little men and women inside, and once more she feels like they aren't quite where they were before, though she can't say what has changed. But she doesn't see anything unusual.

"You see?" he asks, smiling so widely that it scares her. "They're *never* going to find him."

No, there's nothing there. Nothing, no matter how hard she stares.

Outside, the world shakes, her father yells, and her mother and Sintje cry as another rocket goes up into the sky.

And Mieke, though she sees nothing in the wooden carvings, loves Rob so much that she says, "Yes. Yes, I see. Oh, Rob. There he is!"

THE EEL IN THE WELL

~

There is a legend from the Low Countries about a young boy who went fishing for bream in a creek in the woods and unexpectedly caught one of us instead. Terrified, he threw the poor eel into a nearby well and ran off. In the way of children, he soon forgot all about it. Only years later did he happen to pass the same spot and see the well had been abandoned, sealed with a heavy stone. The man felt a deep regret for having killed one of us in such a thoughtless way. Such an awful way to die, slowly starving inside a circular prison! And as the years went on, whenever he had bad luck in his life, this young man wondered if there was perhaps some curse on him. A few times even, he had traveled out to visit the well, fully resolved to open it back up and bury the decomposed body in apology. Perhaps his luck would change? But each time he'd just stand there a while, gazing down, before wandering off having done nothing but poke at his own guilt.

It went on like this all his life. This man lived to be a hundred years old. He never told a soul about the eel in the well until the day he died. His own children had grown old and died by then, and his grandchildren were middle-aged with children of their own. At last the old man whispered the facts of his crime, that he hoped and prayed that the curse would die with him.

And then he did.

Of all the things an ancient man might confess to his heirs on his deathbed, it was one of the strangest ever heard of in their village. His grandchildren took it as merely the rantings of a senile old man, even though he'd otherwise had his wits about him.

But when they repeated the tale to their own children, one little girl was sure that she knew the very well that her great-grandfather had been talking about. She and her friends played on it all the time, out there in the woods, and had been warned to never move the stone from on top of it or they might fall in and become trapped inside.

Soon enough, this girl grew to be a woman. By then the old village had become a small town, full of electric lights and combustion engines. It scarcely resembled the place her great-grandfather had lived in. But she never forgot about his odd confession. And whenever she had bad luck in her own life, she'd consider that perhaps his curse had passed on to her. Nothing bad that she'd done herself, but rather something carried out of the past. She sometimes dreamed about the well, a dark tunnel leading away into blackness, a thing hidden at the bottom still thrashing around, making its wet noises.

At last she organized some friends to go out to the well with her and push away the mossy capstone. Once they had managed to shove it off, the woman secured herself with a thick cable and took a flashlight in one hand and rappelled slowly to the bottom of the hole. The air swarmed with angry flies and spiders, and centipedes crawled all around her. It grew more damp as she went farther down, but in the beam of her flashlight she could see there was barely an inch of water at the bottom. She reached down into the shallow waters with one hand, grasping for anything—expecting at best she'd locate some half-dissolved bones.

But you know what she found instead.

The eel. Still alive. At the sight of that beautiful open sky above, our brethren came to life and swirled onto her arm, eager to escape its prison—ready to return to us. It had been lying in wait, barely moving, almost entirely still, biding its time in the dark, for over a century. The poor woman called to be pulled up. As her neighbors tugged her skyward, she fought the eel on her arm like it was a viper.

But we are not snakes. We are not venomous, nor vengeful. And we are not immortal, either. We are merely patient—so patient, you see.

The very moment the eel sensed the clean fresh air, it leapt gladly away, sliding off as calmly as if it were merely a hundred years late for its last appointment.

The woman covered the old well and never returned. If she lived to be a hundred herself, she would never forget that day. How the span of all those many lives had been, for the eel, merely a brief dark pause between eternities.

—V.S.

GOUDA

~

Will had his go-to story about his father, and it was this. At age six, Will and some friends from the neighborhood had gotten the idea to open a lemonade stand. They took a tub of Country Time powder from someone's pantry and a jug and some cups. Will had spelled LEMONADE in bright, attractive colors. They'd been out there the better part of the day, and business had been good. Just before five o'clock, when the mothers began sounding the call for dinner, Will had tallied their earnings at $7.50, or $2.50 each. He'd already begun deciding which comics he was going to buy that Saturday when a man rushed toward them from the trees. He was wearing a dark blue bandanna over the lower part of his face.

It was Will's father, no doubt about it, with a bit of rope in one hand that had been tied into a lasso. He didn't snag anyone with it, but he did whip it around in a sufficiently terrifying way that Will's friends fled, leaving him there alone. Dumbfounded, Will watched his father grab the $7.50 and mime shooting guns into the air.

"That's ours," Will tried to say, but he couldn't make the words form. Not because he was scared—it was just his dad, after all—but because he could not understand what was happening.

"You've been robbed by the Blue Bandit!" his father hooted. "That'll teach you a lesson!"

Then his father pushed the stand over and ran off into the woods with the money.

Will's friends wanted to know what the hell was the matter with his dad. He said that he had no clue. He helped clean up the mess and went home.

There he found his father standing in the kitchen, grinding fresh hamburger for his famous meatloaf—acting as if nothing had happened.

The blue bandanna was gone. His father didn't look up, even.

He just said, "Hey, buddy, wash your hands. Dinner should be ready in a few minutes."

"We want our money back."

"What money, sweetie?" his mother had asked.

"My friends and I worked hard all day and then Dad came and took all our money."

"Me?" His father was affronted. "Why would I do that?"

"Come on. You did. You had on a blue bandanna, and you took it."

His father went wide-eyed. "Are you telling me that you were robbed by the *Blue Bandit*?"

"Stop it!" Will yelled.

"I heard he'd been spotted around these parts!" his father whispered. "You and your friends should have brought some protection."

His mother's face: trying to hide her embarrassment, unsure what to say or do. Will doubled down. If this was a lesson in toughness, fine. He could be tough.

"Give us our money back—*right now*."

"The Blue Bandit is a piece of work," his father continued. "Sounds like he did you a favor, teaching you to watch your back."

"It was *you*."

But his father shook his head, baffled. His mother pulled out the seasoning for the meatloaf and did nothing.

All through dinner, Will had begged, cried, and finally thrown a fit. In the morning Will found the missing money slipped under his pillow. But nothing ever got his father to admit that he'd been the Blue Bandit.

Later Will would search for the bandanna, but it never turned up.

"COUNTRY TIME . . . COUNTRY Time . . . tastes like good old-fashioned lemonade . . ." Will sang the old jingle under his breath as he pushed an oversize shopping cart through the Sports Drinks aisle of Costco. The gigantic 82.5-ounce tubs they sold still had almost the same design as the one he remembered from his childhood: the canister made to look like it was a curving fence of wooden slats painted yellow; the logo centered in a brown unpainted section. A little green circle declared that one could make from it a staggering *thirty-four quarts* of lemonade. Lemonade forever! Lemonade eternal! Never again shall you want for lemonade! Everything in the store was like this, and Will was in a general awe—he had gotten used to the smaller city grocery stores, not people buying thirty-packs of mac and cheese, six bottles of ketchup yoked together, and three pallets of bottled water, as if the apocalypse was nigh. As if the apocalypse was always nigh.

But clearly his oma loved it.

She moved confidently beside him, leaning hard against her own cart, breathing heavily, after dismissing his offer for one of the motorized scooters the store provided. Eagerly she pointed to the items she wanted him to lift down into the basket. Thirty-six rolls of triple-ply toilet paper. Seventy-eight ounces of dish detergent. Eight jumbo tubes of toothpaste—Colgate brand, of course. He did his best to help her, even as he did so mostly with one usable hand. How did she ever manage to shop here without help? Everything in the store was bulky, and also often quite heavy.

Will thought sometimes about the way the grocery stores had been in Düsseldorf. He and Teru would stop by the store together after they were done at work, to grab just what they needed until tomorrow. He found himself, more and more, longing for that simple moment in their lives. Days lived one at a time. Love abounding and everything else in reasonable quantities—a one-room apartment with two hard-backed chairs and a lumpy futon; a teapot for heating water and a pantry with three shelves; a grocery store the size of a tennis court, with blessedly only a few options for each item.

In any case, his grandmother would be better off shopping at a little local place or even having things delivered—but it seemed important to her to see the ample choices, to seize the wrapped-together boxes of family-size Cheerios in her hands. The promise of so many breakfasts to come.

"So I'm definitely making you my enchiladas . . ." Will said, grabbing a mesh sack of bell peppers and another of avocados. "And I can do a veggie lasagna if you're into that."

Oma nodded at each of these, excited at the prospect of a packed freezer.

Will thought about how, while he was growing up, his friends would always talk in school about these incredible traditional family meals: Feasts of the Seven Fishes, or Passover seders, or Lunar New Year banquets. Sauce that took all Sunday to cook. Dumplings pressed by their great-grandmother's method. Recipes handed down from generation to generation. His own family had none of this.

He turned to his grandmother then and asked, "What about something Dutch? Should we make some Dutch food?"

She frowned. "Kroketten take forever. So much oil wasted to fry them all . . . such a pain."

Just then Will felt a buzz in his pocket. Thinking it might be Teru, he checked, but it was a message from his mother.

I called your office. they said you weren't in this week?

He sighed and texted back. Took a few days off. I'm down at Oma's.

The reply was quick. She's OK?

Twisted ankle. A couple stitches. Fine otherwise.

Will caught up with Oma, who had rolled on slowly without him.

"How about *ten pounds* of beets?" he joked as she came to the edge of the produce section.

"Absolutely not." She laughed, waving at the mesh sacks of purple lumps.

That morning, as Will had nursed his hangover away with large cups of coffee, she'd told him more about the final year of the war. About Crazy Tuesday and the fascistic neighbors and the sudden disappearance of her uncle, the professor. Will had known vaguely that she'd lived through the end of the war, but he'd never asked much about it, had never cared. He'd never thought much about being Dutch, or half Dutch. It had never meant very much to him. He remembered being grateful at school that no one had ever teased him for being Dutch.

Because what would they even say?

He recalled a line from a movie: *Austin Powers*—one of the sequels. He'd been dragged to see it during college. Michael Caine, playing the British spy's snooty father, snaps at one point, "There are only two things I can't stand in this world: people who are intolerant of other people's cultures, and the Dutch."

Will could still remember how the audience had *howled*. The joke, he'd realized, depended on the contradiction between the two things, but also on the absolute benignity of Dutchness. If Caine had said Mexicans or Polacks or the Chinese or just about anything else, the joke would have been repulsive. But it was fine to hate the Dutch because it was plainly absurd. Being Dutch meant nothing. How could someone hate nothing?

AFTER A WHILE Will and his grandmother moved to the corner of the store where the refrigerated goods were stored, and she moved straight to the case filled with dairy products. She seized four wedges of orange-blond cheese encased in rich red wax. *Gouda*, which Will knew instantly. He'd seen it as a boy, being sold from a cart in Delft in wheels the size of his father's chest. The monger had sliced some thinly for them to eat right there on the steps of the Oude Kerk as Will's father had told him about his great-grandfather who had done the elaborate inlaid woodworking inside the Hague, where they tried war criminals. The following day they'd gone to see the International Court of Justice. People called it the Peace Palace. And up in the vaulted ceilings were these immense intricate puzzles of wooden pieces, shades of reds and browns that formed vast scenes: hillsides covered in tulips, thoroughfares populated by burgomasters and farmers and boatmen. So vivid that they seemed to move about on their own. Hundreds of thousands of pieces of wood in harmonious assemblage. Like the cheese, this masterpiece was a part of him. Deep inside his DNA, before he even knew what that was. *This is who you are*, it said. *You are made of this.*

"DO I EVER remind you of him?" Will asked his grandmother suddenly.

Mieke, who had been inspecting an eighteen-pack of eggs for cracks, did not realize what he meant at first. But then she saw the wan look on her grandson's face.

"Not so much," she lied, reaching up to tousle his hair. Her hand found the feathery locks at the base of his neck—even this was just the same as her son's had been at Will's age. And it didn't help that he had borrowed a flannel shirt that morning and a pair of old blue jeans that she'd thought at first had once belonged to her husband. But now she was seeing them in the store's fluorescent lights, she was beginning to think that maybe they had been her son's. There were things up on the second floor she hadn't seen in years.

"You're taller," she said finally.

"Sorry to bring him up."

"That's okay," she said, closing the egg carton up. "You're allowed."

"Teru was asking about him last night," Will said. "How old he was when—"

Mieke interrupted. "I thought I heard something last night. Was she upset about something when she left?"

"Just—" Will said. "This thing came up and we've been—it's sort of complicated. We'll work it out after she lands in Japan."

And Mieke said, "I see," as if this were the most natural thing in the world, and not a crisis that Will seemed to be strangely oblivious to—that's what it would have amounted to if she'd ever left Rob to spend ten weeks by herself, halfway around the world. Yes, times had changed; the culture today was different. People weren't marrying at seventeen anymore or having babies at twenty. Mieke had been a new mother in a city halfway around the world from her own parents, barely speaking the language. Alone all day in the apartment while Rob worked at the Colgate offices, practicing reading and spelling, feeling those mysterious squeezings and squirmings inside her, day by day. To pass the time she'd started to walk down to the movie theater on the corner, which was playing *Gone with the Wind*. She'd watched it once a week, repeating the dialogue to herself the whole way. Soon her English was good enough that Rob bought her the book. Different from the movie, but still she could match up many of the words to the lines she knew by heart from the film. "Frankly, my dear, I don't give a damn," as Clark Gable said it, and in the book, originally, "My dear, I don't give a damn."

Suddenly she realized that Will had still been talking the whole time, but Mieke couldn't understand what he was saying. She tried to nod and smile as if all this about Japan was clearly exciting news, because that's how Will seemed to be presenting it, even if she could see all the worry in his eyes that he was trying to hide.

"Can you hear me okay?" he was asking.

Mieke looked at him and shook her head, tapping at her hearing aid, which was producing a low white noise and nothing else.

Will leaned close. *"There's a desk on the other side of the store where they'll adjust those!"*

They'd moved on to the next aisle, Will struggling to lift a fifteen-pound bag of flour into the cart before Mieke moved to help him.

"Between the two of us," she said, "we're almost capable!"

"I was reading last night," Will said loudly. "You can actually mix up your own sourdough starter. What do you think? It takes about a week, but then we can use it to make real bread, right at home. Just like your father used to do."

Was he planning to stay a *week*? Why?

"Don't you need to be back at your office?"

"I'm taking a few days off," he said. "My partner can keep things running without me."

He seemed less than confident in this assertion but kept talking.

"I want to make sure you're okay. And I want to hear the rest of your story anyway," Will said, busily nestling a sweaty rotisserie chicken into the cart. "Where did Opa's father end up?"

"Who?"

"The professor. Naaktgeboren. I'm assuming he wasn't really living in the trunk carving."

Mieke looked down at the cart, at the plastic spinach container, the bag of celery, the fat black package of asparagus.

"Groente," she said.

"What's that mean?"

"Vegetable."

"What about vegetables?"

"No. There was a town," she said, "in southern Holland, called Groente."

"There was a town called vegetable?"

"It wasn't really even a town. Just an area where they farmed carrots and onions and cabbage. And there was a little prison out there that the Nazis turned into a camp."

"Just what kind of camp are we talking about?" Will asked.

But she could see that he already knew.

Before they'd left for Costco she had been flipping through

the book Shoshana had given her, which so far had been mostly odd stories about eels, but in the next chapter she'd seen this word, over and over—Groente. Groente. Groente. But she'd been too scared, somehow, to read more. All this time she'd been saying she wanted to know what had really happened to her uncle. To solve "The Peculiar Disappearance of Professor Naaktgeboren" once and for all. Only now that an answer was possibly close at hand, she found herself near-petrified.

Mieke was aware they were standing in a bustling Costco produce aisle on a busy Saturday afternoon, their cart blocking people trying to get by. Already it was welling up inside of her. Dizzyingly. How long had she pushed these thoughts away? How long had she stood there in front of them pretending, saying over and over, *Frankly, my dear, I don't give a—*

Her grandson moved to help her stay on her feet. "Hey, let's pay for all this and get you home," he said quickly.

Mieke walked slowly with him, holding one hand against the cart to push and wrapping the other around his elbow. As she touched the sleeve, she was more certain than ever that the flannel shirt had been her son's. Before.

What else of his was up there? What else might Will find if he went poking around?

THERE WAS A long line at the checkout, and as Will and his grandmother came to the back of it, he heard someone calling out her name. "Mieke! Mieke!" She did not seem to register the voice, and Will wished they had time to stop and have her hearing aids checked, but he wanted to get her home before she got too tired. So he tapped her on the shoulder and pointed toward the man calling to her from the next line over.

"Giancarlo!" she said happily. "Oh, hi. Hello!"

"Good to see you!" the man called back, his own cart full of prepared foods from the back counter area, along with a very large case of red-and-white Budweiser cans.

"This is my grandson, Will," she called. "I showed you his picture. Remember?"

The man waved at Will and Will waved back, smiling, studying the man with the powdery-gray hair. "Your wife is Asian," he announced.

"She sure is," Will said, not entirely comfortable.

"Giancarlo is the one who took me to the hospital," his grandmother explained.

"Oh! Very good," Will said. "Thank you so much."

He suddenly felt unwell again, but he couldn't think why. "Thank you for doing that."

"No problem at all," he said. "Your grandmother is very nice company."

She blushed and Will suddenly felt a strange dizziness coming over him. The whole warehouse suddenly swimming before his eyes, and a strange chirping noise that didn't seem to be coming from anywhere or heard by anyone else. He rubbed at his ears, then his eyes.

"Oma," he said suddenly, "I'll be right back. I just need to use the restroom."

AND THERE, SOMETHING passed over him. A wash of cold air, as if some specter had slid right through the place he'd been standing. When it passed, he was sweaty and lightheaded, about to throw up. He thrust himself into one of the stalls and locked it tightly behind him. There were, he was vaguely aware, a few others in there: a father in a Cubs hat with his two sons, washing their small hands in the sink. An old man by the urinals. Will closed his eyes and tried to steady himself, ashamed to be vomiting in front of strangers, unsure if he could keep himself from doing so. He sat there a while. "Hey, buddy. You okay?" someone was calling. The jagged letters etched into the painted wall seemed to be shifting around, spelling words he couldn't parse. *You've been robbed by the Blue Bandit!* He heard his father's voice like it was beside him, but he knew it wasn't.

"You okay in there? Buddy?"

AFTER A FEW deep breaths, Will felt steadier. There were still thin flashes of light against his closed eyelids, swirls of shapes and colors, but his chest was untightening. Just a little panic attack, he told himself. A pair of nerve bundles called the amygdala fires off a signal to the hypothalamus, which relays it to the adrenal glands. The bloodstream floods with cortisol and adrenaline. Breathing rate increases. Blood diverts to arms and legs. Cellular metabolism prioritizes glucose to the brain. *Fight or flight?* Whichever way, you'll be ready. Will remembered the lecture hall, the sweaty teaching assistant going over the diagrams, the scribbling of his own pen on his notepad. Will reached into his jacket pocket and found the pregnancy test inside, still in its purple box. He took it out and read the words on it, over and over, until he felt himself settle down. *Manufactured in Düsseldorf,* he saw for the first time, in fine print. *Schwangerschaftstest.*

It felt like a sign—or enough of one that at least he forgot, for a moment, that he didn't believe in signs.

BEVEL

~

Mieke's father wants them to bake Truus a birthday cake, so he sets aside some time from his afternoon breadmaking, when Mieke and Rob get home from school. Her mother takes Sintje and the other children out for a walk so that father and daughter can get down to work. First, he shows Mieke how to spread some butter around on the two round pans and then to toss a small bit of flour onto the greased surface. Gingerly, then, she lifts the pan and taps it like a drum with her fingertips, revolving the tin circle at an angle so that the loose flour tumbles around and becomes suspended on the buttered surface. Together, he tells her, the flour and butter will keep the cakes from sticking and add an extra bit of crispness to the edges.

"Eggs. Three raps each," her father says, and demonstrating how to break the first. "Never crack on the edge of the bowl, but tap, tap, tap—flat against the table. Good! That way no itsy-bitsy shards of shell go inside to pierce the yolk."

Now he cups her small palms in his larger ones and shows her how to separate the whites between her fingers, letting the boogery goo fall through into one bowl so that the tighter yellows can be set down gently in another. Next they take turns violently whisking the butter and sugar together until the lumpy mass joins with the air to form something unexpectedly fluffy and off-white. At last it is time to sift the flour and the Droste's cocoa with the bicarbonate—only when her father looks in the cupboard for this final ingredient, it is missing.

"Sintje keeps using it to whiten her teeth," he says, clucking his tongue in disapproval. "I bet she left the box in the bathroom."

"I'll get it," Mieke promises, already hurrying off down the apartment's hallway. As she runs, she can hear her father singing to himself, one of the old French tunes he learned during his apprenticeship in Paris, before she was born. Songs he hasn't sung since the bakery closed. *"Parlez-moi d'amour . . . Redites-moi des choses tendres."*

In the bathroom, Mieke hunts around in the cabinets for the little box of bicarbonate powder where Sintje keeps her other cosmetics. There are rouge powders and eyeliners and paints for fingernails. Mieke has never been terribly interested in these things before, has never wanted to look like the grown-up women she knows who wear them—Mrs. Meijman gets done up almost like a clown some days! Though Mieke does think fondly about Mrs. Smit sometimes. The way all those beautiful shades seem completely natural on her.

The funniest thing is that Mieke never sees Sintje wear them, and she wonders why her aunt has them at all. Looking nice never seems to be on her mind. She wears all dark colors, never makes up her face, and seems so sour all the time. It is hard to imagine her, all dolled up—

THE ROAR OF a rocket blast. Off to the north, the second one that hour. With each eruption of noise outside from the rockets, Mieke sees, in her mind's eye, the white columns of heat and smoke rising into the chilly blue air. She hears the little window in the bathroom rattling. Outside there's a sharp hiss and then a slow fading rumble.

When it goes wrong, it sounds different. There's silence, then. The hiss cuts out too soon, and that's when everyone drops to the roadway or the floor. If the rockets fail—they fall. Hopefully somewhere out in the North Sea, but when the winds and the angles are right, they come back toward the beach or the forest. Last week there was a fire that went on out there for hours before it burned out, and a dense woodsmoke filled the streets for a day. And if a rocket can land in the woods, miles out of town, then it can land on them. That's what Mieke fears most.

Each time the roar diminishes as it should, she whispers a little prayer of thanks. It's only then that she imagines the rocket coming down, instead of on her, then on some British girl in a place called London, living in a cold dark hunger.

"ARE YOU ALL right, *liefje*?" her father calls from the kitchen.

She realizes that she's been just standing there, frozen in place, for a minute or two, holding the bicarbonate, breathing shallowly, a cold wetness on her forehead.

"Yes, Papa," she yells back and then carries the bicarbonate down the hallway, feeling her hands begin shaking.

"I thought you fell in," her father jokes when she comes in.

She does not answer. Carefully, smiling less now, she helps add the bicarbonate and stir the dry ingredients into the wet ones. As she does, she slowly stops shaking. Everything begins to feel normal again. *Whatever that means.*

LATER, WHEN THE cake has been assembled and frosted in a beautiful rose color, the others come home and Truus is happy and surprised. They gather around the table as her father lights a little blue candle for the top of the cake. Mieke stares wordlessly at her aunt, just standing there in the kitchen like always, singing and pretending to smile for Truus's sake. The orange glow of the candle flitting across her features in the darkness as she sings the familiar birthday song.

Lang zal ze leven,
lang zal ze leven,

lang zal ze leven,
In de gloria,
In de gloria,
In de gloria,
Hip, hip, hip, hoera!
Hip, hip, hip, hoera!
Hip, hip, hip, hoera!

THE FOLLOWING AFTERNOON, Rob rushes ahead of Mieke in his eagerness to get back and have one of the remaining slices of cake before anyone else can. Normally Mieke would bolt after him, unwilling to let him win, even if she is not particularly in the mood for cake, but that day she is so lost in her thoughts that she hardly notices him taking off at all. But just a block or two later, Mieke looks ahead at their corner and sees Tante Sintje holding a large black bag, getting onto the tram that runs up the center of Laan Van Meerdervoort. Sometimes she takes it east, farther into town, especially if she has some business to deal with over at the government offices. But Mieke notices that this time her aunt is boarding on the other side of the street, getting on a westbound tram instead. It is unusual to see anyone going out in that direction, where there is little left in the way of shops or stores. The Germans have razed most of the properties between them and the dunes to make more room for launching the rockets.

Mieke runs up quickly and hops onto the tram at the very back, just as it begins to pull away. She's not sure what she's doing—she has no ticket, no money. There's almost nobody left in the back car except a few German soldiers who look at her dismissively and resume their conversation.

The tram creaks along for another mile until it reaches the final stop before turning around. Mieke watches her aunt step out of the car and lug the heavy bag along out toward the edge of town. Mieke leaps down lightly, trying to hide, though there is not much cover and no one else out on the road at all. But her aunt is not looking behind her, clearly determined. At last, Sintje stops at the side gate to one of the gardens belonging to the Ockenburgh estate. It is the last big house before the woods begin, and beyond the edge of it are the places where Mieke and Rob once built their houses for the fairies. It all feels like ages ago, now. Mieke had learned all about the enormous white villa at school, which had been built in the seventeenth century by a wealthy physician. During the last war, Belgian soldiers had camped out there and built a long airstrip on the grounds. And when this war had started, the Germans seized it and began using it as one of their bases of operations.

Or at least that's what they said.

Mieke thinks back on a summer day last year, when she and Rob had gone there at the urging of his father. It had been dusk— not really a safe time to be moving about, but back then the Germans had been more accommodating. The professor had brought a pair of binoculars with him and told the children that they were going birdwatching. But he was not watching the little sandy dune birds at all. Instead, he told Rob to train the glasses on the airfield, through the fence, from across the clearing where the three of them had been concealed in the trees.

Rob, who loved identifying the different kinds of German planes with his guidebook, was excited to gaze at them up close. And when he first looked out, he was whispering all their names.

"Fokker G.Is! A Messerschmitt Bf 110!"

"Are they?" his father had said back, smiling. "Look closer."

But Rob could not see whatever it was he was supposed to see. In the end, Mieke had yanked the binoculars from her impossible cousin so she could see for herself.

Through the round eyeholes, she saw great green and silver wings of airplanes. Propellers and cockpits and landing gear. But there was something *off* about them.

It took a moment to really see clearly.

"They're . . . pretend," she'd whispered finally. "Painted. It's all made of wood."

And the professor had stifled a giggle as Rob reseized the binoculars from Mieke so he could confirm what she'd seen.

"A whole fleet of fake airplanes!" the professor had exclaimed.

"But why?" Mieke had asked.

"They want the Allies to think that this is where they have their planes. These are decoys, so the British won't bomb the real airstrip, farther inland."

"Will they fall for it?"

"We'll see they don't."

Mieke had laughed, not sure what else to do. And what had he meant by "we"?

"I wanted you two to see this," the professor said. "To remember. The Germans are extremely dangerous, don't get me wrong. But in the end, they're as hollow as these planes. Fakes through and through. They make big speeches, claim they believe in high and mighty things, but it's rot. Lies. And whenever you see one of those soldiers marching around and you feel scared, I want you to think about these toy planes out here and remember: they are the same."

MIEKE REMEMBERS THESE words now, as she waits, watching Sintje from the same place across the clearing where she had been hiding that summer day. Her aunt stands at the gate, waiting, the bag at her feet. Eventually a German soldier comes to the other side of the gate. He looks around behind himself a few times, to be sure he is not being observed by any of his compatriots. Then he begins to rifle through the enormous bag. Without the binoculars, this time, Mieke can't see everything, but she is able to make out most. He pulls out two brass candlesticks, a few silver picture frames, and a small pink marble obelisk that the professor got in Ankara. Mieke recognizes the objects from the Japanese trunk—some of the few things that the Naaktgeborens brought with them from Rotterdam, the only treasures that survived the fire. Then there is some jewelry that Mieke cannot quite make out, but she thinks they are things of Sintje's. A long golden cigarette holder. A filigreed hand mirror with a mother-of-pearl lotus design on the back, which Mieke has held covetously many times—an anniversary present from the professor.

The soldier considers these items and then takes out a fold of bills. He hands a few to Sintje. She pleads for more. He sighs and relents. One more. Then he shoos her away, taking the bag and all the things in it with him back inside the gated garden, which locks behind him.

Sintje does not take the tram back. She walks slower, her eyes fixed on the buildings in the center of town. Mieke trails behind her reluctantly, looking back over her shoulder at the withering gardens behind the iron fences. The Germans don't take care of any of it now, and the rosebushes in there are overgrown and dying, brown. Sometime last year they got rid of all the pretend planes. Mieke wishes she could ask the professor why. If "we" saw to it in the end? Or if he had been wrong about the Germans all along?

AFTER SEEING SINTJE selling off her treasures, Mieke can't shake a sad feeling. That somehow it means that her aunt believes her uncle will never return. Mieke misses him badly; she is lonely so often now. Rob spends most of his time sitting near the Japanese trunk with three books open at once. If Mieke asks him to read to her, he grumbles and refuses. He is never interested in spying on the neighbors, does not want to go to the dunes or the woods anymore, either. The way that he smiles and sometimes whispers little things—maybe to himself, but maybe to the father in the carving, who she still cannot see—all of it worries her. And it leaves Mieke on her own now to complete her daily reconnaissance. Not as much fun sitting up in the dark and cramped attic all alone, squinting down through her peephole at Mr. DeVries. Many days he puts on records; she can hear the music reasonably well through the loose boards, but she never knows what she's listening to. Beethoven? Handel? All day she thinks about climbing up there to listen to the trilling of piano keys, the soaring of violin strings, the piercing cry of invisible brass horns. How can all this be contained in the thin black discs he places so gingerly onto the player, each time clasping his hands over it as it begins to spin, as if praying?

Next to the record player, also spinning, is a striking red fish in a cut crystal bowl. It flows this way and that, seems almost to be dancing along to each sonata and concerto. Does the creature have ears like her? Can it hear the cascading notes as she does?

And then one day, as Mieke lies there, her ear to the vent, watching the fish swirling as a trembling guitar plays sweetly through the long brass horn, she hears someone speaking.

"Oh, *liefje*," the voice calls gently, so close it seems to be beside her. "Oh, *mijn liefje* . . ."

Is it a ghost? Or is she hearing things? Maybe, like Rob, she's going to start seeing things.

"Come down, *mijn liefje*," the voice calls gently. "I don't mind your company, but perhaps today we can sit in the same room."

It's DeVries—she squirms back from the hole in the attic, knowing it is too late. She's been spotted. Or heard. For a moment she sits, hugging her knees in the dark. Not sure what to do. If he tells her father, she'll be in loads of trouble. Downstairs there is movement. Mr. DeVries is old, but he can wait at the bottom of the ladder all day if he wants. She's trapped, she realizes. There's no other way out. Breathing as softly as she can, she waits, and waits some more. Eventually the movement ceases and the music resumes. Only after some time does she dare to slip down out of the attic. When she does, she sees the door to Mr. DeVries's apartment has been left open. From the shelter of her own doorway, she gazes through his. He's sitting inside, legs crossed at the knee, in a long beautiful red satin robe, like one of the emperors on the cedar trunk, only Dutch and bald and pale, clutching a bowl of plump green olives in one hand.

"Would you like one?" he asks, holding one out. His voice is high, reedy. Mieke shakes her head. "They're gordal, from Spain. Stuffed with piquillo and Marcona almonds."

Mieke shakes her head, unfamiliar with most of the words he's just said.

"Come in anyway," DeVries suggests. "I won't bite. Leave the door open. That's fine."

Slowly Mieke steps inside, hoping that if she does, then he

won't tell her father about the attic and her spying on him. And so that she can see for the first time how beautiful the apartment is.

The room is breathtaking—far more than she had been able to take in through her little peephole. There are enormous green ferns and little sculptures of animals made from brass, and couches in lilac print with arms that curl grandly. In a gilded frame, a painting of loose shapes and looser colors that seem to be a sad clown, only if someone had taken him all apart and re-assembled him inside out and upside down. An enormous opera score sits open on a golden, claw-footed dresser. In a clear globe, the bright pink body of an octopus is suspended, its eight suckered arms coiled beneath its blobby head. There is a typewriter beside it, a page sticking out of its bronzed platen cylinder—somehow he had kept it all from being confiscated. Everywhere she looks, another treasure, another artwork, another marvel.

And something wonderful is bubbling away on the stove in a beautiful purple pot—her nose pricks up at the smell of rich-ness and smoke. Peppery, as bright as pure sunshine. "Chicken paprikash," he says, "it's delicious, if you'd like to try some. Old Hungarian witchcraft at work."

The cooking at her home is done by her mother and Tante Sintje, and it's never this elaborate. She has little knack for it herself, but she's told she'll learn. Someday she'll have her own mouths to feed, they tell her. But she's hopeless at even scrambling eggs or toasting bread. And yet here is Mr. DeVries, with a kitchen filled with finery and a shelf of wire gadgets for mixing and blend-ing, and this incredible-smelling thing there on the stove—better than anything her mother or Sintje could ever dream of making.

"You didn't think a man could cook?" he asks dryly.

Mieke shakes her head in a way she hopes is polite enough.

"Your father is the best baker in the Hague. Couldn't he cook if he wanted?"

This seems a fair point.

"I live by myself, so I do it all," he declares. "I bake and cook and clean and care for my little jungle and—so much more." And he gestures like a magician then to the room around him.

She looks over to appreciate the fish more closely. It swirls furiously into a tight ball of red as she approaches, just the size of her thumb, but then it stops and explodes—its scarlet plumage spreading out into the water until it almost fills the bowl. She presses her hand to her chest, feeling the hard beating. Imagines the fish as her heart, pulsing in the water.

"Why is it all alone?" she asks.

"*It* is a she," he says. "And *she* is alone because she is a mean old thing."

"She is?"

"She is a Siamese betta fish."

When this fails to clarify things, he continues. "Sometimes they call her a fighting fish. For centuries the courtesans of the Ayutthaya Kingdom bred them for a combination of beauty and aggressive behavior. They'd put two of them in an aquatic arena together and watch them battle. If this little beauty gets too close to anyone else, she will rip them to pieces in mere moments. And if you put something reflective near her—a mirror, say—she will think the reflection is an enemy and bash herself against the glass, trying to kill it."

"What would happen?"

"She'd die trying."

Mieke is sure her eyes are wide as dinner plates, and she backs away from the fishbowl slowly, as if she might set the creature off. And still, she looks so gentle, so regal.

A moment later, Mieke spots an immense painting of the golden dunes and the violent seaside, resting above the fireplace. Her heart nearly stops when she realizes she's seen it before.

"That's Mr. Akkeringa's!"

DeVries is impressed. "I thought I was dealing with Mata Hari, not Peggy Guggenheim."

"He used to come to the bakery when I was little."

"I followed his career for years. He certainly had a spark in him. This was, I think, his finest work. I should have sold it ages ago, but—"

He gazes at it and doesn't finish the sentence.

"Do you see him ever?" Mieke asks softly.

DeVries looks at her, not unhappily, but as if she ought to know he doesn't.

"Is he gone?" Mieke asks softly.

"Oh, *liefje*, yes, I'm afraid so."

"*Onderduiken*?" she asks hopefully. Disappeared?

But he shakes his head sadly, then offers her a seat on the lilac couch across the room from him, and she sits in silence, listening to the record he's now playing for the third time.

"What you hear is called the Spanish guitar," he explains to her finally. "A tremendous piece by the equally tremendous composer Francisco Tárrega, titled *Recuerdos de la Alhambra*, 'Memories of Alhambra.'"

"Who's Alhambra?"

"Not a *who* but a *where*. A cliffside palace in a city called Granada in Spain."

Mieke's eyes widen. "Have you been there?"

"No, never. My mother's family came from there, long ago. Or that's what they told me. During the Inquisition, they fled and settled here."

"And you've never gone back?"

"No but I would love to."

"Maybe once this is all over."

The music is low and peaceful; Mieke imagines an enormous fortress on the sea, with white walls and long thin flags flying in the Mediterranean breezes, trembling like the strings of the guitar in the song.

Only then she notices that Mr. DeVries has taken a glass bottle of blue pills from the pocket of his red silk robe. As he hums, he tips one of the pills out into his hand and then uses a folding knife with a tortoiseshell handle to cut the pill in two. He tucks one half back into the bottle and then swallows the other.

"They give these to the soldiers. To help them sleep. Blue 88s. Isn't that a lovely name?"

Mieke nods. He is studying her with now-sad eyes, and she's about to ask him what is wrong when he speaks.

"They don't tell you children what's going on, do they?"

Mieke shakes her head.

"I suppose if they did, they couldn't pretend not to know."

She wants to ask who and what he means. But she remains silent.

"Mr. Akkeringa was a tremendous man. One of a kind. Generous, bright. Beautiful. And once in a while he had it. *The touch of the poet*." He gazes at the painting above the fireplace. "But he was also a Jew."

"Like the Meiers. Downstairs."

"Correct."

DeVries closes his eyes and leans back in his seat, letting the last few chords of the music wash over him before the record stops. The tone arm makes a clicking noise as it lifts. Slowly the disc stops spinning as the arm moves away and comes to rest.

"Why do the Germans hate them?"

"Blame the other . . . this is the incandescent fiber inside of every monster. And the Jews have been the capable *other* for monsters since times before time."

Mieke wants some remedy for this. "My father told me the Dutch rail workers have gone on strike," she says—though she doesn't know what the trains have to do with the Meiers. With the Jews. "The Germans are very angry about it."

DeVries laughs. "Oh yes. Ze Fuhrer *ist verwoed*."

"But why?"

He studies her a moment. Like she is another one of the beautiful things there in his apartment—a vase or a mirror, and what he'll say might break her.

"They use the trains to take the Jews," he explains. "Away to their work camps. Well. They *call* them that, but really they are vile prisons. Grotesque, muddy hells, where they'll slave away for the Germans, and—eventually die."

He says it calmly, a simple fact. Mieke is breathless, waiting for him to continue the story—there must be something else. There's always something else.

"Why?" Mieke asks, softly. "Why will they die?"

"Well, I am sorry to say, *mijn liefje*, but they'll murder them."

Mieke sits there, numb. Thinking, in her father's voice, that it's *impossible*. Knowing, as wrong as he's been every time, that it isn't at all.

DeVries hums. "It's no miracle they haven't come for me yet. There is a soldier I know, from before the war. He's a captain now. Nachtnebel. Isn't that lovely? 'Night dust,' it means. German isn't all so vulgar, as a language at least. In any case, once upon a time we were very close. Very close friends. This was in old Berlin. Before. We would sit in the café and listen to the most beautiful music . . . he's kept an eye out for me. It won't last now. He's been transferred somewhere in the countryside. When I heard you up in the attic, I thought, *Aha! Today's my day.* But no. They'll come through the front door, won't they?"

"Are you also a Jew?" she asks, her eyes moving to the red fish in the tank, alone in the corner, its every motion a stunner.

"No." DeVries sighs. "Something else they don't care for, though."

He peers at her with one eye only for a moment. What is he, then?

What does it mean, to be forbidden?

But she senses that she cannot ask. That he could never answer if she did.

Instead, she asks something else, scratching at something like hope. "If the rail workers are striking, can they not take you—or them, now?"

"This is the idea, yes. To at last refuse to go along any further. It is years past since we should have. All this time we've looked the other way. God forgive us."

When he says "God," he doesn't cross himself, the way Tante Sintje does. Instead, he gazes out at Mr. Akkeringa's painting, as if God is somewhere in there.

"Beauty reveals us," he says, and Mieke recognizes the phrase. *Schoonheid onthult ons.* From Fostedína and her Golden Helmet. The fairy book, has he read it, too?

"And will the railway strike end it?" she asks.

He smiles sadly. "Evil always finds another way. But we may slow them down. Give the heroes more time to arrive before the monsters finish the job. All for a price, of course."

Mieke sits, unsure. Not speaking. DeVries studies her with stern eyes.

"Don't stop asking questions now. Go on."

So she asks it.

"What price?"

"That we'll be next."

Then DeVries bites into one of his stuffed olives and closes his eyes as he chews.

MIEKE TELLS NO one about her afternoon with DeVries, not her parents, and not even Rob. What he's told her makes her heavy inside, as if she's full of sand. Outside, the world goes on as always. Tante Sintje reads about how to let out the waistband of a dress. Mr. Stuldreher works on his car in the alleyway, and waves happily as she walks to school. In her classroom, Mr. Wendelgelst shows them a map of Africa, and they recite the names of the territories there, and the names of the native tribes: here the Fula, and there the Bantu, the Tuareg, the Hottentots. Up at the top, the Berbers and Arabs. Mieke sits and repeats these words, but they mean nothing to her. She looks at Marjo Mulder and Jacoba Kormaan. Do they know? Does *everyone* know what Mr. DeVries has told her? Mr. Wendelgelst must be unaware—the Meiers had two girls, who'd have been in his class a few years earlier. Lenie, she remembers. And Liesl. And what about Ina and Siny? Their empty desks were hauled away, all those months ago. Hadn't anyone else noticed?

She can barely speak the whole day, and doesn't eat a bite at dinner.

Sugar beets, anyway.

THAT NIGHT, IN the darkness, Mieke hears violent sudden noises from down the hall. It is only when she gets about halfway through the shadowy corridor that she realizes someone is vomiting in the bathroom. She comes to the crack in the door and sees Tante Sintje, bent over by the toilet bowl, her nightgown hanging loose. The lights are off inside, and as she stands up and goes over to the sink to wash up, Sintje does not immediately fix her gown, leaving it loose so she can splash some cold water onto her bare chest. Mieke sees this all from the doorway and knows she should scurry back to bed, but then Sintje looks backward over her shoulder, mortified. Gathering the loose folds of her gown, she covers herself up. Mieke starts to run, but worries that if she does, she'll wake everyone else—

"This spying thing is getting tiresome, *mijn liefje*," her aunt says, cinching her gown—too tight—and immediately she inhales sharply at the pressure. Mieke sees in the moonlit bathroom that her aunt's belly is swollen.

"Is that a baby?" Mieke breathes happily.

But Sintje turns away. "It's not your concern," she says as she sinks back down to sit on the edge of the bathtub and begins to hold her head in her hands.

"Your mother knows," she said finally, "but please don't tell anyone else."

She means don't tell Rob, Mieke realizes. Not a month ago she'd never in her life imagine keeping a secret from Rob—let alone two. And to keep a secret for Tante Sintje, of all people? But Mieke feels a new, silent connection beginning. A private thing between two women can be of the most importance, even when the woman is not your favorite. She feels it starting to mean that she is one, too, now, whether she likes it or not.

"Does the professor know?"

Sintje looks very sad at this. "No. How could he?"

Mieke looks briefly at the chest in the hallway and at the perfectly still carvings, wishing what Rob kept seeing in there could see them back.

"It's okay," she says to her aunt. "I won't tell."

Her aunt dries her eyes and then abruptly straightens up. "Go on. Go to bed."

Mieke says good night to her aunt and sneaks quietly back to bed, wriggling down deep into her blankets, already warmed by the pounding inside, of so many secrets all at once.

WHEN MIEKE COMES home from school the next day, she finds, tacked on the red door of their building, a butterscotch-yellow card with familiar bold lettering. At the very top, the word *BEVEL* is largest. WARNING. The rest of the sign she has Rob read to her, and as he does, he places a hand on the back of her head, at the top of her braid. "Tomorrow morning, every man from age seventeen to forty should come out on the street to report for labor. Appear immediately with the described supplies. All women and children must stay inside until the end of the action. The men of that age found in their homes will be punished. Their personal belongings will be confiscated. You must bring with you: warm clothing, solid shoes, blankets, rain gear, a knife, a fork, and a spoon . . . a mug and sandwiches for one day. The daily pay is good food, cigarettes, according to the established scale. For the ones that stay behind . . . we will take care of them. It is forbidden for all occupants to leave the residence. Those who try to escape or hide or try to protest—they'll be shot."

Mieke's first instinct is to laugh. Is this some joke? She tries to imagine it: her father and all the other men in the building standing around down there on the steps in the morning, holding a sandwich and a mug and some silverware. Waiting to be rounded up by the Germans?

And what were the rest of them supposed to do while the men were gone?

Up and down the street, Mieke notices the same butterscotch rectangle on every door. Still, she does not believe it can be real. Not until she and Rob come upstairs to the apartment and discover the pain on their mothers' faces. Her father is sitting quietly in the kitchen, surrounded by all his bowls and pans and such. The sour smell of the day's dough is still lingering there in the air. He is oddly, perfectly calm. He isn't looking at anyone or anything. Even when she sits on his lap and puts her head on his chest, he gently rubs the nape of her neck.

"What do they want *you* for?" she asks, thinking of what DeVries said about the prisons.

"To work in their factories. And make their tanks or bombs or whatever."

"Why don't they make them themselves?"

"Their men are all off fighting. And losing. They can't keep up."

"That's good."

"Yes, but also not good. Because they can't stop. Have you ever seen a rat when it's been trapped? It'll do anything—unthinkable things, until it's finally dead."

Mieke's mother begins to set out some of the items that were on the list. The knife, the spoon, the mug. Her father begins chuckling, softly at first, then harder and harder.

"What are you doing?" he asks her.

"You'll need to be ready."

He's laughing so hard that Mieke slides off his quaking lap. "Put that away. The hell I'll go with them. No. They can shoot me if they want."

Mieke feels a sharp hot pain in her stomach as her mother begins to shout at him and slam the mug on the counter, saying that he's being stupid—that if they shoot him dead there on the steps tomorrow morning, what are the rest of them supposed to do then?

If he goes with them, Mieke hopes, there's a chance he might come back.

Then there is a knock at the door, and everyone straightens up very quickly. Mieke goes with Rob to sit by the cedar chest. Meanwhile, her father walks steadily to the door and opens it. Mr. Smit from downstairs is standing there.

Mieke wants her father to slam the door in his face. Instead, he shakes the man's bony hand and invites him to come inside.

Smit has grown a thin mustache, wider than Hitler's, but, Mieke imagines, each a sick cousin to the other.

"Cora, bring us some coffee, could you?" her father asks.

"Oh, no need. I can't stay long," Smit says. "Shall we make a plan for the morning?"

Mieke waits to see if her father tells him to burn in hell. That he'd rather be shot.

But he nods warmly. "Müeller is too old, I believe. And DeVries as well."

"Him, they'll come for another time."

Silence follows; her father clears his throat.

"I'll go down and speak with Von Fliet. And there'll be Janssen and his son. And Visser."

"Yes," Smit agrees. "So that's seven, including Werner."

"Your son? Is he seventeen already?"

"Last week."

"Well. But he ought to stay and finish school if he can."

The suggestion rankles Smit. "What could be more important than this? Besides, the schools will all have to close. They won't be able to stay open without teachers."

Mieke and Rob shift at this. Mr. Wendelgelst, too? No more school?

"And," Smit says softly, "what about your friend, Naaktgeboren?"

Rob plays gently with the grooves of the Japanese chest, believing his own father is safe already. Hidden away from the bad men and the rest of it.

"He's gone, I'm afraid."

Smit clicks his tongue in disappointment. "They say a man that flies from his fear may find that he has only taken a shortcut to meet it."

Her father twitches. Then he lets out a long breath as if he, too, believes Rob's father is a coward. Mieke wishes she could tell Smit that the professor took on armed guards, destroyed a building full of population records—that he is a hero. But she has sworn not to tell, and she cannot break that promise, now or ever. She has still not even told Rob.

Mieke can't even look at Smit, but then their neighbor claps her father on the shoulder.

"I will go prepare. Tomorrow we will see you outside, at sunrise."

"Yes! At sunrise!" her father agrees warmly and shakes the man's hand. Smit waves joyously at the others and then steps away. When the sounds of his footsteps are clearly away, her father spits at the floor where he'd been standing.

"You should have run like Willem," Rob's mother snaps. "They'll be watching now."

And Mieke remembers seeing so many more soldiers than usual out there on her walk home. Little clusters of them on the corners, waiting. She wants to go to the window to count them all, but her father is coming toward her suddenly with an unexpected brightness on his face.

"My little spy," he says gently, "where is your favorite hiding place in the building?"

So Mieke takes her father's hand and leads him into the hallway. She looks up at the attic.

"I'll show you," she whispers.

HER FATHER GOES down that night to visit with the other men in the building, just as he told Smit he would do. One by one, the men cautiously agree to his plan. That night they eat dinner with their families, kiss their wives, and pack their mugs and sandwiches and silverware. Outside, the Nazi patrols run every few minutes, up and down every street. Mieke strains, listening for sounds through the window: gunshots, footsteps racing. Some will try and escape tonight, and head to the southern countryside to wait for the Allies to advance. Her father believes it will be a matter of weeks. Not so long to wait—if they're lucky.

Then, late, two hours after the lights in the Smits' apartment have gone out, the signal goes out. Mr. Müeller opens his door and crosses the hallway to listen at the door of his neighbors. After a long enough silence has transpired, he goes back to his fireplace.

Gingerly, he extends the handle of the ash broom and taps the inside of the chimney.

Once. Twice. Three times.

He waits. Then come three knocks back from Mieke's father. The coast is clear on the fourth floor.

Müeller slides the lower grate open beneath the fireplace and reaches the broom down toward the Janssens. He taps again.

Once. Twice. Three times.

Janssen taps back, with his own broom, and then repeats the procedure to notify the Von Fliets below him before tiptoeing across the hall to tap on the door of the Vissers. This is risky—he can see, up the staircase, the door of the Smits. At any moment it could push open and Smit and Werner could come out and find them all in the midst of the escape plan.

Each man takes his mug, his sandwich, and the rest, and comes out into the center staircase. But instead of going down to the front steps to be collected by the Germans at dawn, they go up. Slowly. Silently. Shoeless. Step by step, each avoiding the creaks the others have found ahead of them, until they are assembled there at the very top, outside of the Menkes' apartment and below the entrance to the attic. Mieke clings to the shadows inside—she is supposed to be sleeping, but this is impossible.

She watches her father in his stocking feet, standing at the doorway, helping the others up, one at a time. They are so quiet that they nearly float into the attic, men rising like birds. And then they are gone. She looks up in time to see the little hatch being closed from the inside. It is a chilly night, and she is cold in her nightgown. None of them know if this will work, but her father is hopeful. They'll stay up there in hiding, eating and sleeping and waiting for the Allies to come. When there's a sign of trouble downstairs, they'll take the old storm covers and lay them down over the beams at the farthest corner of the eaves.

They'll be safe. As long as Mrs. Smit does not catch on and turn them in.

Mieke and her mother will need to sneak up food and water once a day and clean their clothes once a week. But the bigger job is that when the Germans come back to hunt for them, the signal must go out. Mrs. Von Fliet will send three taps up the chimney to Mrs. Janssen, who will send them to Mieke's mother and Tante

Sintje. And then it will be Mieke's job to go to the trapdoor and tap it with her fireplace poker, so the men in the attic can get into position. The six of them will lie down inside the gap, packed tight, and stay under the boards until the coast is clear.

Mieke glances then across the hall, where Mr. DeVries stands in his dressing gown, behind the open door. In his hand he grips a long golden letter opener—not sharp enough to do much damage to anything tougher than an envelope, but he holds it over his chest like a readied sword. She isn't sure what to do. Her father's life, all their lives, are in her hands now. And in the hands of the Müellers beneath her. And if they cannot be trusted after all?

"Won't you go with them?" she asks DeVries softly.

He shakes his head. "I'm too old to hide in a crevice. But I'm not afraid," he tells her.

She knows she's shaking as he puts a hand on her head to steady her.

"Don't you be, either," he says, turning the letter opener around and passing it to her. It feels heavy and right in her hand.

MIEKE SITS UP by the window for the rest of the night, holding this new golden sword, breathing softly. Outside, the moon is gleaming in the sky. The soldiers march up and down. At last the sun begins to rise. Pinks and purples extend gradually from off behind the shadowed rooftops. The red-and-brown goose begins to squawk and crow. With each minute, the black turns to gray, and the gray turns to the familiar orange tiles.

And then it happens. The door to their building opens and Smit and his son come out onto the steps. They stand there chatting for a few minutes, and then eventually fall into silence. He must be wondering why no one else is coming. She's known this moment would come, but she doesn't know what will follow it. What will Smit do? Up and down the street there are others coming out onto the steps. But not very many. Two or three men from each building. And the soldiers, seeing the ranks are no long filling, are beginning to bark at one another in their German way.

Lists are consulted. Six soldiers march into a building down the road, and come out, minutes later with a man still in his pajamas. He is pushed into line with the others.

The same happens, over and over. And the other men all go, in the end. No one is shot. No one resists very much. They couldn't come out willingly, but they couldn't not go, either.

Big trucks come down the street, green steel monsters, and the men are loaded up into the backs of the transports. She loses sight of the Smits for a moment, and then, there they are, standing in the street. Mr. Smit is talking to the soldiers, furious, pointing inside. It won't be long before they storm in like before, demanding answers. What will they break? Who will they injure? She tells herself not to be afraid. Her mother, all the wives, will say the same as they said about Rob's father before. They don't know where the men have gone. They must have left in the night. They did not say anything to them before leaving.

Will the soldiers interrogate her? Will they arrest DeVries? The boots are coming, loud, up the stairs already. Iron nails studding the soles. The men in the attic should already be in position. If this is going to work, they'll know soon enough. If it doesn't, they will drag her father out and throw him in the truck with the others. Or simply shoot him. She can't tell if the sounds outside are guns firing or cargo gates slamming shut. She risks one final peek out the window. Smit has climbed into the truck; Werner sits next to him. The older boy looks up and their eyes meet, for only a moment before Mieke ducks. He is so small, so scared. She'll see his face in the back of her mind for many months to come. But no more in that moment as she slips the letter opener safely into her pillowcase. The sound of the iron-nailed boots arrives at the door of their apartment.

IN KAMP GROENTE

~

In peacetime, the prison outside of Groente had been a modest affair, run by a man known in the surrounding town as Meneer Woest, which comes to something like "Sir Furious," because of his uneven temperament. He made it less than a week after the Germans took over. No great loss, even if Groente is somehow worse off without him. We have been watching the situation from some distance ever since the arrival of our esteemed author, known here as Vraagteken Schrijver. As we've done for his forebears over the years, we have circled him with our protection; we whisper our secrets in those pinkish seashells he calls ears. And when he can, he writes these things out for us on whatever paper he comes across there in Kamp Groente.

It has been growing rapidly, the camp. From the safety of our somber glades, we've watched the prison expanding outward, the chain-linked fences replaced with high rows of long wire, twisted with barbs. No bother for us to slither over or under, of course. We lurk in the rushing river nearby, come and go as we please. We've been here since the days when these forests were hunted by Henry I, Duke of Brabant. Since the days when a young Hieronymus Bosch lived in the fortified town to the north. And we were here during the town's fiery demise, which he would one day reproduce in his beautiful hellscapes. And we will be here, rest assured, in times to come.

But our author has only just arrived. He fled the rocket-lined beaches of Den Haag, moving on foot by cover of night. Like one of us, he swam and crawled and slid and slithered, past the Hook of Holland, along the branching waters of the Rip and out beyond the ruined docks of Rotterdam. Hiding, sliding, moving in the night, our author came along the river Waal and into the silted Maas. At last he stumbled into the boggy wetlands of Biesbosch and was captured alongside a caravan of Eftavagarja gypsies, brought with them to Kamp Groente.

Now all we can do is watch after him from the river as he stands at the barbed wire fences, staring out at the heaths past the guard towers. It is a bleak sight; we cannot lie about that. Life in a concentration camp, even one named after cruciferous foods, is no laughing matter. There are thousands of people all around. Each day a hundred more arrive and a hundred more are slaughtered: shot over the gravel pits, burned alive. They hung people for a while, but it must have been too slowgoing. In any case, they don't do it nearly as much anymore, we have noticed.

How is it, you ask, that we are so indifferent? It is because we've swum alongside your so-called history for centuries: passing every bloody battlefield, every burned village, the purges of one holy Crusade after another.

But we must admit, this time it has all been more difficult to witness. The timeline of human extinction speeds along with increasing velocity. Each day, more are executed—or are taken away to be executed elsewhere. We don't pretend to understand, nor does our author. Why they kill some now and some later. Why some here, and some there? It is unknowable. Even the Germans do not know, though they like to imagine they know everything. It is laughable, truly, how little they know.

They do not even know who our author is!

You see, as he fled, he was rather stupidly unprepared—for some reason, the only thing he grabbed before scrambling away was a single forged identification card. Worse, one that turned out to be only partially filled out. It listed his name as just "Schrijver" with no surname or address. When the Nazis took him in and came across his papers, they asked him: "Mr. Author? What kinds of books do you write?" But he did not respond. He has not spoken since he left home. Eventually they put him down in their records as "Schrijver, ?" and this, we suppose, was taken literally by some other Nazi at some other point in the intake process, and so now he is officially prisoner number 237040102: "Schrijver, Vraagteken": V.S.

Oh, dear author! You are frightened, yes. You do not know how long it will take them to figure out who you actually are, or if they ever will. What can we do but whisper to you through the walls? What can we do but tell you these old tales? A part of yourself you have hidden back home, to look after your son. A part of yourself, you hide here on these pages. What's left cannot always be seen, cannot speak, cannot feel as before.

If you could feel—if your soul were restored—it would kill you.

Heinousness and fear are numbing. Everything becomes banal with repetition. And yet you hunt sometimes for beauty in this hell. We cry to you: No! Do not. We can hide you from fear, but beauty reveals us. Whenever you find some shadows moving in a pleasing pattern or a half-torn copy of a Tolstoy novel, even the bracing chill of the falling rain . . . these can only reawaken your hidden soul! Why did you think you were captured in the first place? The folk songs of the Eftavagarja, you heard from your haystack—you were revealed.

You believe this is somehow better than being numb. Dead before you are dead. You humans are so exasperating! Must we remind you how an eel survives in a well for a century? Let us implore you, remove yourself from this, you fleshy fool. Wait it out. Do not admire the way the late-day light gleams off the barbs on a wire fence, or the ragged order of the stars above you at night. Do not think about Hieronymus Bosch or Henry I, Duke of Brabant. Be free, we say, of history. Be free, we say, of time.

And yet. You insist! You hum those very same Eftavagarja songs to yourself in the bleak night! You giggle at the prospect of dying in a place called Camp Vegetable. With unbridled appreciation, you stare off at the forests and see the creatures that now-dead medieval highnesses once hunted there. Foxes, wolves. Hares, pheasants. You imagine a new life, reborn as a free creature who, like us, can cross the narrow canyon that splits the landscape, a crack that leads past the straw-thatched roofs of those peasant farmers. It will happen soon enough, we know. Until then, we will whisper on to you, and you will listen on to us, concealed and circling in the waters. We will protect you until we can do so no longer. And, with some quietly tended excitement, you will write our tales down for us as best you can.

—V.S.

VRIJBUITER

~

The tai chi instructor at Sunny Pines Retirement Village was a bright-eyed man in his twenties wearing an olive-green knit cap, in far better shape than Will had ever been in his life or would ever be. Gracefully, joyously, irritatingly, Zak raised and lowered his arms at the front of the Shady Pines recreation room. The walls were painted with snow-covered trees and starry skies, as if trying to convince the assembled senior citizens into thinking they were out in the natural world and not huddled inside a retirement home buried in the asphalt labyrinth of central New Jersey.

Will stood awkwardly in the back, going through the motions, lifting his white cast up high toward the "sun"—or a bunch of overhead fluorescent circular lamps, anyway. He flowed like water, floated, breathed in and out, "being the tide," as Zak explained coolly. "*Hug* the world."

It had been a long sleepless night and an exhausting morning since the panic attack at Costco. Teru's flight had landed, but she hadn't responded to his text messages yet. He didn't know how to be clearer as to what he wanted. Her. The two of them. Together. To try. But he knew her well enough to know that his pushing in one direction only ended up with her going faster the other way. If he gave her space, waited for her to come to it on her own terms—Will still had hope. Only he also still had not slept. He'd stayed up mixing the sourdough starter inside of an old mason jar, combining equal parts 70-degree water and stone-ground flour. Then he'd made the enchiladas, the lasagna, the meatloaf. Charring peppers, mincing onions, smashing garlic. Absorbed in the smells and the sounds and the tastes. Relieved of worry by following ever-more-intricate recipes. What to do—choices gone, instructions numbered and bullet-pointed with coolly imperative verbs. Sauté this, dredge that, drain grease, grind spices. And then in the end, stacking aluminum trays high against his guilt until the freezer could take no more, and finally lying down in hopes of sleep.

Every time he'd closed his eyes, he'd felt nothing—no detachment from consciousness at all. He couldn't shake the notion that his soul was scared to let go, unsure where it would end up or if it would make it back—

"You are a *wave*! Rolling in and going out. Push with your arms. Stay at an angle. Don't forget to breathe."

Zak was still going.

Will saw how well his grandmother was doing with all of it—moving much more fluidly than he was, though he supposed she'd had much more practice.

He began to think about his father again, as if he could go back in time to find some clue as to when it had started.

Most of what he remembered was nothing unusual. His father: driving the carpool to take Will and his friends to first grade; chopping firewood in the backyard; picking out pumpkins at some farm upstate; playing Frisbee with some other high-knee-socked-wearing fathers at a company picnic. All utterly normal.

There were just flashes, then, of the other things. None of which had stood out as all that strange to Will until years later, after he'd learned the truth behind his father's disappearance.

"You are *rolling* the moon. *Caressing* the moon . . ." Zak called, holding his hands in a wide circle, bobbing up and down like a buoy in open waters.

Will watched his grandmother smoothly flowing up and down, moving her arms in the requisite circles, bringing them together. She moved with her eyes closed, he noticed, seeming to be at a kind of peace, to be out of her own body as it moved on autopilot.

Eighty years old. Incredible.

The first aberrant memory: his father standing shirtless in the little ornamental fishpond behind their neighbor's house. Mr. Zimri is out there, too, in his bathrobe, shouting at him: "Please, Mr. Geborn, sir, come out! You are frightening my carps!"

His father is trying to catch one in his bare hands.

They must have all assumed he was a drunk, Will considered, as he raised his arms into a warrior's pose, still half a step behind the instructor. But his father had never been a drinker. They'd barely even kept booze in the house: a few bottles of wine down in the basement, old office party gifts, had sat there for his whole childhood, gathering dust.

"The white crane . . ."

Will wobbled, arms stretched ridiculously.

". . . spreads its wings."

And then, a year later, his father stops all the drains in the house without mentioning it to anyone. His mother accidentally floods the bathroom when the sink overflowed, and water rains down into the first floor, ruining some of the wiring and forever leaving a soggy brown patch in the ceiling of the hallway beneath.

"It's a *system*, Malorie!" his father keeps saying. "You can keep one plug open at a time *as long as you watch it closely*."

"And the snake creeps down . . ."

Then the snowstorm. A nor'easter in the middle of March— this same time of year—in 1993. "The Storm of the Century," they are calling it. Everyone in town loses power for three days, and Will's mother invites the Zimris to stay over because Will's father loves chopping firewood and they have tons. Oma is there, too. At first it is lots of fun, like a neighborhood sleepover, and they all roast marshmallows and cook hot dogs over the blaze.

But then Will's mother notices it has been an hour since she's lain eyes on his father. They look all around the freezing cold house for him, eventually coming to an empty, dark refrigerator. He has removed everything from inside of it—the milk, the butter, the sausage links, the mushroom casserole, the Cool Whip, the cans of orange juice concentrate—and hauled it all outside onto the snow-covered lawn. That is where they find him, too, digging around with his bare hands, no gloves or even a coat on, about to freeze to death. He's been burying the food all over, following some logic known only to him. After they get him inside and warm him up again, he falls asleep. Later, he can't remember any of it at all.

It is a long few weeks afterwards, once the power is restored, waiting for the shoulder-high piles of snow to melt, and finding each day some new thing thawing out on the muddy grass: leftover pot roast, chicken fingers, a jar of olives, a bottle of Dijon mustard, a container of tomato soup, three half-empty salad dressings, three sticks of butter, a pack of sliced bread . . . on and on.

AFTER THE TAI chi class, Mieke brought Will with her to the lunch buffet in the next room, where over turkey sandwiches and mac and cheese casserole, she introduced her grandson to a few of her friends. They were delighted, and Will employed his best bedside manner as her friends called him *Dr.* Geborn and shook his hand, inquiring about their ailments and seeking his second opinion on their various pending operations.

Will commented that he was surprised how chipper they all were about their situations. Abraham had bad arthritis, his hands just about turned into claws, but he cheerfully scooped things up or asked someone to help him. Roxanne had six pins in her ankle after a recent fall; she was focused on an upcoming bingo tournament, showing Will her various lucky charms: a pet rock her granddaughter had brought to life with googly eyes; a troll doll without much of its pink hair remaining; a key chain from

Las Vegas with a four-leaf clover on it. Will's favorite was a man named Bertram who had developed cataracts years ago and still wore the sunglasses they had prescribed for him after cataract surgery.

"Those can't be doing anything anymore?" Will said.

"Yeah, but they look cool," Bertram asserted. "Make me look like Stevie Wonder!"

They were then interrupted by Betty, asking, of an odd blotch, "Is this a mole or a sunspot?"

"I think it's just a freckle," Will said, "but you should really ask your own doctor."

Betty ignored this advice and seemed to forget about the blotch as well. "Can I show you a photo of my granddaughter Susan? She's divorced, but *very* smart."

Mieke watched proudly as Will politely took the little flip phone from the woman's wrinkled hand and pretended to admire the pixelated image on its tiny screen.

"I'm married," he said apologetically.

"Well," Betty said with an overdone sigh, "so was she!"

MIEKE IMAGINED IT would all send him heading back home as quickly as possible, but her grandson responded to every stiff joint and sore toe and tingling shoulder. She was so proud of him, and though she had shown it to everyone already a hundred times before, she passed around the wedding photograph of him and Teru. She noticed him squirming only when her friends asked why they hadn't made her any great-grandchildren yet.

"Oh, she wouldn't like *that*," he joked, glancing awkwardly at her across the table.

At last it was time for Will to drive her home.

"They're all so nice," he finally commented. "I bet they'd love it if you lived there, too."

Mieke had known this would come up. "Four thousand dollars a month! For two rooms, and they don't even let you cook your own food."

"Seriously? For that, we might as well put you up at the Ritz."

"I love my house," she said simply. "What would I do with all my things?"

"I don't know," Will admitted. "I love your house, too. Let's not worry about it, anyway."

But she did worry about it. About what kind of time she had left, and what would happen to everything after.

She fights a great yawn and wishes she could take a long nap. Last night she'd stayed up too long, reading ahead in the little book with the eel on the cover, and she's begun to piece the story together at last. She thinks of her old neighbor. She misses him still—after all this time! Grief is such a strange thing. Last night, as she read those Dutch words to herself, about Kamp Groente and the man who called himself Vraagteken Schrijver, she felt as if the words might change. That the book might somehow undo it all. But no, she had kept on reminding herself. There was no changing any of it now. *History, burdening and constraining, always.* Wasn't that what the eels had said? There was only knowing, finally, what had happened and when.

"I have to stop at Shoshana's house," Mieke announced suddenly as they came down the street, "to feed her fish. She's visiting her sister in Trenton."

Will said he'd be happy to run in and take care of it, but Mieke insisted on doing it herself.

"Stay here and keep the car warm," she said. "I'll just be a minute."

Mieke went in alone. What was inside—it was just that she didn't want Will to see. The alternative. What Mieke's life alone could come to look like if she did break her hip like Shoshana. Will hadn't been over there in years now, not since before. It had happened fast. Piles of books everywhere, too heavy for her to move around more than two at a time. All the dishes stacked on the counter because Shoshana couldn't get up into the cabinets anymore. Deep grooves in the hardwood floors, where she moved around the house with an aluminum walker. Even with the requisite dirty tennis balls jammed onto the bottom, it scratched everything up. But this, even, was not what Mieke feared Will seeing the most.

WILL'S MOTHER HAD called and left a message while he was in the tai chi class. He closed his eyes and lay back as he listened to it.

"Hey, Will. Just checking in. I saw Teru posted a picture on Facebook of the airport in Tokyo! I guess she's not down there with you? Hope everything is okay. You really don't need to stay. Oma will be fine. She's got Shoshana looking after her, so you shouldn't have to miss all this work, you know. That's not fair, if she's asking you to do that. You can tell her no, I just wanted to remind you."

Will knew he should call back and set her mind at ease, but his thoughts drifted. He played with the radio. "Somewhere . . ." Bobby Darin sang on the oldies station she was always tuned to. "Beyond the sea . . ." He clicked it back off. Sat in silence for a minute. Already thinking back on the last time he had seen his father. They'd been sitting outside the A&P, in the family's orange Gremlin. They'd been parked there together, listening to the radio and waiting for his mother to finish the shopping. Will couldn't remember what they'd been listening to or why his father had not gone in with his mother. Had his parents been arguing just before? His mother said they hadn't been, but would she tell him the truth? He had come to accept his memories were not to be fully trusted, either. He recalled a sad song on the radio—but he could fill this gap in with a hundred things. His father singing along . . . "Goodbye, Ruby Tuesday," but also "Nowhere man, can you see me at all?" Why was his subconscious so cliché-riddled? In the end he had no idea what song it had been. What he remembered clearest was his father beginning to cry out of nowhere. His face shot red beneath the eyes, wetness around his nostrils. A low, long blubbering that filled the car.

Had Will asked his father what was wrong? Or had his father simply come out with it?

"I don't know what I'd do if something ever happened to your mother."

Will had become alarmed. What happened to her? Was she all right?

At some point his father came back from the worst of it. Quietly, he added one final thing. "I just don't know how I'd live without her."

And that was it. Will's mother had returned with the groceries and Saturday had proceeded as usual. There'd been no fight, no follow-up. They'd dropped Will off at his swim lesson at the YMCA. After practice, Will had gotten dried off and gone outside to be picked up. He'd waited a while before using the emergency quarter from his swim bag to call home from the pay phone.

"Your father's getting you," his mom said. "He left a while ago."

Will had waited two more hours. Only when it was getting dark had his mother come driving up in the Gremlin. Will had gotten in and asked what had happened to his father.

His mother hadn't answered. The truth was, she'd had no idea.

INSIDE, MIEKE MOVED through the piles toward the side room, where Shoshana kept her fish tanks. Fresh water, salt water, some other thing. Each heated to different but precise temperatures. The room was almost all windows, bright, and the only place in the house that was clean. Shoshana stayed out of there except to feed the royal grammas and the cardinalfish and mandarin gobies— incredible beauties that she had collected and cared meticulously for. She loved them, and yet she kept them apart there in that room for "when the time came."

Everything in the room was for when the time came.

The obsession had begun right after her fall. One wall was lined with medical equipment, much of it still wrapped in the plastic it had been delivered in. No television, but a twenty-disc CD changer, already loaded, thanks to Mieke's help, with all Shoshana's favorites. Strauss and Bach and Mozart and Roy Orbison

and the Bangles and the Beatles. On and on. Nearby, tidily arranged on the table, were devices for the aides she had already
made arrangements with and was keeping on a kind of retainer,
similar to lawyers or accountants, in order to get them to commit
to being there to care for her. When the time came. She had no
children to leave her money to, and so why not spend it on pulse
oximeters, blood pressure monitors, a nebulizer? An oxygen con-
centrator on the floor beneath. You'd think they'd have their own,
but no, Shoshana had learned—these were the responsibility of
the patient to provide, and often there were years-long wait lists,
so she'd begun accumulating them in advance.

Against the wall near the window was Shoshana's pride and
joy—a $2,500 hospital bed, with a wide wooden headboard and
a blue vinyl-covered mattress that could be fully adjusted with a
clicker. Much nicer than the one Mieke had been in just a short
while ago after her fall.

Above it, on a shelf, were well-loved, dog-eared, underlined
copies of the novels of Sholem Aleichem, Bruno Schulz, Isaac Ba-
shevis Singer . . . how long did she imagine she was going to be
laid up in there, waiting for death, with her books and her fish and
her music? Weeks? Months?

It was so morbid Mieke could barely stand it, and yet was it not
very sane, in its way? You met with your attorney about the will,
you made sure the house deed and the car title were in a folder
where they could be found. You built a little room for when the
time came.

Mieke didn't know. Didn't know anything except that she
didn't want this, either. She fed the fish and hurried away before
Will got impatient and came inside.

What would he think of it all if he saw?

WILL REMEMBERED A fairy tale that his father had told him not long
before he disappeared—about a Dutch prince who received, from
the distant lands of Japan, a gift of an ornate trunk carved with
extravagant scenes taken from the histories of the dynastic empires.

In the story, when the trunk was departing Japan, an oni had hidden inside to evade capture—a one-eyed, stubby-horned, hairy imp who ordinarily lived in the clouds above the land of the rising sun. Oni were said to tumble down in strong rains and become briefly earthbound—a hiatus they passed by causing random trouble . . . rattling stacks of dishes, making farmers slip and fall into holes in the fields, misplacing objects around the dining room, and so on.

When this oni was, months later, unwittingly freed by the Dutch prince, it soon set about making its usual mischief all over the palace. Before long, he'd driven the poor regent completely mad. In the end, the Dutch prince tricked the oni into returning to the trunk. They locked it up tight and sent it back east on the next ship. And at last, sanity was restored to the kingdom.

Growing up, Will had sometimes pictured these naughty hairy creatures whenever the dishes rattled unexpectedly or when things became bizarrely misplaced. But had he pictured them or *seen* them? He began to think he really had seen one, or at least the mental picture he'd imagined had been as real as if he had seen it. And if he slipped and fell, he'd looked around for an oni, because they enjoyed becoming invisible and tripping people unexpectedly. And whenever it rained, young Will had stared up at the black storm clouds, seeing those little troublemakers, tumbling down.

Of course, he'd connected the trunk in the story to the one his oma kept below the television. He'd been terrified of opening it as a child.

Would he open it now? he asked himself. Now that he was a grown man and knew that there was no such thing as the oni and that the trunk was just a trunk?

BACK AT HIS oma's house, someone had left a little brown paper bag on the front steps. Will watched his grandmother pick it up, say, "Oh, how nice. A gift from Giancarlo."

The baggie had the logo for his landscaping company on it.

"Something for the garden?" Will asked.

But she did not open it or even look inside. She was so tired and distracted that she just dropped the bag on the table inside the doorway. Again, Will helped her up the stairs. When she got into the living room, she collapsed onto the couch and sat there for a full ten minutes, taking deep and troubling breaths.

Will tried to turn on the television but could not figure out the system of multiple remote controls, a total of ten on the side table, most of which seemed to be vestigial from devices thrown away long ago. He muted the program that he could not change away from, some Spanish-language sitcom called *Vámanos Muchachos!* His eyes moved to the carved trunk—the one, of course, that featured so prominently in his grandmother's stories about his grandfather. The same one in which his opa had seen his own father disappear.

"Do you remember when you fell in the water out there?" Mieke said finally.

She was looking out at the water, down at the empty dock.

Will did remember. It had happened that same day he'd famously eaten the lobster. They all had been up on the deck, talking. Will had been playing down in the yard. He'd gone out onto the dock, alone. Back then, his opa's boat had still been tied at the end. He'd come up to it, sat down on the edge of the dock, and stared down into the swirling silver surface of the water. There was tall green seaweed underneath, waving in the shallow tide, and he leaned over to see if there were any fish. One moment, he'd been up in the world of air. The next moment he'd been gone. Looking up at the same seaweed, in a world of water. He'd fallen in.

MIEKE REMEMBERED THE next part vividly. Rushing down to the dock and seeing him there. It was exactly like in her dream as a girl. The calm expression he had, his butt resting there on the bottom, his eyes open, peering up at the surface still as if nothing strange had happened. He clearly had no concept of being seconds from death. That his next gasp would be a lungful of water and not air.

She'd dived into the water. A moment later, her hands were on him. A moment after that, they were back at the surface, and she was passing her grandson up into the air, safe into his father's hands. It was only at that point, as the screaming of the adults met his ears and the full panic of their expressions registered in Will's mind, that he realized a terrible thing had nearly happened.

There was no time, in that rush, for déjà vu. Her old dreams did not come back to mind until later. And then she could never be sure if she was remembering those properly. The boy in the grasses under the water, looking up at her. How could she have envisioned such a thing, almost forty years before her grandson had even been born? Just a coincidence, or maybe her memory now, of those dreams from so long ago, was unreliable. But perhaps it meant something—she was not so sure that things didn't mean anything.

WILL GOT UP and walked over to the spot on the sideboard where he'd left the sourdough starter in its little jar under the table lamp for a bit of extra warmth. Tiny bubbles of air were indeed beginning to form through its pebbly mass. With some effort, he twisted it open using only his good hand and the grip of his armpit. He was surprised by the swiftness with which its tanginess filled the air. Busily he scraped some of the starter into the sink and fed it with more flour and water. He sealed it up again and placed it on the sideboard under the lamp, taking just a moment to glance then at the chest on which a photograph sat of his great-grandfather, Ambrosius, the man who'd fed the seascape painters, as if the picture could be proud. As if the picture could remember.

"What ended up happening to Opa's sailboat?" Will asked.

"I sold it after he died. I couldn't keep it up on my own. I never knew how to sail."

"*Sintje*," Will finally recalled. "It was named *Sintje*."

"Yes, that's right," she said. "For his mother."

"I want to name mine *Yui*," Will said dreamily, "It means 'elegant cloth.'"

Mieke nodded as if this made any kind of sense at all.

"Will," she said, "would you please tell me what's going on at home?"

She watched as he started to try and deny the charges, but even as he began to say the word "nothing," he seemed to stall out and resign himself to silence.

"Teru and I might be splitting up," he said finally.

It was just what she'd feared.

"We've been trying to have a baby. But, well, you know. It's not working out and she's very, very sad about it. We both are. She's gone to Japan and I offered to come along, but she said she needs to be by herself."

"Can't you just tell her that *you* need her? Need her to stay?"

"It's complicated."

"Everything's *complicated*, Will. You can't just give up."

Will went over to the window where the hyacinths were still resting in their vase. He touched the petals lightly with one finger. A flower made of littler flowers.

"The other night, when we first got here, I told her. About what really happened to Dad."

Mieke sat up straight on the couch, looking reflexively toward the face-down photo on the top of the cedar chest.

"He didn't just leave, right?" he said. "They put him in an institution."

Mieke sat up straighter. "Will, I . . . Look, we didn't want you to have to worry about it."

She'd promised his mother, back then. Not to say anything, and she'd kept that promise, despite the distance between them that had only grown. It had felt just like the promise she'd made to Tante Sintje when she was little, not to tell Rob about the baby. The sort of thing women did for one another, that they had to do for one another.

"But I do have to worry about it. These things can be inherited. You should have told me."

Mieke was quiet for some time. "It's . . . Will, it's just not how we did things back then. Nobody told children the truth. And when I was little? Especially if the truth puts you in danger."

Will laughed. "But I am in danger. That's just it."

Mieke didn't say anything, and Will finally slumped down on the chair across from her.

"Did anyone ever tell you about why I didn't become a surgeon?" Will asked her finally.

She shook her head.

BACK IN MEDICAL school, Will had been doing quite well in his program and had taken residency interviews at a dozen top surgical schools. It had gotten to the stage where it was just a matter of waiting to find out where he had matched, and the outlook was positive from all quarters. But in the wake of all the frenetic hustling and traveling, returning to the routine schedule of classes and rotations, Will found himself unable to sleep. Night after night, he tossed and turned. He pulled all the shades down over the windows to keep the streetlights out. He jammed plugs in his ears. He drank bourbon before bed. He took a few hits from his roommate's sea-green bong. One day he ran six and a half miles, hoping to wear himself out. None of these activities had helped at all, and probably most made things even worse. He couldn't think why it was happening. Everything tasted bland to him suddenly, no matter how well he seasoned and spiced it. Maybe he'd come down with something, a cold or something like that—his sinuses were stuffy. But that didn't have much to do with his lying awake all night, unable to quiet his mind so that he could finally conk out.

It went on. Eight days like this. He sometimes heard little buzzing noises but could not find any insect or anything flying around him. He saw little bursts of light sometimes in his peripheral vision, white, but then strange colors he couldn't name. Sometimes the ground under his feet felt like it was turning to dust and walking on it was suddenly like moving over loose sand at the beach. When he gazed out the windows at the buildings nearby, he felt an eerie assurance that they were just about to blow up. Mid-conversation, sometimes, the voice of the other person would go a little echoey, and he'd have to ask them to repeat themselves. Once or twice, even, he'd had to make up an excuse to leave because he simply couldn't comprehend the other person at all. At a certain point he was walking along, and it occurred to him that God's existence was a provable fact. He couldn't prove it, but he was so certain that he didn't need to. Later, he couldn't think of what any of it had been about at all. He chalked it up to the lack of sleep. It had to be that.

Then came the 6E party. A friend from the surgical program was notorious for hosting raucous evenings where guests were encouraged to come in a revealing or otherwise flirtatious outfit. The apartment number, 6E, sounded like "sexy." It was all very silly. The men came shirtless or in very short shorts. There was a dude in a thong—Will didn't know him. The women dressed like Catholic schoolgirls, with the knee socks, or got into skimpy club clothes, or even wore bikini tops. Will had gone, in a muscle tee and cutoff jeans, mainly because he hoped there might be something there strong enough to knock him out for a few hours.

At the party, things got out of hand very quickly. There was headachy music in every room. Flashing lights and loads of strobing and people dancing wherever you looked. It turned out that so much sexy wasn't sexy at all. A lot of thighs and shoulders and stomachs and false eyelashes and fake nails, and Will remembered walking around the party, calling everyone "ladybug" and then, at some point, everything had started turning to sand. People were simply coming apart in front of him, breaking down into their constituent atoms, crumbling and blowing away in the breeze from the open balcony doors. He kept trying to stop it from happening, hoping to save them somehow, mostly by going out to try and close the doors, and then he slammed one so hard that it shattered, and in the ensuing chaos he'd turned to gaze out at the buildings around him and seen them exploding into flames. He heard fireworks going off, or maybe they were gunshots. Through the streets below he sensed a flow of evil, moving slowly along like an oil spill, coating everything in its path. It was as if the universe itself had begun to shrivel up around him. Apparently, he was screaming something in a made-up language. A lot of it he couldn't remember but was only told later by those who'd seen it. The consensus was that he'd been trying to get up on the railing of the balcony when the host had yanked him back to safety.

Someone had driven him to the hospital, where they'd given him something that—finally—knocked him out.

When Will had woken up almost a full day later, he was still in the hospital bed, restrained. His mother had already flown up and begun reading everyone the riot act and gotten everyone nervous about a lawsuit. Because Will had no history of mental issues, and because his mother had said there was no history in the family, the doctors diagnosed a simple nervous collapse brought on by stress and lack of sleep. They told him to meet with a psychotherapist—but he didn't.

It wasn't true, of course. About the history and what was in the family.

Will hadn't known then what had happened to his father, but his mother had.

When he'd come home to his apartment, his roommate was waiting for him with the sea-green bong and an unrefrigerated six-pack, laughing.

"Stay away from those shrooms, dude!"

An explanation had spread for his antics: magic mushrooms. Will didn't correct the record—it seemed better to have accidentally imbibed some hallucinogens than to have lost his mind. And for a day or two, he believed that it was going to be all right.

But a week before Match Day, when Will expected to find out where he'd do his surgical residency, he received the notice. He would not be taken by any of the places he'd interviewed.

This happened all the time to lots of people, not just him.

Everyone in his program acted like they couldn't fathom what had happened or where things had gone wrong. But Will knew. News had traveled.

In the end, the world was such a small place.

"WILL," MIEKE ASKED, "why aren't you going into the office?"

Will eased back into the couch and took another long sip from his coffee mug.

"A couple of days ago I had a panic attack. Teru had just told me about the Osaka program, so I was a little—I don't know. Thrown off. And then a few hours later, I was in the middle of a meeting with a patient. This new father, he and his wife had just had a baby girl a few weeks ago. He was in for some routine blood work. Cholesterol, that sort of thing. Except the whole time he was kind of freaking out, you know, pacing around. 'I just don't know if I can do this. How am I supposed to *do* this? How does anybody do this?' That sort of thing. All of a sudden, the whole room started spinning. I felt like I was having a heart attack. It just lasted a minute, and my partner, Dr. Mizrahi, she took care of everything. Told the guy it was just low blood sugar. But then, well, she said I should take a little time off. And that's when I, um, punched the door. The doorframe."

"I see," Mieke said. "Well, that's not—really, it sounds like you *do* need a vacation. If you can't go with Teru, why not spend some time on a beach somewhere? Get some *rest*."

"She wants me to start seeing a therapist. My partner, I mean. Mizrahi."

"What's wrong with that?" Mieke asked. "Everyone sees a therapist now."

Will sat quietly, rubbing at his closed eyes roughly with the knuckles of each thumb.

"Not everyone's got—you know, what if they say I've got—"

But he couldn't say it.

"I just don't want to end up like him," was the best he could manage.

ONCE, IN HIGH school, Will had been assigned a report about the Anglo-Dutch Wars in the seventeenth century and learned his ancestors had once ruled the seas, been one of the original colonial powers, which at first he'd figured was pretty cool, until he got to the part where these same ancestors had subjugated the Indonesian natives and captured a half-million Africans and sold them into slavery in the Caribbean and Suriname and elsewhere.

It was difficult for him, then, to square these facts with the kind, gentle tall people he'd met on his childhood visits to Delft and Amsterdam. He wrote the report but felt like turning it in was some kind of betrayal of his people—not that it had ever mattered to him before. He'd read on and on, hoping to find something to explain it.

Then, in the back of one book, Will found a portrait of a man who looked like his father. So much that it spooked him, as if he'd found out that this was where he'd been hiding for years, there inside of a dusty library book. This man had the same dark beard, the same pointed mustache, the same lost wildness in his eyes. And around his neck, a ruff made with blue silk.

Vrijbuiter, the caption read. *A freebooter: particularly a pirate, who would attack Dutch trade ships going to and coming from the Orient.*

Afterwards, in his class presentation, Will told everyone that his family had been pirates—not slave traders or colonizers, but glamorous outcasts, who in their ransacking and pillaging were in some way aligned with the forces of good. As if his ancestors had been on the outside of it all, taking down the capitalist machine, emancipating the enslaved. And while no part of it was true at all, the lie had comforted Will, and he began thinking of his father in those terms. Not absent, just living apart. A freebooter, a renegade, a *vrijbuiter*.

AT THE WINDOW, Will stood looking out at the traffic on the causeway while his grandmother got up and began digging around in her closet for something. When she came back into the living room, she was holding a piece of yellowing paper, about the size of a greeting card. On the top was the word *BEVEL*. It was the piece of paper that had prompted her father and the men to hide in the attic. With it, she also had the order seizing the land where the bakery had been. Then she handed her grandson a square block of wood about the size of a kitchen tile.

"I'd like you to have this. It's something very special."

The wood filled his hand. On its surface a scene had been

meticulously carved in fine detail, the lines a hair's breadth, like filigree on an earring or necklace. It depicted a doorway set inside of an archway of stone blocks. A window was covered by six thin metal bars, as if it were the entrance to a medieval dungeon. Various textures were created by the stippling and scratching in the wood. Will gently ran his hand over the pebbled pockmarks in the stone and the slightly deeper hashing that created a three-dimensional shadowing effect to make the door seem to be a different type of wood than that which it was carved into. As Will moved his hand, the scene appeared to move in time, the shadows elongating, the light increasing, as if some sun was passing over it. What a trick! How had it been managed?

There was also a ledge, going to a short staircase that bent toward his eye as it descended. Each step was shaded and textured perfectly. It was as if someone inside the block could walk up the stairs and push open the door.

"This is where the Archduke Ferdinand was assassinated," Oma explained. "There's a bullet hole there, in the wall."

Will could make out a tiny nick in the stone, amidst the texturing. "Wasn't he shot during a parade, like Kennedy?"

"The assassins tried to use a bomb to blow up the car during the parade, but the gunpowder got damp and it wouldn't go off. The archduke fled here in his car. But as he passed by a delicatessen, just by coincidence—one of his assassins was sitting, just having a sandwich. He walked out on the street and shot him. One of the bullets went through and into the wall."

She tapped on the spot.

"Wow," was all Will had to say. He remembered another history class and a teacher in a navy blazer, explaining how this had been the match that lit the powder keg—beginning the First World War, where soldiers would face mass mechanized death on an unimaginable scale. Machine guns, armored tanks, submarines, dogfights. Pestilence spreading through the trenches, taking as many lives as the bullets and the bombs. And the defeat of Germany leading to the harsh punishments at Versailles, and so to the rise of Hitler, and so right on into the Second World War.

It had all rippled out from this one bullet. That one spot on the wall.

"Who carved this?" Will asked.

"A prisoner," was all Oma said.

"In Groente?"

"Yes."

"During the war?"

Will expected her to nod her head, but instead she said, "No. After."

"What do you mean? This is the place you told me about, right? Camp Vegetable?"

Queasy, still sweating, Will rubbed his finger over the thin marks, going along the stairs and feeling for the bullet hole a moment before pressing on the doorway. It was the strangest sensation; the wood was even soft after all this time. It was like he'd been able to push the doorway open, just a crack. When he moved his finger, he could have sworn it swung back. But it was hard to tell.

His imagination, nothing more.

"Why did they keep it open after the war?"

"For the Germans," she said slowly. "The Germans and the sympathizers."

And then Will felt another wave of nausea coming.

He excused himself to the bathroom, barely making it in before puking. Globs of semi-digested cheese poured out of him. He hugged the cold toilet bowl and pressed his face against the seat. His whole body shook with powerlessness.

As the vomiting ended, Will dropped his hands to his sides and touched the wooden carving in his pocket. *This is who you are,* it told him. *You are made of this.*

GRIJPGIEREN

~

The whole world has gone dark. The streetlamps unlit, the city bathed in grayness, blackness. No power coursing in the electrical lines. No coal in the hearths. No food in the stores. Mieke and Rob huddle on the side of the road before sunrise, each with a long, sharpened stick in hand, watching for the truck coming from the western farms. All they can hear is rain, rain. Every day, rain. Even before the nightly curfews begin, the streets are quiet. It feels like a thousand years since her father and the others went up to the attic, but it has been only six weeks, Mieke reminds herself. "Divers," people are calling them; the city is filled with them now. Filled but emptied. Men quietly waiting in the walls, behind the wardrobes, under the floorboards. *Onderduiken*. Crammed into crawl spaces and closets. At night Mieke hears them in the ceiling. Creaking, whispering, ghosts.

"See something?" Rob asks. Mieke looks out into the dark, wet road, waiting, unsure.

The cars have been taken for scrap, and anyway they'd have no gas to run, so the roads have fallen quiet. It's only the soldiers' trucks going past now. Mid-October and nearly freezing already.

Mieke and Rob are both soaked to the bone; they've been out there for almost an hour. Rob is shivering next to her, even wrapped up in his father's old overcoat. She's wearing the one he outgrew last winter. The shops are all closed. Inside, there are just bare shelves, and if you squint, you can see swarms of fleas, rendering the dust into still more dust.

Money is worth almost nothing now anyway. The other day she heard from Jopie Tideman, up the street, that his father paid *eighty* guilders for a half pound of dried beans on the black market. Good luck cooking them. It's all been taken: pots and pans, drawer knobs and lamp bases. Then the fence posts, the street signs, the traffic lights, the lamp poles. They even took the little jacks that Broodje had bought with his birthday money last year. The bigger problem are shoes, both hers and his, which are wearing thin. If they'd imagined the soldiers would be back for the rubber, they'd have buried Rob's boots in the backyard with her mother's tea set. Too late now.

ROB NUDGES MIEKE in the hip; he sees the truck coming up the road. She can tell from the way the cargo in the back bounces around. This is the one they want. It's coming in from the farms with food for the soldiers and for the soup kitchens. The two children flatten themselves behind the rosebushes outside of Mr. Neijmeijer's—listening. Mieke sees the shriveled gray heads of the dead flowers, browning on the stems. No one's been out to prune them. Mieke's stomach growls. What will be in the truck? She prays for collards or parsnips. Potatoes would be incredible, but she hasn't seen those in days.

They wait, and as the truck rolls past, the children leap to their feet. They pound along directly behind the cart, where the drivers won't glimpse them in their mirrors. At least they hope.

Mieke's lungs sting, trying to keep up. She hasn't eaten since yesterday morning and her stomach is a deflated balloon. Nausea comes in waves but also never truly passes, with nothing inside to expel. With ration coupons at the commissary, each day you can get two pieces of stale bread and half a sugar beet. Unless they run out, in which case you get nothing for your three-hour wait. Even if they weren't also trying to feed six men in the attic, it wouldn't be nearly enough.

"Too much to die on," Tante Sintje says once a day. "Too little to keep you alive."

Like a knight with a wobbling lance, Mieke tucks the hard end of her stick in the crook of her elbow and tries to inch the tip closer to the back of the truck as it rolls on. It's hard enough not to slip on the wet and dirty roadway. And then she has to watch out for Rob and his own pole, jolting ahead of hers. They've gone after two other trucks, and so far, nothing. But this time they've timed it better. They're closer, and the truck's slowing down now, trying to avoid the bump of the tram tracks ahead.

Rob knew this would be the right spot. They raise their poles to lift the netting above the cargo and begin jabbing blindly. And this time it works. Something small falls loose and lands as Rob had hoped, in the black gravel between the discarded track ties. All the rails have been pulled up, hauled away with the pots and pans and bicycles. One by one the ties are being pried loose, too— anything that can be burnt for warmth will be burnt.

First, it is only a few dark shapes that tumble down from the truck, but then suddenly Rob's stick catches something and a waterfall comes. Somewhere up front, the driver jams the brakes.

There's no time. Mieke grabs as many of the hard, rough lumps as she can and rushes toward Appelstraat. Rob does the same, bolting in the opposite direction.

Up Fuchsiastraat, there are alleyways to hide in. Mieke runs and pants and waits for the crack of gunfire, but there is none. The soldier has tossed his fallen load back in and resecured it. Only after he is gone does Mieke finally inspect the bundle she's holding in her dress. Three little lumps, and already she knows what they are from the purple stain they're leaving behind.

Sugar beets.

MIEKE SNEAKS BACK to their building and delivers the haul to her mother. Rob enters a few minutes later, a huge scrape on his leg that he earned trying to get over a fence.

"I dropped all mine," he mutters, eyes downcast.

His mother scolds him and goes to the cabinet to see what gauze or antiseptic they still have left. Not much. "You'll lose your leg if you're not careful, *boefje*."

Rob writhes from the sting of the orange-brown liquid she daubs onto his scratches. They're not deep, thank goodness. Tetanus or gangrene or God knows what else would mean taking Rob to the church basement, where the few remaining doctors are desperately trying to help with their few remaining supplies—this week it is diphtheria going around, and you can smell it, through the walls, and hear it, too. "Shitting themselves to death," or so say Jopie Tideman and his brothers. Snickering bullies, all of them, a little gang of heels and knuckles, apt to come right up and take whatever you've managed to steal. *No honor among thieves*, her father says.

Have you ever seen a rat when it's gotten trapped? It'll do anything— unthinkable things, trying to escape the inevitable.

And in the meantime, they've noticed now. Tante Sintje isn't getting thinner like the rest of them. Her stomach bulges out. No one wants to talk about it. Her husband is still missing and this war is still happening and already there's not enough to eat.

But in just four or five months, Mieke's guessing . . . by March, maybe April at best, she's going to have a baby. What the world looks like then, if there will even be a doctor left in the church basement or if any of the rest of them are still alive in four months—but if they are, there'll be a new *neefje*.

"We'll find more food." Mieke tries to dry off with some old dish towels, even as she stares out the window toward the rising sun. They can't go lancing trucks anymore, not in daylight—but there are always other ideas.

High up on the rooftop of the closed school building, Mieke studies the dark forms, ten or twelve of them, some lining the tiled ridge, a few perching higher, on the chimneys. They're mostly still. Hunched over, looking down for remains to pluck at. Without warning, one unfolds its wings as if stretching out of its slumber and then collects itself. They sometimes put their heads together like they're conspiring. Other times they nip and push at one another, fighting over the same half meter of space as if there isn't tons of room.

Grijpgieren, Mr. DeVries told her they are called. Vultures. Scavengers. They come around all the time now, sometimes the skies are positively thick with them. They don't have to fear people anymore, now that the world has turned in some new way or reverted to an old way. Her mother calls them "rat-birds," but Mieke thinks they're much more beautiful than the horrible gray and brown vermin that climb in and out of the sewers now at all hours of the day and night—seemingly aware that they have less to fear from humans suddenly. The birds circle in the sky, keeping their distance, more or less.

The rats hunt, constantly, like she and Rob do, and on the same plane. But the dark birds wait, perched up there; they know there's plenty coming.

SCHOOL HAD REDUCED to half days and then was gone all together, which was just as well, because scavenging soon became a full-time occupation for Mieke and Rob. The classroom windows were smashed, the desks pulled out, along with anything else that anyone could find to burn. Pencils, rulers, schoolbooks, the maps of Africa. All ashes now. No one gathers in the little park now, and the benches have been taken apart, every wooden board pried loose. And the midnight brigades have chopped down most of the trees. It is illegal to have saws or hatchets, so it must be done cautiously, quickly. Only one big oak tree remains standing there in the very center, too big to be felled by hand. There are slices all around the edge of it, fresh gouges all the time, from people desperate enough to try. The oak just stands, silently wounded, missing all the branches low enough to be stripped off—but alive, nonetheless.

Six weeks. Six weeks for it to come to this.

MRS. SMIT LEAVES during the day at least once to collect her rations. Because her husband and son are members of the NSB, she gets more coupons than anyone else, including the Müellers, and they share extra. Once a week the old Germans invite all the kids in the building to come in for a meal made from anything they have available. In any case, Mieke looks for Mrs. Smit, because when she leaves the building, the men in the attic are free to come down and use the bathroom—her mother doesn't love cleaning up after six smelly men, but they are alive and in good spirits.

They descend and kiss their wives, their children. They exchange their sweaty, stained clothes for clean ones. Sometimes they have an hour, often less. Each day they are thinner, mangier, and complain more about their sore backs and necks. There aren't many spots up there where they can stand up all the way.

"*Liefje*," her father calls as he waits in line for his own bathroom, "Mr. Visser and I carved these for you and Rob."

He hands her a bulge of cloth ripped from somewhere, and inside are a few dozen little bits of wood, some light, some darkened with grease.

"Chess pieces," he explains to her. "The white side have little Dutch caps. The black have German helmets."

Mieke hugs her father, so happy to see him each day that she barely comprehends what he's saying to her. "I don't know how to play chess."

"Rob can teach you."

She does not relish the idea of needing Rob's help with anything else today.

"The soup this morning was *zuuuu-perb!*" He is affecting a French accent. "*Non?*"

"*Non.*" She laughs. "It tasted like horse blankets."

He sighs. "Ah, but *ze* finest horse blankets in all the land."

It is his turn to go use the toilet at last. Before he goes in, he pulls a sheaf of papers from his arm that he's forgotten he's still holding. He turns to his daughter.

"Take these to your mother, eh? I'll be a few minutes."

He goes in and Mieke immediately rushes off to look at what he's given her. Wrapped up in the papers are three forged identity cards for the Vos family. And a sheet of extra food coupons. With tools from his shop that he once used to repair books, Mr. Janssen has been hard at work, counterfeiting and altering documents. With a penknife he can slice the J off the corner of a Jewish person's card. Little daubs of bleach can change a name, alter an age. Extra coupons bring a few more rations for the building. Without a magnifying glass, you'd never know they aren't real.

Mieke delivers it all to her mother and then sits, patiently at the window, watching down the street for Mrs. Smit's return. As soon as she rounds the corner, the men have only a minute to get themselves back up into the attic, where they'll stay locked away until tomorrow.

WITH ROB'S LEG bandaged, he and Mieke head back out. The sun is fully up now, casting a pale gray light. The chill in the air has everyone saying there will be snow early this year. That it will be a very, very cold winter. Out in the western country, the resistance has dynamited the rail lines to keep the Germans from taking more prisoners out to their camps. But it also keeps the trains from bringing supplies in. Every time there's a new sabotage, it means *retaliation*, another word she's learned now from her father. The Germans are taking everything they can.

Which is it? Retaliation? Or desperation? like he said before.

THEN A GREAT blast sounds, off to the north. The same rumble and hiss of the rockets that she heard all those weeks ago now happens three times an hour, V2s launching from the beach, barely a half mile away. With the noise comes a rush of air pressure that cracks and still sometimes shatters the glass in the apartment windows. Not all at once, but, maddeningly at random, around the building. Keeping them open helps diffuse the pressure, but then it gets too cold. Rob's been scrounging for bits of tar paper that can be nailed up in their place. With each day that passes, a little less light comes in from outside, and soon there's almost nothing to brighten the rooms but a small fire they keep low in an old tomato can, and seldom have anything to cook over.

MEANWHILE, THE WORLD belongs to the children. With all the men gone and the mothers in their houses trying to keep things together, Mieke sees the other kids doing what she's doing. Begging, scrounging, scavenging. Some of the older kids lead groups of the littler ones and they squabble with one another over anything and everything. They push around old baby prams and fill them with fallen branches and loose scraps of wood and anything they hope they can barter for food. Soldiers ignore them, mostly, unless someone decides to spit toward their boots or shout something from the alley, and then they chase the kids off. It's a way of creating a diversion, Rob says.

"Yeah, but what if they shoot you?" she asks.

"They won't waste a bullet," he predicts, but not confidently.

Jopie Tideman and his brothers pass on the far side of the tracks. One of them has an axe in his hand, but they're distracted, trying to lift a small tree. It's a sapling, and wet still. All that's left for miles probably. Even if it won't burn well, it could get them through another night.

A cluster of girls, this one led by Marjo Mulder, goes the other way with their fishing poles, even though the river is mostly too cold at this point to snag much. But it gives her an idea.

"Remember the eels?" she says to Rob. "The rivers won't be frozen yet."

He shudders. "You can if you want. If Jopie's gone, I'm going to take Broodje to pick through the alley. The soldiers usually dump yesterday's potato peels about now."

Mieke goes toward the narrow path behind the butcher's shop, where Rob has had some luck finding not just thrown-away food scraps, but also parts of tables and chairs that no one else thinks are worth burning. But mostly it is filled with rats, and the other end is blocked off. She doesn't like that there's only one way out, and if Jopie comes back out in a few minutes to find Rob rooting around on his own, they'll set on him.

"I'll stay with you two," Mieke says.

"Go if you want," Rob snaps. "I'm fine on my own."

Mieke's hands want to clench. "Don't be stupid."

"*You're* stupid. Thinking you can catch an eel all by yourself."

"We'll see. *I'm* not a baby."

"I'm not, either," Rob shouts back.

She storms off to go home and gather up the lines and hooks that his father left behind. Then she heads out to the stream alone, trying to find the spot where they fished the eels, long ago.

AS SHE WALKS through the woods, she thinks back on two weeks ago. The signal had come up through the fireplace, three taps from the Müellers. The Germans were coming. Mieke had only half a minute to get over to the attic hatch and tap at it, to signal to the men up there that they'd need to hide behind the tarps and storm windows. The five of them had practiced over and over, squeezing together into the gap between the eaves and the false wall. Mieke had gotten back in the apartment before the soldiers made it to the stairs—but they turned out not to be there to poke around in the attic after all.

Spying from the crack in the doorway, Mieke had seen the Germans approaching the locked door to Mr. DeVries's apartment. A few days before, he had brought over a box full of food for the men in the attic. "I have to go on a little journey, and this will all go bad," he offered by way of explanation.

"Where are you going?" she asked, but he put his fingers to his lips and smiled.

"Don't sneak inside while I'm away, Mata Hari," he said. "I left out some traps."

"For mice?"

"For rats," he'd answered. "But don't worry. I'll take care of them, *liefje*."

The Germans had broken down his locked door in under a minute. Inside, probably they'd expected to find the same modest odds and ends that they'd been pillaging from the other apartments in the building. Mieke had spied on them as they'd rummaged through the rooms, shouting happily, pulling down paintings, lifting the marble sculptures. Stashing the mother-of-pearl boxes, the silk robes, and the fine rugs. Acting like they'd found the mother lode. Excitedly jabbering in German about how their wives and girlfriends would enjoy the ruby-set jewelry, the gold-framed bathroom mirror, the phonograph. The taxidermied octopus. The typewriter. Bit by bit, they'd taken his beautiful treasures away.

ALONE, IN THE woods, Mieke pulls the golden letter opener from the hidden pocket she's sewn inside her dress. It is still not very sharp, but it brings her some confidence when she is scavenging alone. She tries to stay dry and cuts the lines and gets them set in the ground around the stream, which flows busily through the forest, bearing the browning leaves along its babbling length. She baits the hooks with earthworms and sits in wait, the lines along her fingertips, breathing softly. Praying that the eels have not yet departed the streams for the winter. They travel thousands of miles, according to Rob's father, first to the ocean and then back toward the Sargasso Sea that lies in its untraveled heart, a quiet place filled with the brown seaweed they need for shelter and food. Wrapped up and protected by currents on all sides, it is itself a lost, calm space. She imagines it, an oceanic Luilekkerland, an expanse of still waters, from which you can see waves moving out and across, far away, but unable to touch you. A land that is not land, filled with life and plenty. If she were an eel, she thinks, she would stay there instead of being here.

Though it is peaceful and quiet, the leaves that have not fallen yet are still lit in the sun's shine. Colored red and orange and yellow. Out here it is still as if there are no Germans, there is no war. Here she can pretend that it all is not happening, and that she is not their sole hope of eating anything tonight.

Then she sees a huge form, hunched low across the river, higher up on its muddy bank. Immediately she thinks of Gullin, the fiery beast from the fairy-tale book. No. But an actual wild boar? Hadn't her father told her they'd all been hunted long ago? Only slowly does she realize that it is just a man, with a beard all overgrown and bushy—his eyes are dark and beady as they fix on her. He's soaked, too, trying to keep his head dry under some dark animal skin. She freezes as he parts his mouth. Two teeth set apart by a few inches of absence in the middle. Though the river flows between them, it is not very deep. He could bound over it in two or three strides if he wanted to. She's petrified. She can't get to the letter opener, lying there on the ground, without dropping one of her fishing lines. There's probably no one else around for miles. Whoever he is, he's clearly enormous, even folded over as he is. Whatever he might want to do to her, she could not stop him; she knows this even though she does not even know what it is that he might want. It's the fear in her mother's eyes when strange men come too close. It is all unknowable, but it does not need to be known to be feared. Her survival depends on only one thing now— what is, or is not, inside of this creature.

Only after a tense moment does Mieke get her answer. Disinterest. He turns away from her and busies himself with what he has been doing. He has a piece of a paving stone in his hands and is using it to cut down into the mud. Where he's crouching, the ground is black and dense. Grunting, working, he marks out a rectangular area. Then he digs his filthy fingers deep down into the crevasses and loosens a chunk of earth the size of a cinder block.

Peat, her father will explain to her later, when she tells him what she's seen. He'll slap his own forehead in excitement—*I never thought of that!*

Packed layers of dead leaves and bits of trees that have fallen into the bog. Decomposed, compressing over the years until it becomes dense like coal. Just needs to be dried out. Once the grizzled man has peeled off a few blocks, he sets them onto a skid he's built from an old piece of carpeting and some rope. They'll each take a few weeks to dry out fully, her father will surmise, but then they can be burned in a stove like coal or wood. It is how it had once been done all around the eastern country before they'd been able to depend on coal coming down from the mountains every season. It wasn't as efficient, but it was certainly plentiful. All they'd need was time and a way of getting it back to the house.

Mieke's lines suddenly go taut—one within a second of the other. Her fingers almost slip away, half-numb from the cold. As she grunts and struggles, the bog man sits up and takes a new interest in her as she fights with the lines, tugging and easing in turn, not sure how she can possibly get two at the same time, but determined to try. The one on the line in her left hand breaks the water's surface first. There on the end is an enormous eel, twice the size of the one Professor Naaktgeboren had caught before, and so powerful it could take her arm off. The second is a little smaller, but lightning fast, and Mieke has to dig her heels hard into the muck to gain any leverage at all. She looks toward the bog man to see if he might help, but he watches in curious silence.

It is then that she realizes she has not brought a bucket to carry them home—the one Professor Naaktgeboren had used last summer had been carted away weeks ago. And she has no knife with her, either, to kill them there on the banks.

Desperately, she gathers both lines together in one hand. They cut against her skin until it splits and bleeds, but finally she hauls both eels to the shore. She uses her foot to hold their bodies down, but no sooner does she stomp down than the smaller one coils up her leg, slimy and fast, everywhere at once. Meanwhile the bigger eel lowers itself mysteriously into the mud and becomes so still she wonders if it has gotten free. She releases the lines and grabs at the eel circling her calf. It is tying itself tightly beneath her knee. Vaguely she is aware she's been screaming. Her hand finds some bit of the eel firm enough to hold and flings it off.

As fast as she can, Mieke throws her coat over the eel, and then wraps it all in a ball so it cannot wriggle out. No time to celebrate, she turns her attention to the second eel, digging with her bleeding hands down into the spot where it has vanished, pulling on the line, until the irritated beast at last erupts from the earth. It flies right up into the air, a shocking height, and if it had simply swum off into the dark sky, she wouldn't have been surprised. Instead, it falls back against her arm, and she seizes the thing in two gory hands and jams it into the coat with the first eel.

It is done; she is exhausted.

Only now she must carry her wet coat instead of wearing it, and she's cut and drenched and slimy. Miles from home and it is still raining. Mieke looks around for help, but the bog man has left, and she is alone there, breathing heavily, waiting for her heart to stop pounding. She'd had it in mind to catch a half dozen eels before going home—but she needs to dress her wounds and get warm before she catches pneumonia.

Then, movement from beside her. The bristly bearded man has crossed over on her side of the river, a foot or two away. She cries out and leaps away, heart in her throat. He is so much bigger than she's realized. Where is the letter opener? Has he been waiting all this time to come deal with her?

Mieke slips in the leaves. It is only after she hits the mud and feels his hand on her arm that she realizes he is not trying to steal her food or hurt her.

Mutely, he helps her up. Once she is on her feet, he yanks off his coat and tosses it down on a flat rock. It is far too enormous for her to wear, but he has only removed it so he can pull off his shirt beneath: heavy, knitted, and reddish. In a moment his skin is bare, though so thickly covered in coarse dark hair that she can't believe it isn't yet another coat. The bog man hands her the shirt. It stinks, and though it is warm from his body, it is also damp with his sweat. Still, much better than nothing. Once she is wrapped to his satisfaction, the bog man climbs back into his own coat and grunts a farewell. Silently he trudges away, dragging his mud behind him.

AS SHE STUMBLES home, her hands cut and bleeding, Mieke considers this kindness. If she fails to grasp the cruelty of some people, it's the goodness of the rest that mystifies her most. For what good can last, in a world like this? It makes her miss Mr. DeVries even more.

"Schwarzwälder Kirschtorte!" Mieke recalls the Nazis coming out of the kitchen in DeVries's apartment, carrying it: a perfectly beautiful chocolate cake, circled in ribbons of creamy frosting, topped with black cherries. It had been sitting out for a few days, but it still looked quite moist, with one wedge already cut out such that Mieke could see the thick layers inside, four beautiful brown lines of chocolate, divided with rich white bands of whipped cream, a blood-red cherry syrup oozing out as the soldiers consumed the rest, slice after slice. Chortling, as if DeVries had made it just for them before he'd fled the apartment, a consummate host to the very end, even to those vultures.

BACK ALONG LAAN van Meerdervoort, Mieke finds Broodje and Rob, a clump of potato peels in Rob's shirt, but also a fresh black eye that he doesn't want to talk about. There were probably more potato peels before they lost whatever fight they lost. She's about to show them the eels in her coat bundle when suddenly everything goes dark around them.

Her ears have gotten so numb to the sounds of the Luftwaffe planes going overhead by now that at first she doesn't recognize the difference in the noise of the plane's engines. Rob does, however, and he looks up into the cold gray sky and says, "Amerikanen."

There in the sky is a plane—very low. Maybe a hundred feet

above the rooftops. So low that she can clearly see its different col-
oring, the little badge of red and blue stripes. White stars. A line
of gray smoke, trailing. It is hurt—the plane, flames licking out of
the fuselage.

She freezes. It is coming right for them. Rob clutches at her
hand, unable to move himself away. It hangs in the sky, glittering
in the pale sunlight like a Christmas ornament.

Impossibly, she can make out the face of a pilot in the cockpit,
and then in an instant, the glass around him bursts away and he
is airborne. Him and another man, no longer inside the plane's
shell, as the hollow thing veers away toward the shoreline, away
from the city buildings. She holds her breath as the two forms
twist in the sky, almost dancing with each other as they fall, and
then there is a great puff of parachute that erupts and fills like a
balloon.

"They're too close," Rob mumbles. And he doesn't need to say
more. Mieke shivers as the two bodies plummet, still so fast, toward the ground. In one second their swirling forms appear to be
hitting the orange-tiled roof of one of the apartments on the next
block; then they're lost in the alleyway behind it. The parachutes
follow, tangling up with each other, great beige bedsheets coming
down, and then they, too, are gone.

Silence. Then a massive explosion up by the beach where the
plane slams down—she imagines it has crashed right onto their
pointy little Nazi heads. There are shouts from all up and down
the avenue. Soldiers rush out, guns flapping and rocking around
at their sides or perching there between their hands as their boots
go stomping—some north toward the beach, and others over to
where the men went down. And in the rush of it all, Rob manages
to squeeze life back into Mieke's hands. "Broodje, go home," he
commands, shoveling the potato peels into her brother's bag. The
boy is gone in a flash, and then she and Rob are running, too,
half trying to get to the alleyway first, the other half trying not to
get trampled. They come around the corner where the Meijmans'
butcher shop still sits, boarded up and dark, and then stand at
the mouth of the alleyway, watching, insignificant, as the soldiers

storm to the place where the parachutes now lay out across the cobblestones in muddy lumps. From the uncollected trash heaps, the rats come scrambling out, dozens, scrabbling and screeching. The soldiers tear the parachutes up and push the rubbish heaps over. Looking everywhere for the two Americans. Orders echo around, to spread out, to search the area, to kick down the doors. Then the soldiers scatter, following alongside the panicked rats until the alleyway is empty.

Rob and Mieke stand there, unsure what to say or where to go. It is barely a minute before they see two women duck out of the nearest door. The women seize the parachute and drag it inside. The gray-brown cloud vanishes quickly up the steps and through the door, which clicks shut. What will they do with it? They don't even know. There isn't always a plan.

BUT SOMETIMES THERE IS. The rat poison that Mr. DeVries had laced the cake with had been fast-acting. Mieke saw the soldiers, ten minutes later, clenching at their stomachs, stumbling out the door. One fell over and hit his head on the wall. She heard the sickening crack, watched his eyes widen. Mieke hid inside, unable to watch as he thrashed around, screaming. She had no idea how long she stayed there, head buried in Tante Sintje's apron, her mother huddled beside them, stroking her hair and singing something to try and cover the agonies outside. When the noise finally stopped, the other women were shaking. They told Mieke to stay put, but she snuck to the doorway anyway while their backs were turned.

And there it was, her first dead body. She barely had a chance to absorb it when more noises began outside the building. The second soldier was there, bent over on the curb. Collapsed, twitching, gurgling for help. A third soldier, who maybe hadn't eaten quite as much, managed to get all the way to Meijmans', moaning for help. The men and women gathered on the street just stepped away, watching, but refusing to help him. Others were already eyeing the loot that the soldiers had been gathering, abandoned out there in their truck. Unguarded. It wouldn't be long until reinforcements arrived. Someone dashed over to grab a lamp. Then a second and a third, and soon the whole neighborhood was there, hauling off whatever they could: picture frames, eggbeaters, Persian lamps, a pair of brass sconces with lilac glass. Jopie Tideman and his brothers made off with the painting from Mr. Akkeringa and a table runner made of silk. If they couldn't sell them off, they'd burn them for warmth. When Mieke came back inside, she found her mother and Sintje moving quickly through the already nearly emptied rooms of DeVries's apartment, taking whatever else they could find before more Germans could arrive.

HOME AT LAST, Mieke pulls the eels from her coat like a small, wet, skinny magician. While everyone else backs away, Mieke deals with them just as she's been taught. Hammering the nail through the head, slicing behind the jaw, pulling the wriggling skin back. Removing the organs and then cutting out chunks of meat for her mother to cook. Mieke feels numb, a fuzzy tiredness that holds her tears at bay. It would be too human, to cry, and she doesn't feel human right now. Thinking of the professor, thinking of the fluid-emptied soldier in the stairwell. No one says a word as they watch her work. When it is done, she cleans her hands and finds the bandages and the antiseptic and goes out into the living room to find Rob resting on the chest.

"Get up, lazybones," she says. "We can still go out to the farm before it gets dark."

MIEKE AND ROB head toward the edge of town then, to the grove where they've been hiding their bicycles. The farm is about ten kilometers away. She only half remembers the route, but her father has passed her down instructions, written out in a concerningly shaky hand. He'd taken her along when she was—what, three? Four? Before the war. They'd gone out beyond the edge of the city to where Farmer Stuldreher grew the wheat her father milled to make the flour for his bread.

Mieke and Rob ride their bicycles slowly along the dirt roads, wary of breaking a wheel or popping their tires, for there'll be no fixing these now. If soldiers come by and spot them, they'll take the bicycles—but she has no choice. The men in the attic are hungry. Everyone's hungry.

She guesses they've been riding almost two hours, even if in the spits of rain and the grayness of the day it is hard to know.

At last they come over a little hill, expecting to see the road ahead of them and soon, the Stuldreher farm. Instead, they find themselves staring at a vast brownish lake. It spreads a mile out to the other side, and, too, the other way. Mieke's suddenly worried she's led them the wrong direction, but after a moment she recognizes the farmhouse, still there, half sunk in the middle of the tide plain. Heartbroken, she follows the horizon line and realizes what has happened. The wide seawall that used to be out there is gone. Blasted away. And now this: a flood of mud and muck. The land reclaimed by the sea. It is happening all up and down the shoreline, she's heard. The Germans are blowing up the dikes to swamp any Allied advancements. And the Allies are hitting them, too, hoping to wash out the antiaircraft defenses along the Atlantikwall.

Last night, through the hole to the attic, her father told her the most incredible story, about how the Allies managed to corner a bunch of the German troops on tiny Walcheren Island. They'd bombed the dikes at Westkapelle that sent a flood in to sweep them all away. Her father was happy about this when he came down that morning with the other men in the ceiling, but Mieke spent the night restless. What about the Dutch people on the island? she kept wondering. Had they gotten out? Were they swept away, too?

"It's not too deep here," Rob says, testing the path ahead with a bare foot. Mieke can make out some of the fields, safe above the waterline, up ahead. If only they can get to them. They hide the bicycles off the road a few feet, behind an abandoned tractor, whose unrusted parts have already all been hauled away, along with one of its enormous tires. The remaining one is shredded so badly that it has been ignored. Mieke tucks the bicycles and shoes behind it where she hopes no one will find them. Then, rolling their pants up above their knees, Mieke balances the big straw basket on her head with one hand and with the other she grips Rob's hand before taking their first cautious, sucking steps through the frigid watery sludge. A few feet at a time, trying not to step on the sharp sticks and rocks that hide along the bottom, Mieke and Rob manage to slowly creep out toward the undrowned field.

"Look," she says after a while, pointing out to the deeper water. Near the flooded farmhouse is a little rowboat, being slowly paddled by an old man in a dark hat. There is a woman with him, trying to steady a haul of goods they've pulled from the top floor of the farm. Big rolls of blankets, an old chair, some boards of wood. Sacks of either clothes or food. The man has a rifle, sticking up at an angle from in between his legs. Is it for protection? Or did they bring it in case any of the Stuldrehers were still in there? Maybe both.

Eventually Mieke and Rob slop out onto drier ground. But even as they do, they can see the field is all green winter wheat. It won't become full and turn its final amber color until summer. For now, it waits out the coming freeze, lying dormant for months, before spring's light awakens it. Crushed, Mieke lets her fingers dance lightly through their stunted reach.

"This is too young," Rob grunts.

"Maybe there's more on the other side." Mieke points deeper in at a few taller beige rows, waving gently in the cold wind's blowing.

They crawl between the rows, leaves whipping them in the face. She keeps the basket under her coat, just in case. If they're spotted, she can say she is a friend of Mr. Stuldreher's come to check on him. But he must be gone or in hiding, she's sure of that—the fear is that one of his younger sons also has a gun or that his wife is still in the house, alone and terrified.

They're in greater danger of running into other looters—like the man and woman in the boat, who have had this same idea.

But for now the whole place is deathly still and quiet. Mieke and Rob creep up along the winter wheat until they come to the next crop, all cut down now, whatever it is or was. They shiver, feet wet and freezing. For a few pulsating moments there is no shelter at all, and they are out in the open, and then they are safe—or safer, in the shadow of the wheat. What's left of it, anyway. The stalks have been knocked down, mostly—by deer or some other animals. They're getting bolder now, without people around.

The other day she heard there was a huge wolf spotted strolling up Leidsestraat just after dawn. She grimaces, remembering the end of that story, which was that the soldiers killed it and burned the carcass so that no one could scavenge the meat.

There are a few stalks of wheat they can still work with, and she begins showing Rob how to take them down and separate out the stock. Inside are handfuls of wheatberries, but the chaff around it has to be removed. You can do it by hand, but it takes ages. However, her father had told her, if you give it to the wind, the wind will do the work for you.

She pulls as much down as she can and then holds the wheat stock high into the air, twisting it and turning it in her fingers until it catches the breeze like a kite. A little at a time, at first, the thin papery chaff comes blowing off like thin dandelion wisps and flies away. Soon the gusting picks up and they are cleaning two, three at a time. The trick, her father explained, is to launch it high in the air and then catch it in the basket coming down. It sparkles and glints in the sky, like fairy dust. And Rob laughs, thinking this, too.

IT WAS TANTE Sintje who found DeVries in the bathroom. He'd swallowed a dozen of his little sleeping pills and climbed into his pearl-inlaid claw-footed bathtub. Mieke had not been allowed to see—she would never have wanted to. Now when she closes her eyes at night she pictures him in his red silk robe, asleep in his porcelain coffin, his skin pale and waxy. *Blue 88s. Isn't that a lovely name?* She hears his voice. *They don't tell you children what's going on, do they?* He had been in there three or four days, they said.

And in the living room, the majestic fighting fish. This Mieke had seen herself. The warrior floating belly up in the clear water, her silken fins dangling downward. So still, so peaceful.

Tante Sintje had taken it into the kitchen and dumped it out.

Seeing her niece's sadness, she'd said, "It only would have rotted," and without thinking rested her hands on her stomach as she turned to keep Truus from toddling toward the staircase.

WITH THE WHEAT safely covered in the basket, she and Rob leave the field through the muck and return steadily to the grasses. Their bikes and shoes are gone.

"*Godverdomme!*" Rob snaps, and Mieke glares at him. *Goddammit!* If his mother ever discovered he'd said it, she'd take his books away for a month. But Mieke would never tell.

"*Godverdomme! Godverdomme! Godverdomme!*" she howls.

It feels good, for a moment. Still, she has no idea what to do, or how they'll ever get home with no shoes and no bicycles.

"I hate the Germans," Rob spits as he begins to pry at a rock in the roadway.

"What are you doing?" she asks.

"Making us some shoes."

She watches, thinking. The Germans would have confiscated the bicycles, but not the shoes. That those are missing, too, Mieke thinks, means some other Dutch people took them.

But she just grunts as if Rob must be right. She takes out the golden letter opener that DeVries gave her and uses it to help Rob hack some pieces off the tractor's shredded tire. Then he climbs up inside of the great rusted dinosaur and spends a few minutes digging around inside it, until he comes out with a mess of wiring. After a little bit of effort, he's able to loop the wires through the rubber pieces so that he can tie them to their feet. They're uncomfortable and the wiring rubs raw against her damp, cold skin. But it is better than nothing. Slowly they begin the long walk back. Their bodies have burned every ounce of fat they once possessed. The rolls around Rob's middle have vanished in recent weeks, and his cheeks have pulled inward, like curtains.

IT IS ALREADY dark as they come down the final stretch along the dismantled trolley tracks near their house. There's a clearing ahead that the soldiers have blocked off, in case paratroopers should try to land there. The red sign reads MIJNEN, land mines, and along the wire border, Mieke can see a crowd has gathered there in the dark, which is unusual these days—there are some of the older men, some of the mothers. Lots of children. A few people have little hand-crank flashlights. Someone else has a camping lantern with some oil still in it. But for the most part it is dark, hard to see what is going on.

Two German soldiers are holding back one of the teenage boys, who, she sees in a moment, is trying to get in. She's seen him hanging around with one of Jopie's brothers. His name is Riet—

"Is he crazy?" she asks. "Can't he read?"

"Smell that?" Rob replies, and as she inhales, she does smell something—a terrible burning smell. Like when her finger slipped last year, trying to light a candle. And then they see that a gray smoke is dispersed over the dark field. One of the mines has gone off. It happens sometimes. Birds, rabbits—already the ground is pocked and cratered in places.

But this time, Mieke guesses, a pit in her stomach, it has not been a bird or a rabbit.

Riet isn't trying to get in there because of a bird or a rabbit. *"Zus!"* He's sobbing. *"Mijn zus!"*

Mieke closes her eyes, tears behind them. *Sister. My sister.*

Kormaan. Riet Kormaan, she remembers.

"Come on," Rob breathes. "We're almost home. Let's go."

And as Mieke lets him tug her along, she opens her eyes. See-ing what she'd hoped not to see—a bit of purple coat, there by one of the craters. If she looked longer, she'd see more—which is why she can't. His sister, Jacoba. From the class down the hall. The one she'd wanted to hex.

"WHY WOULD SHE go in there?" Mieke asks Rob later as they take the wheat inside.

Rob doesn't answer. He knows she knows why.

How hungry do you have to get? How cold? How tired? Before the last bit of flame inside you goes out. Will she wake up one day without it? How long until there's no more wheat to steal? No more eels to catch? No more beets to poke loose?

AT HOME, THEIR mothers moan about the bicycles and more over the shoes, but still they take the wheatberries the children have collected and slide them scrupulously into the mouth of Professor Naaktgeboren's old coffee grinder. Fine set, it can crush the bits into a sweet blond flour. They haven't gathered enough for a whole loaf of bread, but mixed in with the grated sugar beets, they can make them into little patties. With a flame going in the aluminum can, they can heat some rapeseed oil in the big pan and fry these pancakes up into something half-edible. They can stretch her three little beets into food for six or seven people. Her eels will feed even more, and then there will be a thin gray soup made from the potato peels that Rob found in the alleyway. And that will carry them all through to tomorrow, when she and Rob can try again at the trucks.

THAT NIGHT MIEKE lies in bed, exhausted and hungry, but not quite as hungry as the day before, and for that she's grateful. She tries not to cough; her lungs are heavy. She's wearing a full set of worn clothes—they crack the windows so the air pressure from the rockets won't shatter the panes.

Rob is snoring, but her mother will be awake, trying to nurse

Truus, while Sintje slowly makes them new shoes from bits of leather and string pulled from their old bedspread.

Mieke can't sleep. There's a lot of noise coming from downstairs, and at first, she thinks it must be more soldiers coming to raid the building. If the Von Fliets aren't awake or if the Müellers are sleeping, they won't send a warning up in the fireplace in time. But when she peers outside the window in the moonlit night, she can see it is Jopie Tideman with more of the boys from up the road. She looks for Riet, but if he's there, she can't find him. They're keeping to the shadows; they're up to something. They bang around downstairs for a few hours, and then it is quiet.

CAREFULLY, MIEKE COMES down the stairs, the letter opener gripped in her hand. She stops at the landing in the dark and sees what they were doing. The Meiers' door, which has been shut and locked tight since long ago, is now completely missing. Someone has taken it right off its hinges—and then pried out the hinges. Probably it is already back at the Tideman house, being sawn to bits, ready to be put on the fire in place of the absent coal. Even with how cold she was last night in her room, having to snuggle together under the blanket with Rob to share their warmth—even then, she cannot at first believe that someone took their whole door off. But a moment later she's wondering why none of them thought of it. The Meiers didn't need it anymore. Who knew if they'd be back? She thinks about what DeVries told her, and how they almost certainly are dead already.

Mieke tiptoes inside the Meiers' apartment, moving slowly so that if anyone is still inside, rummaging, she'll hear them before they hear her. The cabinets are all open and emptied. The drawers have been pulled out and taken away, their contents spilled onto the floor. Even before she looks at what's left, she knows what she won't find. There won't be a scrap of food, not that much could have been edible since the Meiers left months ago, but if there'd been cans or jars of things, they will be gone now. She looks at the piles of junk on the floor. No thimbles, lead weights, anything metal. Books have been pulled off the shelves, too, and it looks like some are gone. Paper burns too fast to get much warmth, but the hardcovers last a little longer. The furniture's all gone; just two cushions remain from one couch. The bed frames have been hauled away in pieces. Suddenly she realizes it isn't just the doors missing, but even the framing of the doorways. It's been hacked off, pried loose, with just nails left, twisted. It must have been a whole crew of them. She can smell the stink of places they've pissed inside, but it may be from the rats.

Hopeless. Clothes, gone. And someone's smashed the mirror in the living room, too, taken the frame and left the broken glass all over the floor. The more she looks around and sees what must have been there, hours ago, the more she wonders how foolish they've been—to have overlooked it all for so long. The hangover of their former kindness and consideration is what will kill them, she thinks—but this idea is so horrible she shakes it away. What if they all thought that way? What if the bog man had? What if the Müellers preferred collecting the reward they'd receive for turning in the men in the attic?

No. There is still good. Right now, there is. For how much longer, she doesn't know.

It's freezing in the apartment. No one's been there to cover the broken glass in the windows as they've been shattering, these past weeks now. But there's light then, inside. She hasn't seen this well indoors in weeks. Mieke is careful, moving past the area with the loose shards. And as she glances down to make sure she's not crossing over any shattered sections, she catches a look at herself refracted within one of them. Silver with winter moonlight. Her hair is matted and knotted. Her face smudged and dirty, worse than her clothes, which are also bad. But it isn't this that stuns her. She's felt these things, seen things turning to rags, all the thread going bare. What she hasn't seen in weeks now is *herself*. Her own eyes. They're dull, dark. Like the eyes of an animal. Her own cheeks, jutting out at hard angles. Her hands, she's seen, are as thin as the bones inside them. But the same applies to her shoulders, her arms, her legs. Biting against the cold, she can't stop herself from looking. She thinks about the fighting fish, how DeVries had warned her. If she saw her reflection, she'd bash herself into the glass until she died.

Slowly Mieke eases her sleeves back, lifts her pant legs. Finally, her shirtwaist, and beneath it, she's all ribs—*that* she's felt— and the blades of her hips, and the hard ridge of her breastbone rising right into a spine masquerading as a neck. She's so thin, her skin's so close to everything underneath. It lifts and throbs with her heart's clumsy beat. She watches it, in there, like another thing, some red fairy living inside of the shell of her, trying to keep itself warm. Only no, she tells herself, it is the opposite. It is pumping its blood to her, thin and deficient as it might be. This is the part of her that's most alive. Each time it swells, it is a defiance. Each time it smooths itself away, it is summoning more force, to be propelled, and to propel—her. In the glass is a girl who is not dead yet, and she's grateful for the reminder.

NACHTNEBEL

~

The new kapo running Groente is a man named Nachtnebel, a human certainly possessed by strange whims. He devotes hours each day to forcing the prisoners to listen to tinny recordings of Beethoven and Schubert over the corrupting prison speakers, and has taken the time in what we suspect is his crushing boredom (parading people around and then murdering them must lose its appeal even to monsters when repeated day after day, thousands upon thousands of times) to arrange for a variety of instruments to be brought in. He postpones the executions of anyone with a nice singing voice or a talent for playing the accordion or the violin. The Romani are frequently quite gifted, and many have traveled all through Austria and Turkey and Czechoslovakia and have mastered a startling array of folk tunes. And so Kapo Nachtnebel, from time to time, demands demonstrations from those whose deaths he's forestalled.

To this end, he has transformed one of the larger rooms of the prison for their performances. We eels have advanced on it in secret, moving silently through water mains and sewer trenches. While the larger atmosphere of Kamp Groente is generally gray, cold, and heavy on concrete and barbed wire, the performance room, known as the Corner, is gaudily arranged. The kapo has hung framed paintings, many of which are of the precise variety normally viewed as degenerate by other Germans:

elongated nudes draped and lounging around. The whole room has the feel of a prewar café.

Nostalgia, a word made of Greek bricks, our author knows. *Nostos*: "homecoming"; *algos*: "sorrow." But despite the Homeric undertones, the term comes from seventeenth-century Switzerland. Invented by a medical student there attempting to diagnose the anxious mercenaries fighting far from home.

Disgusting! To think of Nachtnebel as anxious. Our elongated stomachs twist in knots at granting him any feeling whatsoever. But the Corner brings it to our author's mind, along with all the "homecoming sorrows" of his own. Entwined with him as we are, we feel what he feels, even see what he sees. Oh, it is terrible to be human! You must know. Why must we now long for a brierwood pipe, stuffed with tobacco from Tideman's Tabakswinkel? We are eels and cannot even smoke. Why must we now fantasize nightly over the runny crème brûlée at a school dining hall where our author once taught? Why must we see, in our mind's eye, the look of sawdust to him as a child, hanging in the air during the golden hour? Why must we feel his son's infant weight in our phantom arms? Beauty finds him, even here. And so it finds us, too.

"Better this be a prison of the body," one of the prisoners said to him the other night as they stood side by side out at the barbed wire fence in the cold, "than a mass grave of the mind."

Our author knows Nachtnebel from somewhere. We are not sure exactly; he conceals it from even us. He avoids the kapo's eye, but he still attends the performances. Often they do not even know he is around. And though an hour spent there in the company of Brahms or Schubert is a treat, there is an agony that comes with the sight of Nachtnebel, moved to tears by a partita or a rondeau. This monster feels for notes and chords and songs—just not for anyone else there with him. It is a torture so exquisite that we can't help but wonder if it is intentional.

We wonder. It is all so new to us. We did not think anything could be.

—V.S.

DÜSSELDORF

~

After Will had failed to match for his residency, his faculty advisor scrounged up a year-long research position overseas, to boost the chances for a future match. It had all happened quickly, three days after a five-minute meeting for coffee. The Faculty of Medicine at Heinrich Heine University in Düsseldorf, Germany, would take Will for one of their *forschergruppen*, a research group on *medizinische soziologie*, or in English, medical sociology.

Were it a post in Siberia, Will would have approached it with more enthusiasm. But upon arrival, he quickly took a liking to the folks working in the hospital group, who did not mind that he spoke no German and were eager to practice their English with him. One of the other researchers introduced himself as "Aoto from Kyoto" and on the second day brought, for Will to admire, his glass-encased collection of all fifty American state quarters, which he'd been painstakingly gathering for almost seven years.

Aoto genially showed him the sights in Düsseldorf: the Königsallee and the Aquazoo Löbbecke Museum and an extremely bawdy puppet show. He wanted to introduce Will to the local brew, Altbier, but Will said he did not drink (at least he had not since the med school party). But he did at least pretend to be enthusiastic about going to see Die Sexobjekt, a local Kraftwerk cover band—

and Will heard repeatedly how the *real* Kraftwerk was founded right there in Düsseldorf.

And this fact, Will tried hard to find amazing each time.

Meanwhile, he sank into the field of medical sociology, of which he'd known next to nothing before arriving—his former advisor had given him packets of reading materials: Henderson, Becker, Pescosolido, Fox . . . on and on. Will began dedicating his early mornings to boning up on Harry Stack Sullivan and interpersonal theory of psychiatry "high contact" therapies. The *forschergruppen* was examining bulimia nervosa patients at a nearby hospital. The idea was to see if IPT effectively supplemented treatment of their eating disorders by tackling so-called problems in living: finding the patients stable jobs and affordable places to live, and improving various other quality-of-life metrics. With these stressors reduced or eliminated, the patient would be able to focus more easily on becoming well.

When he compared this to his surgical training, Will found the work utterly alien. And yet he could not deny that the Germans' approach got results. Alleviating the frenetic pressures of ordinary daily life and reducing overall anxiety was far more effective in helping the patients with their disordered eating than he'd have ever imagined. At the same time, he felt this same thing working for himself—life in Düsseldorf was easy. Simple. He had only a few new friends, no family to worry about. Barely three weeks into his stay there, Will was happier than he could remember being. He was even thankful, for the first time, not to be back at Duke or Emory, being fed into the meat grinder of surgical resident life.

Will spoke on the phone with his oma a few times to report he was alive and well. She urged him to hop on a train across the border, into Holland, to see Den Haag again, since he was so close by. She even seemed a bit unhappy with his being in Germany at all. Will kept promising he would get out to visit the Hague, and sometimes even looked up the train tickets, but he couldn't quite bring himself to do it. He was so detached, so free, in Düsseldorf. He couldn't say why, but while there was some comfort at being nearer to his homeland, he felt more intensely that he should stay in this new place, where he could be a new person, one who had never been crazy, who did not have a father who'd bought him Gouda cheese in Delft, and who had never seen reality dissolve in front of his eyes while wearing jorts. Will began trying to figure out if there was some way for him to stay in Düsseldorf permanently.

And that's when Will met Teru.

Düsseldorf was headquarters to many global companies, including several Japanese ones. Aoto explained that Germany and Japan had quite a strong business relationship, and when Will laughed at this, his colleague did not seem to understand why it was so humorous. *Axis powers together again? Was Italy not available?* Will did not say this, though. He'd already noticed that there'd been little mention of all that dark history in his explorations of the city. He realized that the fact of it was everywhere in what was not there. Barely any buildings existed at all from before 1943, when the seven-week bombing campaign had obliterated nearly all the old city. There was a memorial museum, he'd read in his guidebook, in an old air raid shelter, dedicated to better understanding the role of the German anti-Nazi resistance, Die Mahn und Gedenkstätte für die Opfer der nationalsozialistischen Gewaltherrschaft, which came to something like Memorial for the Victims of the National Socialist Tyranny, and Will had it on his list of things to do at some point—but like going to the Hague, it somehow never felt like the right time.

In May, Aoto invited Will to join the rest of them at Japan-Tag, an annual festival of Japanese culture in Germany, the culmination of a whole week of themed events. Will had already noticed large displays of martial arts happening in the nearby church square, and men and women milling around in droves, often dressed up as anime characters, as well as in more traditional Japanese clothing. Will agreed to come and at least see some fireworks on the final day and to take part in some sort of regional cooking class.

A real chef from a local Japanese restaurant would take them to the Fischmarkt on the Rhine and teach them about finding the best quality seafood, before returning to the kitchen for a two-hour class on how to prepare authentic Japanese dishes.

Will went along, not realizing until he arrived that everyone else there would be coupled up. Young people, backpackers and tourists, holding hands in the spring sunlight, tending to their own private gossiping and bickering and cuddling. For the first time since he'd arrived, Will felt homesick. Then Aoto messaged him to say he was not feeling well and had given his ticket to a friend, so sorry, and Will decided he should just quietly leave.

But then Teru appeared. Through some hidden law of magnetic rearrangement, they shuffled around the other paired nuclei for a few moments before ending up near each other. Will said hello, introducing himself as Aoto's friend, and asked if Teru was also originally from Kyoto.

"I'm from North Jersey," she said. "But my parents grew up in Osaka."

"Oh, nice," Will said. "My grandmother lives near there. North Jersey, I mean. She's more central. Near the shore."

"Listen. I hope you brought your A game," Teru said as the chef began leading through the market stalls.

"I think I did," Will said quickly. "Why, though?"

"I want to crush this cooking class. I need a win today."

Will almost asked why, then thought better of it.

"You do this sort of thing a lot?" he asked.

"Well, my boyfriend's the cook, mainly. And if you think *I'm* competitive . . ."

Will frowned faster than he could cover up. "Where's he, then?"

"Belgium."

Then the chef began to lead them around the booths, describing in well-rehearsed detail what to look for when buying sturgeon and what one does with skates and shad. How did you treat herring and trout? And what were the differences between the pink salmon and the Danube variety? And of course, though Will had made scant notice of it at the time, there were eels—eels everywhere: live ones ready to become unagi rolls, frozen eels covered in icy crystals, and pre-smoked eels that smelled heavenly even through their plastic packages.

As they gathered ingredients, Teru told Will how she worked at the Japanese International School in the Oberkassel district. Most of her students, she explained, were the young children of businessmen and -women from Japan, who often came through Düsseldorf on five-month contracts. She was there to teach English. "Points of location. 'To be' verbs. Stuff like when you use 'tell' versus 'speak' versus 'say' . . . 'They *tell* me to go to the conference,' not 'They *say* me to go to the conference.' That sort of thing."

"These kids are attending a lot of conferences?"

"They want them learning business English." She laughed. "And you know, I get it. My dad is still like that. SONY, SONY, SONY. It's this whole corporation mindset."

They walked together then, scribbling down occasional notes. Will admired her neat, perfect handwriting, but also tried not to stare. Teru was left-handed and standing to his right side and so kept bumping him with her elbow, or maybe he was bumping her with his, he couldn't tell.

He had not realized that the Fischmarkt would have so many other things besides fish: heaps of local flowers and beeswax candles and croissants the size of car headlights and sacks of hand-roasted coffee beans and beautiful vegetables.

Teru told him that her plan was to get out to Osaka, probably later that summer, where her parents had been born. She wanted to teach English there. When she asked Will how long he would be in Düsseldorf, he said he hoped forever.

When the group finally came to the restaurant kitchen with all the supplies they'd been gathering, the chef at last began to lead them all through the preparations. Will got to work on fileting salmon as Teru stained her hands purple, removing the skins from a pile of beets. Most of the couples were by now deep into the gratis wine, but Will turned it down and Teru did as well. She was all business—dicing, sautéing, salting water. He found it impossible not to stare as she worked, but he did his very best.

"So what's in Belgium?" he asked finally.

She seemed not to know what he meant. "Chocolate?"

"Sorry," he said, "I meant—you said your boyfriend was there. Is it family?"

"Nope," she said flatly. "Postdoc. He's a researcher. Epigenetics."

"Oh, cool. That's . . . very cutting edge. Environmental factors and trauma affect DNA—"

But she interrupted him with a cry of frustration. "I'm sorry, this knife is driving me *crazy*!"

She was holding it right at the top of the hilt, fingers on the side of the blade. Just then, the chef came over and said that this was correct, but instead of pulling *back* through the carrots like he had demonstrated, she was trying to push forward.

"This is the Japanese knife," the chef said dismissively.

"What does that mean?"

The chef waved his hand at her. "You use a western chef's knife, not a santoku like this."

"Why?"

"Because you're not Japanese. Your knife has a different shape. Goes the other way."

"No, no. My parents are from Osaka," she said. "This is just like the knife I use at home."

"Then you're doing it wrong at home." The chef shrugged and moved off to help one of the couples trying to get a burner started. Will watched as a series of emotions played over Teru's expression. She tried chopping it the other direction, but the carrots refused to be even, would not slice "on the bias" as the chef had instructed them, and her teeth bared in real anger then.

"I'm going to just see if they have the other kind of knife over there," Will said, getting up quickly and crossing to the supply shelf.

When he got back, she was gone, her notebook still there on the table.

They'd tell this part of the story many times in the years since: the story of the judgy chef, of the complicit knives, of Will getting Teru's address from Aoto and then fighting his way through a literal parade of costumed anime characters so that he could deliver her lost belongings, along with all five finished fish dishes, carefully wrapped up. The story of how she'd kissed him in the doorway before he'd even explained himself. The story of how she'd lied and said that there'd been an emergency, a phone call from Belgium, she'd had to go. The story of their feast on cold fish. And that night they'd stayed up to see the fireworks, in celebration of currently-less-problematic German/Japanese relations. And sometimes they included the footnote in the story of Teru breaking it off with the postdoc, or maybe it had been called off already—this detail changed somewhat, depending on the mood.

And then, never mentioned but felt, the story of what didn't happen: how Will never went to visit Holland and Teru never went to work in Osaka and neither of them ever went to the Memorial for Tyranny or whatever it had been called—Will could never quite remember. There'd been no time for history, no time for backward. Only forward. They crashed at his place, crashed at hers. Two bare white rooms with lumpy futons and a teapot. Three shelves in the pantry. And in a few months, Will, happily bumping elbows with Teru on their flight back to the United States, reentering, unafraid. That was all—all that mattered, truly.

NOW, IN THE darkness of the guest bedroom of his oma's house, Will thought back on those happy days like something out of another life. Again, he could not sleep. He had a fever and seemed to cycle between wild sweating and intense chills, every twenty minutes, back and forth. He again chastised his panicking amygdala and his hypothalamus, but this time it wouldn't stop. Adrenaline, cortisol. Glucose to the brain. Adrenaline, cortisol. Glucose to the brain. Adrenaline, cortisol. Glucose to the—at two in the morning, he'd taken some Nyquil, thinking it might knock him out, but it just made his head swimmier, gave him the sense of things being stretched too far: shadows and objects and light and sounds. He heard music, bits of Schubert and Beethoven, elongated in his ear. Songs he'd played on the piano staggeringly badly as a boy, but there was nothing playing now, of course. It was all in his head. There was much too much in his head. Guilt, sorrow, loss, history. *Yui.* Elegant cloth. He felt a texture to the air where he knew there was none. Will could not escape the smell of the sourdough, though he had fed the little jar hours earlier and washed his hands and even changed his clothes. It was alive, he kept thinking. The dough was host to a vast conglomeration of bacterial life, consuming and dying and fermenting and flavoring en masse, single-celled blobs, a micrometer wide, covered in wriggling pili and taillike flagella. Tooth decay, the black plague, pneumonia, yeast, bifidobacterium, lactobacillus. Each barely more than a few strands of DNA, floating in circles of cytoplasm. A trillion or two inside him right now. More residing in just his own mouth than there were human beings in all the world or had ever been alive since the dawn of time. *Yui.* Elegant cloth. He and Teru had agreed not to think about names until— But *Yui Geborn. Yui Geborn. Yui Geborn.* Will could not shake the name from his mind. He turned the slim purple box around in his hands, listened to the pregnancy test inside rattling around. *Manufactured in Düsseldorf. Schwangerschaftstest.* Now it was five A.M. Where had the time gone? Will lay alone in the guest room. He saw snow falling against the window. A few flakes at first and then *wild, rushing waves of it!* As if he were belowdecks on a great ship, looking out at a white, roiling sea. A dark cloud had spread across the night sky. From above, the snow came down, and then without warning, it gusted back up in rocketing volleys from beneath the window. Will watched the wind catch in the corner of the neighboring house, swirling around like a trapped animal. As the air blew in great squalls, it screamed—a shrill and monotonous agony. High, almost like the wailing of a child. It was the middle of March! It had been sixty degrees just a few days ago. But his phone confirmed it: a rare late-season blizzard. Winter Storm Stella. A weather system that had begun five days ago as an "extratropical cyclone" way out in the North Pacific, coming down out of British Columbia, *an Albert clipper,* they called it—

like the old three-masted trading ships he'd read about as a kid,
packed with all his imaginary *vrijbuiters*. The storm had come
across the Great Lakes and then fallen all the way down to Geor-
gia before swerving back up without warning. Over the frigid
Atlantic waters, it had undergone a rapid strengthening trans-
formation called bombogenesis. They were predicting twenty
inches of snow by morning, and more up north. He texted Teru.
It's snowing here. No answer. She was living thirteen hours in the
future. In Osaka now, it was the next evening already. Will paced
in the bedroom, studying the world outside the window, already
utterly blanketed in ivory. Slopes a foot high, maybe more, and
with the winds so powerful, it was blowing up in veritable mountains against the easterly sides of each identical beach house. All
down Sand Dollar Street he could make out the domes of white
on the covered barbecue grills, great piles of powder on top of the
sagging awnings, immense mounds pressing against the sliding
glass doors. A pair of noble Sea-Doos sat on their trailers in the
backyard of Oma's nearest neighbor, encased in icelike sculptures that belonged in the Guggenheim. In his grandmother's
own yard, all the little delicate purple and yellow flowers that
had begun spiking above the ground were buried beneath the
ill-timed snowfall. Beyond everything, Will searched the roiling bay, lines of deadly whitecaps crashing in, and every gust
and bellow sending spray up into the air to be frozen and fall
back down in stinging droplets of ice. The water in the bay was
very high. The causeway dark, maybe already underwater. He
couldn't see that far. How long had it been since he'd slept? He
didn't care, suddenly. If this was another episode or the beginning of a breakdown, what did it matter? He had forgotten how
powerful he'd felt the last time it had come upon him like this.
Bombogenesis. Whenever his forgetting had failed him, Will had
looked back on that night at the med school party as a disaster,
a lapse, a weakness. An error that had instigated the long collapse of his plans and dreams. All overwriting the true feelings
that had overtaken him that night. A sense of pure oneness with
the entire world—its evil, its good, its past, its future. Limitless

belonging in all of that, and more—of his purpose within it. And so, standing there by the window, watching the ice storm raging outside, Will decided. Just welcome it now. Working so hard to seem regular was not working out very well anyway. And when there was so much more?

MOST OF WILL'S life he hadn't known what had become of his father after the day of the swim lesson. But after med school and Düsseldorf, he'd begun digging around a little online, reaching out to colleagues with access to older medical records, and come up with a picture, if a bit of a fuzzy one.

While young Will had been waiting for a ride home from the YMCA, his father had been across town stealing a motorboat from a Public Works Department dock—the sort of little runabout they used sometimes to maintain the channel markers and buoys. It was just tied to some municipal dock somewhere, bobbing away; nobody had ever bothered to chain it up. But according to a court transcript, Will's father had interpreted its free availability as a sign. From God. A command to receive the boat as his own golden chariot—and Will remembered those boats had always been a warmish shade of yellow. His father had gotten the thing out past the causeway and about two miles out into the open ocean before he'd been stopped by the Coast Guard. Will's father had told them quite calmly that he was on his way to a holy spot in the distant waters, that a great prophet was there, waiting to be born. A celestial beast with the power to restore the river of time. That was the word he'd used, according to the official report. *Restore* it to its proper flowing. Time had been dammed up, the past accruing exponentially in the now, unable to drain away. All of us, everywhere, stuck circling endlessly. He'd cheered the coming of a new age, a free age, a return to the wilderness. He urged the Coast Guardsmen to come along. That they had only to follow the whispers to guide them there.

Instead, his father had been arrested and placed into the

care of a psychiatric facility, where he'd stayed for at least a few months. Possibly several years. After that, nobody seemed to know what had become of him. But Will had a growing feeling that his grandmother knew and that she wanted to tell him before it was too late. That all this historical retreading was part of it.

Where was he? Disappeared? Stuck in a well? Hiding in a wood carving? Off in a prison camp somewhere. Huddled in the attic. *Onderduiken.*

THIS WAS WHAT he had confessed to Teru that night before she'd left. They'd been rooting around in his grandmother's kitchen. She'd gone into the pantry to find flour to make the sourdough starter. It had all been her idea. Instead, she'd emerged with a little circular tin of traditional Dutch windmill cookies—the sort of timeless thing Will had seen at the airport gift shop, leaving Amsterdam. Teru had popped the thing open and found a stash of the crisp, tasty speculoos cookies that Will had enjoyed so much as a kid. But mixed in with these was a small card with a printed message: HAPPY BIRTHDAY MOM!

"How old are these fucking cookies?" was Will's first response.

But there was no way they were twenty-five years old. He knew right away they were fresh, new as of a week earlier, probably. They smelled incredible.

"Will," Teru said, excited. "Will, you know what this means?"

He'd turned the card over numbly in one hand, but the other side was blank.

"Will, baby, she knows where your dad is."

Slowly he placed the little card back on its bed of cookies and sealed the tin back up. He took it and put it back into the pantry where it had come from.

"Last I heard he was in a mental hospital down in Cumberland," Will said, not sure why he was saying it. Not sure why he had never said it before.

"I'm not supposed to know. I figured it out a while ago. No one ever told me."

He told her then. Everything. About the stolen boat and the great beast waiting to be born.

Teru took his hand and squeezed it so hard it hurt. "Babe, I'm so sorry. That's terrifying."

"I'm fine. It's fine. It's—you know, it's better," he said.

"How's it better?"

Will could not quite articulate the rest: that it meant his father had been sick, that he had not abandoned them out of careless-ness or an absence of paternal love. That beyond this—the thing three therapists had tried to tell him before he turned thirteen, but which Will had never fully believed—it had never been Will's fault.

"Babe," she said slowly, "I really wish you'd said something. Before. I mean. This kind of mental illness has genetic factors, right?"

Swiftly Will had found himself growing angry. How could she be so blunt about this? Or was he upset at himself for hav-ing said anything at all? Was he getting mad now just to be ahead of her far-more-justifiable anger? *Selfish. Careless. Cannot be trusted.*

"It's complicated. There's no direct determinative . . . It's in-heritable, but it's maybe, I don't know, one in ten?"

Hardwired. Deep in the lizard brain.

"One in *ten*?"

"Maybe. But that's not, you know—that's not that bad. And I don't even—I've never had any real issues. I don't know."

It was a lie, and she knew it. But he was desperate—what else could he do? He was losing her. Even if she was standing right there, she was going. She was already lost. It was all his fault.

"Will—"

"This isn't a *sign*," he said.

She then said nothing.

"It doesn't make anything meant to be or not meant to be. I'm *fine*," he'd insisted.

She'd continued to look away.

"Believing in signs and stuff being meant to be or not meant to be—*that's* crazy."

"Yeah, well, believing nothing means anything isn't a testament to sanity, either, Will."

"I don't believe *nothing* matters."

She waited for him to explain what he *did* believe mattered. But he found he couldn't say.

"How old was your father when it started?" she'd asked.

Will had said he had no idea.

She said nothing for a while. Will, still hurt, barely registered the fact that she was rubbing her side a little, feeling more cramps.

"Look, I'm fine. It's nothing to worry about. I'm sorry I ever said anything."

But Teru had stared soberly at him. "*I'm* not. You get that, right?"

That's when she'd gone to the bathroom. And discovered that she had gotten her period after all. And then she'd left.

SERIOUSLY, IT'S SNOWING? Teru wrote back, around six in the morning.

Will felt a warm swell all over him. An envelope of joy, a trembling all along his nerves. He'd missed her so much. Then in an instant everything inside of him quieted down. The whisperings, the music, the obsessive bacterial cataloguing. It was all gone, so far away now that it seemed to have all been some sort of fever dream in the first place.

Thought maybe I was hallucinating at first, he typed—but did not hit send. He added a smiley face. He did not hit send. He deleted the message. She wouldn't think it was funny. Or she might, but it wouldn't be, anyway.

How is it going so far?

There was a long pause and then the phone rang. He picked up and heard Teru's soft hello on the other end, almost lost in the echoey noises behind her.

"I'm still jet-lagged as hell," she said. "Up all night and crashing by noon."

"Ugh," Will said.

Will watched the snow rushing outside the window, flowing over the bird feeders and filling the kiddie pools. Washing over the sides of the boats that stood wrapped up in blue tarps on their trailers. In the wildness and the dark they were like ghost ships, moving through a stormy white sky. The *Flying Dutchman*, the legend said, a great trading ship captained by a man who had sold his soul to the Devil. Gone down in a storm, only to emerge, phantasmagorically, in bad weather, a sign of bad luck, a curse—visible only to those sailors whose ships were about to be sucked into the sea forever.

"How's the school?" he asked.

"It's a total mess. Everything's disorganized and nobody seems to know what we're supposed to be doing there. It really isn't what I was expecting."

Will tried not to feel happy at her disappointment. He bit back the urge to beg her to get back on a plane immediately and come home.

"It'll get better. You're probably still just getting adjusted."

"Yeah," she agreed. "Probably yeah."

WILL LOOKED AT his laptop, where the tabs of the medical journals he'd been researching were still open and shining brightly at him.

Bastiaan T. Heijmans, Elmar W. Tobi, Aryeh D. Stein, et al., "Persistent Epigenetic Differences Associated with Prenatal Exposure to Famine in Humans," *Proceedings of the National Academy of Science of the USA* 105, no. 44 (2008): "[. . .] individuals who were prenatally exposed to famine during the Dutch Hunger Winter in 1944–45 had, 6 decades later, less DNA methylation of the imprinted IGF2 gene compared with their unexposed, same-sex siblings."

Laura C. Schulz, "The Dutch Hunger Winter and the De-
velopmental Origins of Health and Disease," *Proceedings
of the National Academy of Science of the USA* 107, no. 39
(2010): "As discussed by Rooij et al.,[2] CNS structures are
formed in the first trimester of pregnancy, and changes
underlying mental illness, altered appetite regulation cen-
ters, or even later declines in cognitive function likely oc-
cur during this period."

These were just two of the medical studies that Will had found
examining the DNA of children who had been in utero during the
Hunger Winter, both early or late in gestation, and the way that
the stress and near starvation of their mothers had impacted them.
Low birth weights were to be expected, but the longer-term impacts went well beyond. Certain genes in the unborn children had
been silenced. As adults, they had higher levels of triglycerides
and LDL cholesterol. Were more likely to experience diabetes,
obesity, depression, and more.

Will didn't remember everything from his epigenetics course
back in medical school, but he'd seen studies like these before.
Quebecois women, pregnant and trapped in an ice storm that had
left them in forty-five days of cold and darkness—they'd found
increased levels of mental illness in the babies born afterwards.
Worryingly, the other women who survived the storm and then
became pregnant a decade later *also* saw impacts. The damage—
the silencing of those genes, had left permanent scars. Worst of all,
it carried on in the DNA of the children of these children—to the
grandchildren of those originally traumatized.

In short, to Will.

And perhaps now, to the hypothetical future children of Will.

"IT'S WEIRD TO feel, like, *homesick*," she said. "I feel like I'm twelve
years old again."

"Back at Camp Lakota?" He laughed.

The name of her childhood summer camp sprang from his

memories, some old stories she'd told him, years ago. Terrible food. Narcoleptic bunkmate. Chicken pox that had erupted on her back from one shoulder blade to the next, like a pair of red, rashy wings.

"The time will fly by. I'll see you in ten weeks," he said.

When he closed his eyes now, he could see the smooth softness of her skin. The places it was still scarred from when the itching had been irresistible.

"I'm so sorry about everything," Will said. "I wish we hadn't left it all on such a bad note."

"Telling me the truth finally wasn't a bad note."

"I'm just really sorry," he said again.

Will felt sick. He didn't want to have to hang up just to rush off to the bathroom. He took a deep breath and tried to hold it together.

"Will—"

He closed his eyes as she said his name. *Will. Will. Will.* He could hear her getting scared.

"I'm sorry, Will. I don't know. Maybe this is a big mistake."

He didn't know what to say. Yes, it was a big mistake. Yes, she should be home with him. Yes, he had lied to her, but—

"Come back?" Will whispered, chewing his lip so he wouldn't cry. He gripped the purple box in his hands, twisting at it like a rolled newspaper. "I'm sorry. I really want you to come back."

She took a hard breath. "Do you ever feel like you don't know who you are?"

"You don't think you know who I am?"

"No, I don't think I know who *I* am. Don't you feel that way ever?"

"Basically all the time."

"It's been just *eating* away at me lately." She was crying; he could hear her trying to hide it. But there wasn't much point. "I don't know why. I need some more time. I'm sorry. I know this is lousy. I wish I'd done this before we got married. I should have. I didn't think—I thought if I focused on the future, you know?"

That she wouldn't need to figure out what was in the past. Will wished he could explain that he knew exactly what she meant. But where to begin?

"I need to be where my family came from," she said, "for a little while. I just can't put this off forever."

Of course she couldn't. And neither could he.

She promised to call more often, as soon as she got used to the time change. He said that he missed her; she said she missed him, too. She had to go. He hung up the phone.

WILL CAME OUT into the dark living room. His eyes fell on the Japanese trunk, and he walked toward it as if he could not stop himself. Slowly he began clearing the photos from the lid.

He had to do it, finally. *I just can't put this off forever.*

It was time to open it, oni or no oni. If there was some imp around, it wasn't hanging out in there. It was wrapped around his ribosomes. Tangled in his G-T-A-T-A-C-G-G . . .

The lid was incredibly heavy, more stone than wood, he reminded himself. Inside was nothing special, just a pile of blankets and more old photo albums. He'd seen them all before.

But he pulled them away now and felt inside, reaching all the way to the bottom of the trunk—only the bottom of the trunk wasn't at the bottom of the trunk.

Hidden compartments. The *magisch speelgoed* specialty.

He'd been puzzling over his great-grandfather's escape. "The Peculiar Disappearance of Professor Naaktgeboren." Rob—Will's opa—had said he saw his father climb into the chest. But when he'd looked in afterwards, his father had been gone. Mieke—Oma—had thought he'd lost his mind. And maybe he had. But maybe there was a logical explanation in the end.

Will pressed and banged around on the trunk, not caring now if he made noise and woke his grandmother. In fact, he soon heard her calling out from her bedroom. He pushed and tapped until at last he found a little knot in the wood that moved, released, and fell away. Using this as a fingerhold, he could then lift the base of the trunk, revealing the secret compartment beneath.

The professor must have hidden in there while the soldiers had been in the apartment looking for him and then slipped away later when the coast was clear. Maybe he'd lain there a full day, until the following night, Will wondered. How?

And now inside this same space was a heap of plain white envelopes. Hundreds, their triangular flaps still sealed, but the tops carefully sliced with the golden letter opener that Oma kept on her desk. He reached and pulled from inside an envelope, a letter handwritten on plain, blue-lined notebook paper. And folded up in it, photographs. Will lifted one up. It was dated in jagged black ink on the back.

February 19, 2017.

Not even a month ago.

And in the picture was his father.

An old man now. Heavyset, especially in the face. Bald on top, but with long mullety lengths of badger-toned hair on the sides that wisped down to his shoulders. His father stood proudly, both arms draped like a sweater around the shoulders of a woman with a pasty face and stringy blond hair. She looked younger than him, if not a lot. And in front of them, two grinning boys. Will noticed that around his father's neck there was a bright golden cross on a chain, much too thick. The woman had one, too, but a bit smaller. And the kids wore matching T-shirts from something called the Blue Ridge Bible Camp. But the real thing Will couldn't get past was the look of beaming pride on his father's face.

Then he heard his oma come into the room behind him.

"Will. What are you doing out here in the middle of the night?"

"I'm sorry," Will whispered. She was in her bathrobe, holding it shut with one hand while the tie hung tangled to one side. In the same hand she held the red book with the eel on the cover, her thumb still holding a place inside of it.

"I was up reading—" she started to say, but then came a long pause when she'd finally seen that the trunk was open, and what he was holding in his own hands.

"I didn't think you'd want to see those."

He stood up, not looking at her, not sure what to say.

"He writes you a lot, I guess?" Will managed, pointing to the letters.

"Every month," she said. "I know I should have told you."

"So he's down in . . . the Blue Ridge Mountains are, what, Tennessee?"

"They live in North Carolina, about an hour south of Asheville."

"Okay. How long?"

"About six years now."

Will sank down to the floor, his knees no longer structural. "I thought he was crazy or something."

Slowly Oma reached out and put a hand on his shoulder.

"He was, for a long time. But he's made a lot of progress. Treatments these days are better than they were back when you were little."

Will made a strangled noise and then stopped. Slowly he drew himself back up and dropped the photo back into the chest like it had burned his fingers.

"Well, good for him. Everyone deserves a fresh start, right?"

She didn't answer at first. "Everyone deserves a chance to get better."

"That's good, then," Will said. "Good for him. Well."

And then Will rushed to the stairs and hurried down to the front door. He didn't care about the storm. He needed to get away. He had to get to Teru somehow. He threw open the door and plunged out into the freezing night, not thinking, not able to think. Bits of ice stung at his cheeks and drifted gently in the darkness in front of him. Night dust. The road ahead was covered in drifts of snow, the fine powder kicking up before coming back down again in nauseating, spiraling motions. Will reached back into the closet and pulled out one of his oma's coats, fuchsia-colored and too small and with a furry lining around the hood. He yanked it on as best he could, knocking something off the hallway table in the process—the gift Giancarlo had left, before. Will hurried out into the pitiless white world. Was he out of his mind or heartbroken or in love, or all three at once? In the end, he supposed, it didn't matter. There was only what he did or didn't do. There was only what he chose or didn't choose. There was only the great waste ahead of him. The frost biting at his earlobes. The car was still out there, not so deep in the snow. He thought maybe he could get it out still. He would set things right. Restore the proper flow of the river of time. He had to get away. Everything was dammed up. The past refusing to go. Stuck circling endlessly. He would follow the whispers to guide him—

Then Will's foot came down on the last icy step from the landing, but through the drifting snow he misjudged the depth and badly. He pitched forward and fell hard, sideways, off the steps. His head whooshed into a slope of wet snow and there was a brilliant bright burst of lights all around him and then everything went dark.

MIEKE DROPPED THE book on the floor and moved after Will as fast as she could, cursing each of the stairs in turn beneath her breath. *Godverdomme! Godverdomme! Godverdomme!* By the time she reached the open front door, she could not see Will anywhere outside. He couldn't have gotten far, she was sure. His car was right where it had been before. But she could not make out his silhouette in the snow or the darkness. How could he have just disappeared? She began trying to yank her coat on and then her boots, thinking she would go after him. She wanted to cry, but she couldn't seem to start. Oh, she had ruined everything. Just when she and her grandson had begun to find their way together again. She had been reading in bed, just before, woken by the storm and unable to get back to sleep. She'd been reading in her old tongue, about Nachtnebel and Groente. It was undeniable now—this book had been written by Rob's father, and he had died in the camps. This was what she'd always believed, and yet now, to know it for sure . . . it hurt more than she'd ever expected. But then, as she'd lain there, she'd thought of Will, and of the trip they'd taken to Holland together, long ago. How she'd brought him back to the beach there, out by the dunes. One more time, she wanted it. The feeling of moving lightly along those familiar grasses, with her descendant at her side.

Godverdomme! Oh, they had tried to kill her. With bullets, with cold, with hunger. But she had stood there fifty years later, alive and well in spite of it all, with that innocent boy at her side, who knew nothing of any of it. A boy soaking in the world around him as she had once. All of it just a free, open fairyland that she'd lost sight of long ago.

Mieke came out onto the icy steps, looking into the darkness, shouting her grandson's name only to find her voice silenced in the wind.

Back when he was young, they couldn't have explained what was happening to his father. Then, as he'd become older, she'd watched him moving happily through life, despite everything, and all she'd wanted was to keep that from shattering.

When she first began getting the letters from her son, Will had been a teenager, on his way to college. Full of promise, full of brilliance. She'd told herself that it was all fine now, that he was fine. That they should not disturb him with all of this. And even when she began to hear from her son that he was better, that he was in the care of a local church group, that he had found Christ and begun to train in carpentry—it all seemed too perilous. Too wobbly to trust. But year after year, he'd remained stable. Well. She'd been so, so happy.

Of course, she should have known that Will must be wondering, must have been wondering, all this time—if his father was somewhere, if he was even alive. If the things that had happened to him would happen again.

And now he was gone, off in a violent storm, alone.

She still had not been able to tell him about the worst of it.

About the Hunger Winter. All the very worst things, that had left the deepest scars, the hardest calluses. She had been thinking about those months all week. Wondering how to explain. Unsure if she would ever be able to put words to the memories that she'd swallowed up and hidden away so long ago. They had such a dark power over her still, and she did not know what speaking them aloud would do. To her. Or to him. It was all hopelessly wrapped up with what had happened to her son. Neither she nor Rob had ever explained to him what they'd been through, but it found him anyway. And all that silence had caused his madness. It had passed from her nightmares, crawled out of the woodwork, and found him.

And could words hope to unravel the tangle of horrors, even now? Even if she could find the strength to say them.

COLD AND WET and scared, Mieke went back inside, wondering if she could get her phone to call the police. Would a signal even go out? As she fumbled for the light switch, she almost tripped on the little bundle that Giancarlo had left on the step for her the other day. It had fallen to the floor, a small brown bag from the garden center. She'd never opened it, but now she did. Inside were a handful of little brown papery bulbs.

She dropped them to the ground with a cry from another time.

Tulips.

Sitting there, round and unassuming. The little tendrils of roots coming from the bottoms, almost like an onion's.

She reached into the bag, pulled each bulb out, and hurled them out into the storm.

THE HUNGER WINTER

~

Mieke stares into a gutter blocked with ice and snow, at the detached head of Mrs. de Witt's dog. *Manfred*, the name resurfaces in her memory, as if from a hundred years ago. Mrs. de Witt used to walk the dog up and down this same block in the mornings, and Mieke and Rob would pass her sometimes as they walked to school. A gray Keeshond with long dark fur and triangular pointing around the cheeks. He's always struck her as a happy animal, even if Mrs. de Witt herself was an eternal sour-puss. The sort of woman who wore furs year-round and had pearls on her necklace the size of oyster crackers, and whose shoes were blockish at the toes and raised an inch in the back.

So how did Manfred's head come to be in the gutter? And where was the rest of him?

Asking these questions is like asking thirty more questions all at once, questions whose answers are all basically the same. Be-cause it's the war. Because there's nothing to eat anywhere. Be-cause people have all lost their ever-loving minds, according to her father.

No way to know if it was Mrs. de Witt herself, of course. Most likely she let Manfred go free, without spare food to give him.

And someone had gotten to him from there.

Up and down Laan van Meerdervoort, there is not a soul anywhere. Just snow, fresh and still falling over everything. In the cleared area across the street, even the Nazis are huddling inside their encampments, invisible.

Would she eat a dog? Mieke asks herself, standing there in Rob's old clothes, doubled up, and still cold deep down inside of every bone. If someone handed her some odd piece of meat, greasy and warmed from the fire, cleaned and beautifully pink? And if it meant the men up in the attic would sleep with bellies filled, and that her mother and Broodje and Tante Sintje would experience even a moment's happiness that day?

But still. She wouldn't *kill* a dog. No. And she won't touch what's left of it here, just the head anyway. Slowly she moves some old boxes over it and whispers something in the shape of a prayer to it once it is hidden away.

HUNGER. EVERY MINUTE. Every day. It is like there is a living thing inside her, pulling on one organ, pushing on another, prodding her from the middle out. And at the same time, she is empty. Weaker than she's ever been in her life. Her muscles sting in all the places they attach to her bones, as if they might just snap loose. When she walks around she feels stabbing in the bits between the bones in her feet. When she lies down, the pain is there between the discs in her spine. Her head throbs like a thumb struck by a hammer, and it hurts as well just to breathe. Each lungful of air pressing against her tightening rib cage, and she fears soon they'll just—

Pop.

There are teams of clergymen, helping to gather and evacuate children to farms out in the countryside. The Germans are allowing it, but they must go without their parents. To live with some other family somewhere, for who knew how long. Tante Sintje's friends at the church have encouraged her to send Rob, but she doesn't want him all alone, and Mieke's mother won't agree to send her. "Who knows if they'll even take them where they say? If they'll ever be brought home?" Mieke is glad of this. She can't think of anything more terrifying than being shipped to the countryside, separated from her parents for months. She'd rather starve than live all alone, somewhere else.

By now she's seen a boy her own age passed out in the street from hunger. She's seen other ones lined up by the stalls, ration cards in hand, their legs as bony as birds. Waiting hours in line for a ladleful or two of thin gray broth, not even warm. It's all that's left. Children half her age walk around the city now, barely clothed, with spoons in their hands, in case someone has a little extra. In case there's half a mouthful of anything, anywhere, to share.

MIEKE SEES TWO women coming down the street carrying little bags filled with tulip bulbs. Lumps, hard as rock. With a thin brown papery layer on the outside, almost like a fat head of wild garlic. Little hairs of root coming down from the bottom, just the same. But inside there is no softness to speak of. None of an onion's eye-stinging moisture. None of the nostril-prickling scent of garlic, either. Only a hard white rock, so compacted that she and Rob cannot get through them with a knife on their own. Their mothers crack down at them with the sharpest thing they can find. It must be done, to pry the yellow core out. The flower's bud has a poison in it that a bite leaves you doubling over with cramps, so dizzy you can't tell the floor from the ceiling. You vomit for hours. So out it goes, leaving the rest. Thick, fleshy scales of white that taste like the foulest onions imaginable. Dried up, they milled into a bitter but usable flour. The better thing to do was to boil them down and pray that it burned off the worst of the flavor.

SLEEP AT NIGHT is the only thing Mieke looks forward to. The blessed oblivion of it. Her brain lacks the energy to even dream, so there are no nightmares until the hunger wakes her in the middle of the darkness. She desperately misses the unfelt painless hours. And then as each day creeps along, coldly, slowly, the nightmares continue. Even as they happen, she forgets them, but as she does, she knows that each will come back to her, decade after decade.

A BODY IN the snow, a soldier belonging to one side or the other. She can't see his identification through the crust of ice. The skin of his neck is blue, but his head is inside out and frostbitten, frozen and filled with pure white.

DOWN THE AVENUE, clip-clopping, a horse, gotten loose from somewhere, lost and confused. Silenced with a crack of gunfire. And then, doors opening, people coming out with dull knives. Her mother slides her back from the frost-flowered window. *Kijk niet*, she says. *Don't look.*

THREE BODIES LYING against the wall of the church, their faces covered with white sheets. The man on the far left wears a white shirt still tucked into his dark trousers, with a limp necktie. His hands are folded across his waist, where someone has removed his belt—if he ever had one. The same goes for his shoes. Both are gone, along with one of his socks, but not the other. Mieke expected his bare foot would be waxy or blue, but it appears almost normal, pinkish and unrigid. Almost as if it were still alive, attached to a living body. But it isn't. The two smaller forms beside him are harder to see; the sheet covers more of them. Their pants are light-colored, flecked with mud, and their thin shoes have been left alone. It is their legs that creep into Mieke's mind, thin as poles and locked straight. The one all the way to the right is twisted over, his left arm reaching over his body toward his right, as if it had been trying to crawl somewhere when it decided to rest.

THE NEXT DAY, outside the commissary, Mieke joins Rob and Broodje as they go at the empty steel vats with their spoons. Rob leans over the top, reaching in with his long arms, scraping blindly against the edges inside. Pulling up a mouthful or two at a time, pausing to pull away so that he can train his eyes inside, to see what he might have missed. Mieke's job is to keep lookout—they'll have only a few minutes at best to get what they can before someone else comes by and hoards in on the find. She looks about nervously as she holds Broodje by the waist—he's thin enough and small enough that he can get his whole top half inside the mouth of the container, allowing him to scrape around at the insides with his hands. When he's done, she pulls him back and he's covered in bits of the mushy cereal. Mieke scrapes some off his face and combs it from his hair. He giggles and then goes back in for more.

They trudge through the deep snow to come home and try to warm up, though there's nothing left to burn and their blankets do little good. Already they have pried off every other step from the staircase—any more and they won't be able to get up to the apartment or down to the street. Huddled by her window, Mieke watches the soldiers across the street. They pace around. Sometimes they look back at her and scowl. Sometimes they wave. On the streets, old men travel together, draped in discarded tarp and burlap, sixty or so in a pack, moving from door to door, begging for anything anyone has to spare. The last time she saw Marjo Mulder she'd been with her older cousin, pushing a pram by the river, a boy's dead body inside. Heading God knew where or why. There are paths running through the snow from where they've dragged other bodies. Mieke avoids any streets where she sees pink trails left by the bleeders, the ones who've been shot for helping the resistance or for stealing or for being out past the curfew, or for any reason—or no reason at all. These trails all lead to the same place. They form a grotesque spider's web that goes out all around the town, but its center is the old police station. People drag the bodies there, pile them up. Four this way, four that way. Ten or twelve high, if the base is stable. Corpses thin as rails, skin taut, clothes removed and given back out. Their bare feet blue and white, the toe bones knobby, sticking out at neat angles to one another. The ground is frozen, too hard to dig a pit to bury them in. Mieke doesn't know if anyone's keeping track of which ones will go where once the thaw comes. If the thaw comes. If anyone's left when the thaw comes.

A DAY LATER, a week later, a month later. Mieke can't order these events. Can't find herself inside the hellscape around her. She sees herself sitting by the window and staring at the snow. It could be a hundred different days. Across the street, one of the soldiers stares at her from his station, and as always, she waves at him. But on this day, he does not wave back. Instead, he lifts his gun, his eyes blank, his motions stiff. She drops to the floor and screams, just in time. A bullet hits the wall next to the window. She can feel the impact from the other side. There is another shot, and then a third. She hears glass shattering and ducks, but nothing happens. It takes a moment before she realizes that he did not hit her window, but some other one. There is a shout from the next room— Rob's voice. Low and throaty, annoyed, as if someone has ripped his book. She scrambles across the floor, still not daring to stand, and moves out into the hallway and peeks into the living room. There, Rob is sitting on the chair, frozen as he's reading. The window beside him is just gone. He's covered in tiny sparkling bits of glass, and so is the floor. He doesn't seem hurt. He goes to brush the glass off his clothes, like it is some sand that's been thrown at him. Mieke calls out for him to stop. "Don't! Rob!" she cautions, and he freezes. In a moment her mother is there, rushing in from the bedroom. She screams and moves across the room, in plain sight through the window, and Mieke is sick, thinking that there will be a fourth shot any moment. But none comes. Her mother reaches Rob and uses the edge of her dress to brush him off. When she is sure he is okay, she tells him to get up and go with her. Within the hour they have some old blankets up over the window, and the floor has been swept six times. Her mother tells them that they cannot play in the front rooms for a few days, so they have to sleep in the bathroom for a while.

A FEW DAYS later, Mieke dares to walk outside the building for the first time. She can see the places where the other bullets hit the brick; there are bits missing from the masonry on the ledge below the window, about where she'd been hiding on the other side.

SEARCHLIGHTS GLEAM THROUGH the windows at night sometimes. Yellow sweeping circles on the ceiling, laced with the delicate patterns of the frost, enlarged above. They dance, alive and beautiful, as long as they last.

FOR CHRISTMAS, ROB brings home a rabbit he's caught in a snare in the woods. It looks more like a pine marten or a large vole—but no one is complaining. They wait until Mieke's father can come down safely. He is skin and bones already; tenderly he slices the fur away and helps Mieke carve every last bit of muscle for a stew. In the end, there is a whole cupful for each, warm and satisfying and filling. There are no presents, no tree for them to sit under. They do not set their painted wooden shoes out for Sinterklaas to leave candies inside. But Tante Sintje has gotten two half-used candles from someone down at her church. They light them in the windows, and for a few hours they enjoy some light and even a gentle warmth. Up and down the street, Mieke sees, there are other candles, flickering, in other windows.

That night Mieke reads from the fairy-tale book for the first time by herself, as Truus and Broodje and their mothers huddle around. Rob sits near, ready to help if she gets stuck, but she does not. Mieke reads each word of the story of Gullin the boar, without making a single mistake.

"By and by," she ends the story as her father always does, "the wild boars were all hunted, and today there are no more in the forests here. But the Boar with the Golden Bristles was painted once on the shields of the men who protected these lands and can still be found on our feast tables each Yuletide as Mother Night passes and we sing carols of Christmas and Sinterklaas."

TANTE SINTJE LOSES the baby on New Year's Eve. Mieke finds her in the bathroom, in the night, and there is blood on the floor and something—they won't look—wrapped up in Sintje's robe. Mieke helps her mother boil a little clean water, and they warm rags for her forehead.

"We should have a doctor come," her mother says.

"From where?"

There's an absent look on Sintje's face, and Mieke watches her mother swipe aside the sweaty locks of hair.

"It's a relief," Sintje says finally. "God strike me down for saying it."

"Damn Him if he does," Mieke's mother says, kissing her sister-in-law's cheek with such love it hurts Mieke to see it. "With all this going on, how else should you think?"

Together they care for Sintje, mother and daughter, through the night, moving silently in the dark, so that when morning comes, it will all be gone. Like it had just been a strange dream.

THE KNOCKS ON the fireplace come daily now, more than that. Mieke never needs to tell the men to hide because they always hide now. There are no more chess sets. No more forged coupons. No activity of any kind. It is easier to all lie there, not moving, burning less energy. Wedged between the roof beams. Slumped behind the false wall. Alive in only one sense now.

JOPIE TIDEMAN'S NEWEST scam is selling cigarettes to the German soldiers. He's gotten his whole crew together to scoop up the butts from the ground where the patrols linger between their rounds.

They unroll them and gather the tobacco together until they have enough to make a new cigarette, which he sells back to the Germans for a few bits of bread or whatever they have. Mieke finds a few of Jopie's smokes that someone has dropped near the corner by the Meijmans' and unrolls one gingerly in her fingers. She's wondered where he'd been getting the papers: most people by now have had to burn their books for any scant heat they produce; that's what's happened to her Sherlock Holmes, to the Tolstoys and the Dostoevskys that Professor Naaktgeboren left behind. "Russian novels. At least they're big" is her mother's only comment.

But inside the cigarettes that Jopie has been peddling, she finds a verse from a Bible he's been tearing up, page by page: "Take counsel, execute judgment; make thy shadow as the night in the midst of the noonday; hide the outcasts; bewray not him that wandereth."

AN OLD MAN passes, his foot gone, leg ending in a blue stump. Some, if they've been stuck in bed too long, have dropsy, their hands and arms swollen, turning purple. Rob told her to be careful not to come near anyone who's got the red blotches that mean typhoid. Sometimes it's scabies, which will just make you itch, but you don't want to risk it.

"*JE HEBT GEEN honger, je hebt trek*," Tante Sintje says to them at night when there's nothing left to eat. "You are not hungry; you only have appetite."

SOMETIMES THE SOLDIERS will take pity. Most of them didn't come here to starve anyone to death. Some of them will show Mieke photographs, kept in their breast pockets, of children their own age, back home in Germany—whom they miss and pray to see again. It is not their fault, they say. There was a conscription. This is nothing like what they were told. It is not their wish to see any of this happening. Then they give a scrap of bread or some old jerky from their packs.

THEN NEW YEAR'S Day, 1945. One of the rockets goes up, screeching like always, and then stops. There is a silence and a shadow passes overhead and then—the whole city shakes. Mieke and Rob are out, on their way to the *gaarkeuken* with their pans to get the day's ration of the gray liquid the Germans call soup. Now the air suddenly becomes smoke. Coughing, blind, she and Rob drop to the street and wait in the pandemonium. It is several minutes before they can get up and begin moving slowly, bent half over, eyes tearing up, to find out what has happened. One of the rockets launched from the dunes and almost immediately had some failure. The cold winds off the sea pushed it back, had carried it right over their unexpecting heads. Now the broken missile had come down on top of an apartment building on Indigostraat, barely a kilometer away. For the first time, Mieke can see for herself the thing she's imagined guiltily for months. What must be happening three times an hour, when the rockets land over in England.

Glass in the road, glimmering and sharp under their feet— Mieke tries to be careful where she steps. Her shoes now are not even shoes. Her mother took the stitching out of an old purse and wove each half back up into a pair of coverings, not even very thick. Up ahead, there is a dining room chair, randomly sitting upright and fully on fire. Dark shapes begin to emerge, all different sizes. Mieke knows they must be bodies. Or parts of bodies, in some cases. Smoke curls off them still; cold as she is then, she feels their warmth. Beside her, Rob points in horror at the blackened shell of a Nazi transport van—uniformed bodies hang limply out of the melted windows. And there are living people, too, sitting on the curb, crying, holding hands. Bleeding from the ears or from the places where arms used to be, or legs. Some are screaming. Some are sitting, taking in the horror, while others scramble and run. Mieke peers down at the road, wet with the melted ice and snow that the rocket has not fully vaporized. There is blood everywhere, and something gray and grisly that could be burned flesh, draped over the loose bricks. From the dust there comes the sound of guns firing, and all around them, people leap back down to the ground.

Sheltering among the rubble. Mieke lies there on her side, breathing heavily, vaguely aware of blood in her eyes, a metal taste in the back of her mouth. On the ground in front of her are the fluttering remnants of a hardbacked book bound in red leather, the pages singed at the edges. Darkness moves around her in waves; billowing smoke blots out the sunlight and then drifts away, only to return twice as thick a moment later. She can't tell what is real and what isn't. She hears something almost like single notes of music, underneath the rumbling and running. Ten yards away there is an enormous piano—the great instrument has spilled onto its side such that the lid is open. Inside, something has splintered, is still breaking. One by one, the strings are snapping loose.

Mieke stares up into the smoke, at the black hole in the side of the building, flames shooting out of it on all sides.

Her eyes stinging, she sees something impossible.

The golden boar, Gullin, there in the very center of the destruction. He snorts and whips his great tusks this way and that, every motion sending off streams of brilliant sparks. Wailing, furious, steam rises from his black, wiry fur and fire seethes from his mouth. He looks right at her. His giant hooves scrape at the cobblestones, sending off sparks, leaving great ruts in the earth. One of his golden tusks swings over and collapses part of a nearby wall. The boar lifts its head and snorts into the darkening air, and Mieke can see row upon row of yellowed teeth inside of its horrendous mouth.

She can't help but look away, and when she finally looks back, the beast is gone.

No. She's imagined it, she tells herself. But it was so real. She cannot explain why she is so sure that she's seen what she's seen.

Where is Rob? She's lost him in the madness—he had been a step or two behind her. And then his hand presses against her back. He helps her up, and stumbling, coughing, they find their way out of the chaos.

"You saw it," Rob sputters, spitting up ash everywhere.

"I didn't," she answers.

"Yes, you did."

And she can't lie again, so she says nothing.

BY DAYBREAK, THE scene of the explosion has been picked over. Everything burnable, everything edible—it is all gone. The bodies have been brought over to the church to join the others in the pile. The building becomes one more crumbling facade; the rubble in the street is covered in fresh snow and then encased in ice.

IT IS A week later when the weather has warmed a little, and Mieke and Rob have gone back outside to find some more things to burn or eat, buried under the snow, which has fallen deeply all over.

They're down near the river, which is frozen solid, looking around in the darkness under the bridges for logs or branches that may have piled up there, and finding little.

Fields of cold snow cut by paths of mud. Bare chestnut trees jutting high above the naked branches of the linden trees. A slice of gray sky runs upside down along the river's black surface, reflecting nothing—the sky is a wall of dark clouds and cold wind, and there are no fishermen and no boats. If there are bodies in there now, they aren't swimming and won't be found soon. Another field of dead stalks. Circling vultures, eyes already trained on her, waiting.

Mieke and Rob work in silence, with nothing to say now, afraid of attracting attention, saving their words for the future, saving the energy it might take to say them. Then Mieke sees a soldier on the other side of the overpass, approaching Rob. The soldier wears the usual gray Nazi uniform, has a rifle over one shoulder, a scared look in his eyes. Mieke notices his round, owlish glasses and remembers him. He was with Captain Schneider, who'd come in hunting for Rob's father, months ago. It feels like years. Mieke is about to call out a warning to her *neefje* when she sees he's handing something to Rob.

Mieke comes over and sees it is a loaf of bread that isn't even stale. They tear off a few pieces of it and save the rest for the others.

"Hoe oud ben je?" he asks in rough Dutch. How old are you?

Mieke answers him and he looks away a moment, as if choking.

"I was your age," he says softly, "in Düsseldorf, at the end of the last war. In Germany we had nothing, just like this. It was so incredibly cold, and they called it Steckrübenwinter. The Turnip Winter. Because that's all we had to eat. If we were lucky. I nearly died."

Mieke investigates the circles of the man's glasses and tries to imagine him as a boy, Rob's size. He survived, she thinks. Survived to do this, anyway.

In thirty years, she imagines herself grown, handing bread to someone like her now.

"I hope you can go home soon," Mieke says to him.

"It's all gone anyway," the owl-eyed soldier says and rushes away, scared to be seen.

A WEEK LATER, a truck comes around with a loudspeaker attached to the roof, barking in its tinny tone that everyone from each household must bring clothes and blankets to the schoolhouse in exchange for a certificate guaranteeing against future searches. Mieke's mother and Sintje argue about what to do—already there is no coal or electricity. Without clothes or blankets, they might all freeze to death in the coming days. But with the certificate, they'd have that much better a chance to keep the men in the attic from being discovered. Perhaps it is a trap. Perhaps if they don't take their blankets over, they'll become that much more suspicious. Mieke and Rob protest as their mothers go through everything in the apartment, trying to get enough together, hoping they can split the difference. Keep enough to stay warm through the weeks ahead. The children shout as their mothers fold the blankets, sweaters, pillowcases, and tablecloths—beginning with the ones left behind by their husbands and then moving to their own. Sintje has a checklist, with numbers that she adds up, her bony fingers shaking. They pile on some of the children's clothes. "You two share this blanket," she says. They'll still be warmer than their mothers. Warmer than the men up in the attic.

ONE EVENING IT gets so cold that no one can move. The weather outside so frigid and fierce for three days, with snow coming horizontally at the windows at all hours. They've slowly gone through all the wood they had stored up and now, even after the weather eases, it might be days before they find anything out there that isn't frozen solid or soaked.

Everyone sits silently in the apartment, having run out of anything to say a day earlier, each entombed in their corners, hidden under whatever they've been able to find. Tante Sintje has on one of her husband's moth-eaten bathrobes and plays with Truus on her lap, trying to keep the pale, squirming child warm underneath an old bath mat. Mieke and Rob are not far off. It is too dark to see well, but she is slowly reading something from the old fairy-tale book—one of the few that they have not yet burned, so thin and little that it wouldn't accomplish much if they did. With a quavering voice, Mieke recites more than reads the tale of the Golden Helmet as her *neefje* coaches her through one word at a time.

> *"In days gone by, when forests covered the land and bears and wolves were plentiful, the people worshipped Woden, whom the Frisians called Fosité. When someone was ill, they laid the sick one at the foot of Fosité's holy tree, hoping for health to come soon.*

*And if the patient should die beneath the tree, then the sorrowful
friends were made glad when the leaves of the tree fell upon the
corpse. It was death to any person who touched the sacred tree
with an axe, or made kindling wood, even of its branches."*

Mieke stumbles along slowly, as a singer from the southern
lands who comes north to entrance the wild people with his sad
songs and then falls in love with the king's beautiful daughter,
Fostedína, meaning Lady of Justice. Mieke loves to imagine her:

*"The pride of her father, because of her sweet temper and willing
spirit, while all the people boasted of her beauty. Her eyes were
the color of a sky without clouds. No spring flower could equal
the pink in her cheeks. Her lips were like the red coral brought
from distant shores. Her long tresses rivalled gold in their glory."*

Fostedína is imprisoned for falling in love with the south-
erner and made to wear a thorny crown as punishment. Then
everyone sees the way she endures the pain without tears, and the
people fall to their knees and forge her a beautiful aureate head-
dress with ornate leaves that covers her forehead like a helmet,
hiding the scars left behind from the thorns. On the final page
there is a glorious illustration of her wearing the Golden Helmet,
at the end, the Frisian warrior princess. Even now it helps bring
Mieke some hope. *Schoonheid onthult ons*, the fairies say. Beauty
reveals us.

Only she never gets that far into the story, does not even turn
to that final page, before Rob's mother abruptly stands. She's shivering so hard she can barely speak, but her tone is soft, as if she is
simply having a conversation with someone the rest of them cannot see—her eyes fixed at some point in the middle of the room.
Mieke's mother rushes over to take Truus before Tante Sintje
drops her mindlessly to the floor.

"This is not real," she says blandly, like someone might say,
"That shirt is not blue."

She continues. "Because this is not happening. I am not even here right now. This is all nothing. And I am finished with all of it. I won't, I won't, I won't."

And then Sintje does something that even seems to surprise her, crossing to the cold fireplace and lifting the iron poker—one of the only metal things they still have left.

"*Zus zus . . .*" Mieke's mother is shouting, concerned enough to set Truus down now beside Broodje on the floor. But by the time she gets her hands free, Sintje is already halfway to where she wants to be. Or where something else wants her to be. Rushing across the room to bring the tip of the poker down hard on the lid of the Japanese trunk.

There is a tremendous crack, as if thunder has burst right there in the hallway, and Mieke sees Rob rushing over to stop his mother. Only no, she realizes, he is stupidly about to jump on top of the trunk. Thinking he can shield it with his own self. Thinking his mother will not bring the poker down if he is there. Thinking his mother is still in command of her own body.

Mieke manages to catch one of Rob's ankles and pulls hard. He falls sideways and hits the floor like a trout on the bottom of a rowboat.

His mother brings the poker down on the trunk, again and again.

Later, she'll claim that it was all because she was so cold. That she'd wanted to break it into firewood. But Mieke won't believe her; she'll remember the look in her eyes now. In this moment. "A murderous rage," they'd call it in a Sherlock Holmes book. A wish to kill, a wish for destruction. The way a child might zealously kick apart an old box on the street for the sheer thrill of seeing it come to pieces.

Only the trunk does not come to pieces. The crack they all hear is the poker itself, the metal fracturing below the hooked end. It must have been damaged already, her mother will say, but without even believing it herself. And there, indisputably, on the trunk itself—not even the smallest scratch. It is as if Sintje has tried to hit a mountain with a fallen branch.

Soon they have her lying down. Soon Mieke's mother is pressing her own body against her sister-in-law's, warming her with what little warmth she still has, holding her until she calmed. That night Sintje sleeps for ten hours, but Mieke cannot keep her own eyes closed.

THE NEXT MORNING there is a knock at the door to the apartment, a desperate wrapping of knuckles on wood, and Mieke knows immediately that something is very wrong. As her mother and Tante Sintje go to answer the knocking, Mieke instead takes up her position near the window, looking outside for signs of trouble. And she sees it. A line of gray vehicles coming down the snowy avenue in their direction, three blocks down. She looks back through the bedroom doorway next, to find in the hallway the last person she wants to see.

It is Mrs. Smit. She stands there, weeping, begging something of Mieke's mother. Even though she is the enemy, Mieke can't help but be struck by the beauty of this woman. Her hair, golden and curled up against the back of her neck. She wants her own to be like this someday. Ordinarily, Mrs. Smit's face is a thing of porcelain beauty, cheeks pink as a doll's, nose sculpted perfectly. Only now there are tears streaming down her cheeks, and she wipes frantically at her nose with a lace handkerchief. On the corner of the white cloth, gripped in her hand, are two embroidered flags. The orange and green flag of Holland, and next to it, the red and black of the Third Reich, the black swastika next to her thumb. Mieke has seen these before, favors given out to the wives of the *landverraders*.

But she is crying into it, hard now as the line of gray trucks stops outside of the building.

"Werner," she's saying. Almost gasping. "Please. Help me."

Mieke's mother, still supporting the woman's panic-stricken weight, moves to one side, and then Mieke sees Werner is there, too.

He is half the size he used to be, and his face is patched and unshaven with scrapes and a blackened eye, mud all over one side of his forehead. He looks twice as scared as his mother.

"Please," the woman begs, "you have to help us. They'll take him back."

"No, Cora," Tante Sintje snaps from the kitchen, "it's a trick. She's clearly lying."

Mieke gathers what her aunt means. It might well be a trap. If they help Werner—if they take him up to where the other men are—he could reveal them all to the soldiers. Then in ten minutes they'd all be in the backs of the trucks outside and be in the prison camps by nightfall.

"Her husband," Tante Sintje snaps, "turned them in. The Meiers. Those beautiful little girls. Cora. Please. You can't."

Mieke feels something new. A freezing-up inside herself. Her head aches, as if someone has dropped something heavy onto it.

Mrs. Smit whispers. "I'm so sorry. I didn't—please, I'm begging. Please. Help my son."

And Werner looks up helplessly, his eyes lost, until they meet Mieke's. She hears the doors of the trucks slamming outside as the knocks rise up inside of the fireplace, passed up from the main floor, then to the Müellers, and now to her, in warning.

She's supposed to go tell the men in the attic to lay low. But how can she now?

If Werner has fled his post, then they'll see him and take what they've come for. They'll leave her father and the others alone.

And if he is there to double-cross them all, then he won't know where the men are.

The best choice is to let them come for him.

To say nothing, do nothing.

It's easy to do nothing.

Then, before her mother or her aunt can stop her, Mieke is a flash of light. Through to the doorway, grabbing Werner's hand in hers and pulling him to the hallway.

"*Liefje!*" her aunt says, but it is too late.

Mieke lifts the fireplace poker and pulls the ladder down for the attic, and no one speaks. Her mother, her aunt, even Mrs. Smit, stand there, frozen in a kind of horror.

Mieke doesn't know yet why she's done it. Why she trusts him. Or if she even does.

All she knows then is that she can't be silent, can't be still. Can't obey the rules and do as she's been told. And if it costs her life and the lives of everyone there around her, then she'll have been brave and a fool in the same instant.

Werner clambers up into the attic and closes the hatch behind him. It is done. Then the door to the apartment building is being taken down from the outside by the angry soldiers, unwilling or unable to wait to be let in. With a sick crack of wood, the front door of their building is split in two, and they are coming, stumbling over the missing stairs that they've had to burn over the past two weeks. Mieke sees the familiar face of Captain Schneider at the head of the line.

"Wo ist dein sohn?" he demands as soon as he sees Mrs. Smit. He tries switching to Dutch instead. *"Waar is uw zoon?"*

And Mrs. Smit is crying too hard to answer him. Mieke watches her intently for even a sidelong glimpse at the attic hatch—that would be enough to give them all away, whether she means to or not. Unable to breathe, Mieke stares over at the men behind the captain on the stairs. In a moment she recognizes one of them—it is the same owl-eyed soldier who gave Rob his ration under the bridge the other afternoon. When his eyes meet hers, she sees the width of his shoulders slump. There's as much fear in his eyes as in hers. Mieke shifts her gaze back to the captain. *Fake, through and through.* He's a fake airplane, nothing more. In her mind she turns him into wood, his features nothing but gouges and lines carved into a board. And as he speaks again, Mieke finds she is not afraid.

"Where is your son, Mrs. Smit? He abandoned his post without leave. We followed him here. We know he came to see you."

The woman shakes violently, and Mieke is sure that this was no trap.

"What is up there? Does this open?" the captain shouts, and Mieke thinks he has seen the pull string, still swinging gently.

And the captain begins to order one of the other soldiers to go up and look, but Owl Eyes steps up and yanks at the cord himself.

Mieke's heart sinks—there is no way the men have had a chance to get into their positions—to move the false walls out. And the moment the soldier sticks his head up there, he'll smell them anyway. The men are all unbathed, and the old bucket they're all sharing as a chamber pot hasn't been emptied yet today.

The soldier comes to the top of the ladder and sticks his head and shoulders up inside. Then he comes down and shakes his head.

"*Niet*," he says, pinching his nose. "Just a lot of dead rats."

Captain Schneider glares at Mieke then and says, "Where is he, little girl?"

Mieke wants to spit at his boots. Wants to scratch out his black beady eyes.

"*Het raam*," Tante Sintje answers coldly. "He burst in here and then left out the window."

"*Please*, let him alone," Mrs. Smit begs, still sobbing.

But the captain is not listening to her—he pushes into the apartment, past the smelly blankets and the pile of book covers they've been slowly burning. He storms around, knocking things over, going to the kitchen window and shouting at the other men. They make the usual show of turning over cabinets and opening closets and then, in a few more minutes, they are gone without a word of apology to anyone or a moment of sympathy for the weeping mother of the boy they're trying to find. The last to file down the stairs is Owl Eyes. She wants to thank him. He avoids her eyes, but she can see on his face that he is miserable. Was it for some glorious vision of a better world that he was deluded into joining? Or was he forced, the same as Werner? She wishes she could ask. She supposes it doesn't matter. The whole world, every inch of it, each day of it, is one mistake after another. But on this day, on this inch, she's done something good.

ONCE THE COAST is clear, Werner comes down from the attic and curls up in his mother's arms. Now that they need not fear Mrs. Smit, the other men come down, too, slowly, one by one, their bodies stiff from being hunched over up there, day in and day out, for weeks now. They're filthy and need to shave. Mieke can see the cage of her father's ribs; all the meat of him is gone. He hugs her tightly, and she runs her fingers lightly over them, as if apologizing.

"I'm so sorry," Mrs. Smit cries over and over, sobbing as she watches the wives from the other apartments go to their husbands and sons. Knowing that it was her, in some sense, who consigned them to this condition.

"What happened to your husband?" Mieke's mother asks Mrs. Smit gently. She does not answer, but Werner speaks for the first time in her place.

"He was killed in Loobeek," he says. "The British shelled Overloon while they were liberating Venray."

Then he looks around at the children, his eyes falling on Rob, who is sitting not far off, in the lap of his own mother. After a few more minutes together, the men begin to climb back up into the attic, and Werner now behind them.

"One more mouth to feed," Tante Sintje says bitterly, toward Mrs. Smit.

"They give me extra rations," she confesses.

"We know."

"I'll share them."

"Yes," Tante Sintje says. "You will."

JOPIE'S GANG USED to be more careful. They'd steer clear of the black-market salesmen, who are beyond cutthroat, but eventually there is not much else to hit, and so one day they try their usual play of bum-rushing a baker who's selling wet, dark loaves for twelve guilders apiece. While some of the boys pummel the man with rocks, the others pry the cart open and yank out everything they can. They take the man's money. And they break the wheel on his cart before they disappear.

But the men who sell on the black market kick a bit back to the soldiers for protection. The next day there is a loud shouting outside as Jopie and three of the other boys are marched out, hands bound, holding signs they've been made to write themselves.

Ik ben een plunderaar, they say. "I am a looter."

Just children. Just her own age.

The soldiers parade them around the little square three times and then they go off.

And she never sees Jopie Tideman again.

MIEKE LEAVES HER body one day in April. One moment she is inside of it, as she always has been, and the next moment she is not. It is like remembering being born inside of a dream. Suddenly it all changes. She's in the room; her body is breathing there, below the blanket. She's looking down at this and, at the same time, up at the ceiling through another pair of eyes. Those eyes are looking at the ceiling, at the cracks—and then it all rips apart, as if it was a painting of a ceiling this entire time, and someone or something has pierced it. There's blinding light inside the fissure, cold and bright, like the moon on a night so clear that you can't stare directly at it. How can she be looking at the moon if she's inside? How can she be looking at herself looking?

Her lips are moving. The small bud of her tongue wets them, barely. She's asking a question—asking it to Rob? Asking her self, above her self?

"Ben ik op het strand?"

Am I at the beach?

The light breaks. Like a window made of stained glass, it splinters into colors she's seen before but forgotten, trembling colors that have never been given names in this universe. Her body that is not her body anymore is shot through with such an intense warmth and pleasure that she thinks she must be dying, and yet she doesn't mind it in the slightest. And this is when the voices call out to her, high voices that jingle like a million tiny sleigh bells all sounding at once, speaking something without need for words. Buoyant embers. A flickering of wings. And there's a lingering scent of hearth cookies. And maybe it is Luilekkerland, or maybe it is heaven, or maybe it is the gasping of her brain shutting down; she doesn't know—she still doesn't know—only that the freed part of her was moving toward it for some number of endless moments. And then it is all gone. And she is back in her body, and someone is holding it up. Rob is. His arm moves around her. He's talking to someone, but she can't turn her head to see them.

A warm hand, a woman's hand, comes to her cheek and guides her face upright. It is Mrs. Müeller. She's come upstairs to share an extra roll of bread. She takes a piece off with her fingers and presses it together before sliding it into Mieke's mouth. It takes all Mieke's effort to even swallow the hard, tasteless fibers, but she does, and after a little time, the lights begin to blink out as the color slowly comes back to Mieke's face. Inch by inch, the ceiling rejoins itself and becomes dark and cold and ordinary. The sun is gone. And she cries because it can mean only that it all continues.

But then Rob is there watching her. And his relief is all the reason in the world to stay.

THE LAST VIOLINIST

~

Snow and rain have been coming down for days, swelling the river alongside Kamp Groente where more and more of us are gathering. Eels from far and wide journey here now, moving deep beneath the icy coverings of the river. Inside Groente, the prisoners and the soldiers grow increasingly listless, stuck indoors together far too long. We all feel it. Something will give, and soon.

A contest is being held with the special permission of Kapo Nachtnebel. One of the guards in our author's section, Trinkenschuh, remarked to another guard named Buhle that one of the Sinti, a violinist named Jeroným, was the finest musician that he had ever heard. Buhle, who played the flute, took umbrage at the notion that a gypsy could be superior to him. And so a wager was made and Nachtnebel arranged the contest.

If Buhle is to win, then Trinkenschuh must buy him a flagon of ale. If Jeroným wins, then Buhle will buy one for Trinkenschuh.

Of course, in that event it is also quite likely that Jeroným will swiftly be killed.

"He'd better make sure he doesn't win," says one prisoner.

"You've heard Jeroným," his friend answers. "He couldn't play badly if he wanted to."

"Anyone can play badly if they want to."

We all hope for Jeroným's sake that this is true.

"Although," the man muses, "if he plays too badly, they might kill him anyway."

In any case, our author soon finds himself following a small crowd into the room where the contest is to take place. He carries a little pen and some loose paper. He scribbles quietly as we eels creep as close as we are able to—eager to watch what will happen through our author's eyes.

After a brief wait, Nachtnebel and the others settle into the corner section. The kapo fishes out his thin green pack of Eckstein No. 5 cigarettes, lights one, and signals that the contest may begin.

The room falls silent as the squat little Nazi, Buhle, clears his throat, licks his sizable lips, and raises his gleaming silver flute.

"Zeee Sonata Appassionata," he croaks. "Composed by zeee late Sigfrid Karg-Elert."

Damnably, the sounds he begins producing are gorgeous, sweet. Quivering and then long and leaping. At times soaring high, trilling like a bird singing, and we think of the pheasants out in the icy heath, the way they leap about and shoot through the air in graceful arcs against the white sky. At times the music falls downward in a way that is so gentle it is heartbreaking. It slows and becomes humble, calling to our minds the kinds of furtive little steps through the snow taken by a family of foxes in the morning's first light. Our author closes his eyes as he listens, unable to bear the fact that these sounds are flowing forth from such a grotesque man. That he is hitting each note with such perfect clarity, without a single stumble. We feel ourselves borne back in time a thousand years, to the wild days before humans ever spread out across these plains. Our author listens and weeps inwardly as he writes, not least of which because he is certain that Buhle will succeed and win the contest and Jeroným will be all right in the end.

Then it is over. There is cheering and Nachtnebel himself seems quite impressed. We watch, eel and man in one, as more drinks are poured and the kapo waves a hand toward Jeroným.

The gypsy violinist was a reedy fellow even before coming to Kamp Groente—now he is but a whisper. We had seen him in the Sinti encampment, though none of us had ever heard him play the violin.

"This is a piece of my own," he explains softly, "inspired by a tale I heard many times in my youth. My grandmother, may she rest in eternity, called it, 'The Man Without a Soul.'"

Indeed, it is a tale we eels know quite well. One of our favorites of all.

Jeroným brings the bow to the strings gently, and then in an instant begins his performance with a strike so fierce that Nachtnebel actually falls back in his seat.

No! We cry out wordlessly. We try, we try to warn you. But it is too late. The intensity—Jeroným cannot help himself in the end. It is as if he knows full well that he is making a mistake and that this knowledge causes him to play even more powerfully. His entire body flexes out and bunches up with each line of the music. He soars, he clenches, he seems to float an inch or two off the floor. Over and over, he produces his jagged and uneasy chords. They accumulate in fiery bursts. As he plays, our author sees colors that he has not seen in many gray months. The linden green of the trees outside his childhood window. The soft pink bellies of the starfish washed up on the shore, carried to his four-year-old feet by a kindly wave. Yellowhammers gathering beneath a park bench to peck at the seeds his grandmother dropped for them. The sound of his own voice, which he's impossibly forgotten.

Lines of ink move out in flowing scribbles from his pen.

Jeroným races along, playing too fast, truly, in certain sections. His hand trembles and his face twists up until it becomes nothing more than a map of all our aching. It is mystical. Melancholic. Capricious and sweet. We recall again why people once believed in wizards. Still believe in God. Fiendish and ecstatic, it goes on and on until it becomes simply unbearable.

Out in the river, we eels writhe and swirl, circling and entwining one another, faster and faster, performing an ancient dance known not even to us—we have only heard of it from our elders long ago and have been told that in some moment, it might come upon us. And here, now, it has. While we twist about, the waters of the river roil and rise steeply. As we move this way and that, we create a series of small waves that go crashing out over the riverbanks, moving outward in growing increments. Toward Kamp Groente.

At last the song ends. Through our author's eyes, we look and see

Nachtnebel remove his cap from his head in shock. In honor. He does not cry; we don't know that he is capable of it anymore. But lacking this outlet, it seems as if the sorrow inside of him is breaking through his very pores. His lips shake, his Eckstein No. 5 burning on obliviously.

We continue our thrashing, our tempo increasing. The waves grow larger and larger now.

For it is in this ecstatic and terrible moment that our author's entirety returns to him at last, just as we've feared. We have tried! To warn you.

Beauty reveals us. Nachtnebel's dreamy eyes fall onto our author's. There is a flash of recognition. The present moment collapses into the past, as all moments do, as all moments must.

The kapo has seen our author before. Some years ago, when the war was new.

Our author once came to the door of an apartment belonging to the kapo's friend, just across the hall. The kapo was visiting that night. Our author was asking to borrow a bottle of gin. Through the door he saw things he should never have seen.

We move faster still, pushing back and forth in the waters, sending them swelling, ever higher. We cry out in the name of Abai, the destroyer. We are igat and utsubo. We are a sky, a void. We are an absence touching everything.

With the final notes of Jeroným's song still lingering in the air like ghosts, no one has yet applauded, lest the noise of their earthly hands chase away the power of what has just transpired.

Now Nachtnebel places his hat back onto his head, takes a long pull on his cigarette, and rises to his feet in the corner, a goblet of dark red wine in hand. As he comes to attention, so, too, do the men around him. The prisoners rise as well, almost automatically.

"Stupendous!" the kapo declares. We all see the blood on Jeroným's fingers as he releases them from the strings at last.

"The violinist," Nachtnebel announces happily, "is our winner."

He licks his lips as if to say more, then does not. He seems to be in some distress for a moment, but then corrects himself a moment later.

As the room hangs in silence, he turns to the others and says solemnly, "To Groente!"

The soldiers lift their mugs and drink and begin to babble enthusiastically. And as they do, Jeroným walks back into the crowd, a marked man, heading now only for his death.

And it is in that moment that the first waves crash into the barbed wire fences, and someone up in a tower sounds an alarm. The soldiers in the room begin to murmur and organize. Kapo Nachtnebel whispers to one of his lieutenants and urges him to see what is going on.

The waters rise higher and higher. We cannot stop it now if we want to.

"They've blown the dam!" one of the guards says, rushing away.

The flood begins to move in beneath the doors, rushing waters soon taking down fence poles and eventually even guard towers. It is true, the Allies are approaching, and 's-Hertogenbosch will surrender to the incoming forces by morning. It will be bloodless; the Germans there have already left it unguarded. Nachtnebel and Trinkenschuh and Buhle will evacuate the flooded halls of Groente in a matter of hours. Before they do, they will murder Jeroným and a hundred other men—alas, our author included.

But as the waters rise and the guns are loaded, and while the other prisoners begin trying to flee and become picked off by the barbed wire and the soaring bullets, our author waits patiently in his cell, setting pen to paper. There is enough time for one last tale.

—V.S.

THE *FLYING DUTCHMAN*

~

Will's head ached. Cold rushed around his body and washed swiftly through the padded fuchsia coat he'd stolen from his grandmother. Chilly water seeped into the neck of his sweater and under the waistline of his pants, jolting him upright from what he'd believed, at first, was a large puddle. But it turned out to be much more than that. He was in some kind of icy river, gushing down the roadway. But he was also right outside of his oma's house, where he'd fallen in the dark. His fingers were numb but not frostbitten. He had not been out there so long, then. Daylight was just about to start breaking. Gray water buoyed massive white snowy floes past him at an alarming speed. He had landed just a foot to the left of the stairs, onto the bank of snow that had been covering the front garden. Only the snowbank was mostly gone now—washed away in the flood.

Will sat up the rest of the way, head still aching, and began to wade through the ankle-deep water. Around the side of the house, he could see out to the bay, where the wickedly high winds were sending the seawater roaring up and over the rocky edge of the land. It took him a moment to take in the full size of the waves curling toward the house now, crashing down as they came into the yard and moving with frightening speed. Where was the dock?

Completely gone. Broken into pieces, now indistinguishable from the debris all around him. Will turned back and ran inside to find his grandmother, discovering as he pulled open the front door that water had already gone under the sliding glass doors in the back. Just an inch or two so far, but enough to soak the carpets and the walls. He found his oma down there, struggling to move a heavy sandbag that she'd pulled out of the garage. Will pushed by her, grabbing the bag with his good hand and rolling the thing over toward the leaking door.

"You're all right," she said, gripping his arm. "I looked everywhere. I couldn't find you. I was trying to call the police, but I couldn't get . . ."

She clutched her cell phone in one badly shaking hand.

Will said. "It's okay. Let's get back upstairs."

"You hit your head," she said, looking at the side of his head above his ear.

"I'm fine," he said, brushing away some blood that was wetly there.

"We lost power," Mieke said. "The generator must be flooded."

Will helped her up the stairs, got her to the couch, and then rushed to the bathroom, grabbing all the towels she had, throwing three over her before starting to remove his sopping clothes.

"You're blue," his grandmother said. "Will, you're freezing."

"I'll be fine," he said, not sure why he thought so. "Give me a second."

He rushed to the guest room. Shaking too much to dig around for dry clothes, he instead grabbed the down comforter from the bed and wrapped it tight around himself. Then he stumbled to his grandmother's room and got hers and pulled it out for her. Barely had he stopped moving before he thought of something else.

"Is Shoshana still over in Trenton?"

Outside the wind was howling and the water was spraying so fast and hard that it was difficult to see much at all. He couldn't find the causeway at all anymore, couldn't tell where the dark waves ended and the purple sky began.

"I don't know," Mieke said quietly.

Will hurried to the stairs and climbed them two at a time to reach the old upstairs bedroom. There he began getting himself into some more of the clothes that he'd been borrowing since he arrived. He pulled down a pair of rubber hip-wader boots that he recognized immediately. If they weren't the same ones his father had been wearing during the ice storm, when he'd buried everything from the refrigerator in the snow, then they were the same kind, even down to the shade of green in the rubber. Will found some heavy yellow foul-weather gear, unused since the sale of the *Sintje*, and climbed into it. Last, he groped around on the high shelf for a scarf or something to hide his face in. He felt something— and pulled down a crumpled bandanna. Blue. And even in all his panic and fear, Will had to stop and laugh. *There it was.*

In another minute, Will was heading back outside, wading into the water, which had already gotten much higher. He was being stupid. What if his grandmother's house collapsed? There could be fallen power lines. Certainly there was all kinds of debris— bits of wood and garbage, bumping off his boots as he took what he hoped were cautious steps. Streaks of oil, odd chunks of ice. Something slid past his left leg, but he couldn't see it and then it was gone. Will imagined eels slithering by, circling him. He closed his eyes and pressed ahead, a foot or two at a time, trying to make sure he didn't slip or lose his footing. When he turned to look out at the bay, he saw greenish seas and white-capped waves in endless lines, rising up into the air. He wiped the rain from his eyes and tried to focus on inching toward the lightless edge of Shoshana's house. The wind howled in his ears, his head ached and throbbed where it had hit the ground before, and his feet kept tangling on things he couldn't see. He looked up at the sky thinking that, at the very least, Teru was far away, safe on the other side of the world.

There was still time to set things right.

At last he got to the front door. It was unlocked, so he pushed inside the dark house. The water had gotten into Shoshana's house as well, a chaotic mess of things floating everywhere—papers and books and chairs, all knocked over in some frenzied rush.

"Shoshana?" he shouted. "It's Will, Mieke's grandson. Are you in here?"

He moved through the kitchen into a library, then finally into a large room at the far end. When he went in, he saw that it was perplexingly packed with medical equipment. A rack of oxygen tanks, a blood pressure monitor. Everything floating or half-submerged, surely ruined. And there lying in the water at the foot of a hospital bed was a woman his grandmother's age, wrapped in an old pink ski parka. He knew before he reached Shoshana that she was dead.

Her eyes were open and cold. Lifeless. Her skin was pale and her lips were dry despite the inch of water on the ground. Each hand was mottled and purple, though her nails had been newly painted, a warm red color. Will touched her body gingerly, shaking her shoulder a little, waiting for something to happen. When it didn't, he tried lifting her. She was not heavy at all, but because he was working with only one hand, at first it was difficult to raise her up. Once he got his second arm around her, the rest was easier. He held her body until the water fell away, then placed her on the hospital bed.

As he caught his breath, he looked around a little more. He saw that there were six kitchen pots on the sideboard, each filled with water. Were they catching drips from some kind of leak in the ceiling? No. Inside each pot were five or six little colorful swirls. Fish, moving about, surely confused. Safe for now.

Will didn't know what to do. The storm was still going. He was cold and wet. His head still hurt. He would need to get it checked out soon. Nevertheless, he sat beside Shoshana's body.

The cadavers he'd trained on in medical school—those stiff, days dead, preserved figures—were nothing like this. Back then he'd learned to detach himself. To focus on the operation to be performed, the procedures to be followed. You didn't want to think about them as a mother or a child or an uncle—really, you didn't want to consider them even to be a whole body. Not a heart, but a coronary artery that needed bypassing. Not a liver, but hepatic tissue that required resection. Not an eye, but a retina that needed to be reattached.

Now Will looked at the body of this woman and wiped her wet hair away from her face and dried her cheeks and forehead with his sleeve, though this was still soaked through. If he had to guess, she'd probably had a heart attack, panicked by the flooding. Trying to save her fish. *The bloodstream floods with cortisol and adrenaline. Breathing rate increases. Blood diverts to arms and legs.* It didn't really matter now. He hunted around a little until in the closet he found a blanket to put over her. Then he found another one and threw it around his own wet shoulders. Was it his imagination, or did the fish seem to be watching him as he moved around? He wondered how long they'd last in their pots. Their water must need regulation, heating, aeration. He didn't know much about fish, or generators, or really anything at all.

More and more lately, Will had been missing surgery. His med school rotation had been just eight weeks, but for the handful of simple procedures he'd felt perfectly at ease. He'd been able to do them as if he'd performed them for years. Others had panicked, quivered, fallen apart, or worked too slowly. They had not been able to get out of their own heads. To stop second-guessing everything. But to Will, it had been like following a recipe, as crazy as that sounded. Lost inside of a mental flowchart, in control of the entire chain of events, Will just detached from himself. He'd go out of his own body for what had felt like hours. Pure thought and motion, as little feeling as possible. And more than anything he missed the *certainty* of it. The belief in what was correct and what was incorrect. A heart beats, or it doesn't. Cut here, cauterize that. Three-centimeter margins. Tumor versus healthy tissue. People talked about the way surgeons could get a God complex, having that sort of power over the insides of another body. But to Will it had come entirely from the confidence attendant in every motion, every moment.

It wasn't like that in his practice now. Not at all. Every day, he dealt in percentages and odds. Second opinions. Third opinions. Prescriptions were like darts thrown at a board in the dark. *Let's give this a try for a few weeks, and then let's check back in to see if things improve.* And then they'd improve a little or not at all, and he'd go on to the next possibility, spending his days in a murkier world of constant unknowing.

Will, in the world of gray areas.

But that was the world, wasn't it?

The surgeons were the ones with the complexes, not him. They had delusions of grandeur. Hallucinations of certainty. But that's all these were in the end. Certainty was death. The past. History. Even if you didn't *know* for sure what had happened—that thing *had* happened, and would never have happened any differently. But up ahead, uncertainty was all there was. Life branches infinitely, the future arrives in secrecy, and this would always be the most beautiful and terrifying thing about being alive.

Shoshana was free of it now, he thought. There must be prayers to say, over the body. Something he could do. She was Jewish, he remembered—but he didn't know if she believed in Judaism or what their prayers were if she did. He thought of the Meiers. Girls that age, who ought to have been women this age now. Up on her bookshelves he saw novel after novel, but no holy text that he could discern, which made him think she must not have wanted one there, which made him think that this meant they were all holy texts for her. So he might as well pick any of them, read any page for her. But all he could do was to keep on fixing her hair, straightening her pink robe, as if he might bring her a little dignity now that it was too late.

IT WASN'T LONG before the water began to recede. Will finally got a call through to a 911 operator, who said they'd send someone out to Shoshana's as soon as the roads were cleared. He walked slowly back to his grandmother's house, through the calmer waters. Oma knew what had happened the moment she saw him carrying the pot with Shoshana's fish. Still, he told her, and she sank back to the couch and closed her eyes and cried.

He sat with her until she stopped.

"How many more fish are there?" she asked.

"A bunch," Will said. "But I don't know what they need."

"There's a binder on the shelf next to the tank. I promised her I'd take care of them when the time came."

"Why?"

"What else could I say? To be honest, I hoped I'd go first, and it would never come up."

Then Mieke cried some more, although not for too long this time, and Will sat with her until she was all right again.

WILL MOVED THE rest of the pots one at a time, located the binder, and found the requisite food pellets and equipment. It was all organized, all ready. As he was getting the last of it over, a truck plowed through the remaining inches of icy water—a landscaping company logo on the side. It turned out to belong to his grandmother's friend from Costco. Giancarlo had come out, against the stay-at-home order, to check on her and make sure everything was all right.

Soon Giancarlo began working on clearing the water from the downstairs of Oma's house. There had been a lot of damage, but the man seemed to think it could be repaired soon enough. Will did not feel like watching the EMTs arriving down the street, so he tried to help Giancarlo remove the buckets of mopped-up water. Giancarlo said not to worry, pointing out that Will had only one good hand and all, but Will didn't listen, and as much as it soon began to feel like his left hand would fall off, he kept apace as they got the water steadily back outside again.

The man worked busily for half an hour on the generator—the water levels outside continuing to inch down as the storm moved farther up the coast and high tide passed. The skies lightened and became a white-gray color. Will tried to help where he could, holding things, passing things from a toolbox.

"Thanks for coming by," Will said.

"Praise Jesus," Giancarlo said, crossing his chest.

Will hummed in a vaguely agreeable way.

"You don't believe in God?" he asked.

"Not really," Will said, bracing himself for some kind of weird sermon. But Giancarlo just laughed as if this mystified him and pointed up at the house toward Oma.

"Her, either. And yet I see her at the hospital, checking her horoscope."

"Oh yes." Will laughed. "*That* she takes very seriously."

"But not you."

"No," Will said. "Although lately I've been wondering if I'm cursed or something."

Giancarlo laughed and looked out at the water, which was still rough, but far calmer now.

"Where I grew up," he said, "everyone believed these things. Curses and magic and ghosts. It didn't matter if you were a teacher or a doctor or a gardener. We all knew it. If you took seashells from the beaches—very bad luck. My mother refused to *ever* put her purse on the floor. It meant you would end up being poor. And my great-grandmother, God rest her soul, knew the day she was going to die. One morning she woke up and saw her rocking chair moving on its own. She came down the stairs and said to us, '*Hijos míos, moriré antes de que se ponga el sol.*'"

"What's that mean?"

"She said, 'I'll be dead by sunset.'"

Will tried not to smile. "And?"

"That afternoon, she collapsed! Right on the floor. Gone in an instant."

Giancarlo looked as if this certainly proved his point, but Will was unswayed.

"Coincidences happen," he said. "It's all still just random. I think."

The man moved back to his work silently.

"No offense intended," Will said. "It's just not what I think is going on."

But even as he said it, he knew he wasn't sure. He knew he was saying only what he'd always said before, and that nothing now would ever be like it was before again. He looked up at the clearing sky at the sound of a plane going somewhere overhead.

He wished Teru was there. She'd come back when she was ready. He believed this, and he did not know why.

Giancarlo cheered as the generator at last puttered to life. Minutes later, power was restored to the house again.

ON THE WAY to the hospital, Will thought about his grandfather, Robert Geborn, a smiling gentleman with a wide jawline and swept-back hair, who always called young Will "Boefje." *Boo-fee*. Although, as a boy, Will did not know that's what he was being called. He did not speak Dutch, and nobody had explained the nickname to him. He'd believed his opa, with his thick accent, was calling him Goofy, like the large lanky dog-man in the Disney cartoons. He'd say things like, "Come here, you little Goofy," and "Where is that Goofy hiding?" and this always delighted young Will.

He'd passed away when Will was still little, only six, from leukemia. So for many years no one called him Goofy anymore, but Will still remembered. When they'd gone to Disney World for the first time, a few years later, he'd continually picked out Goofy-themed items: a T-shirt, a hat with long ears, and a fanny pack with neon lettering that his mother insisted he wear at all times to prevent pickpocketing. More likely it was because she did not want him to lose his trinkets on the log flume or something. In any event, Will picked out Goofy paraphernalia whenever possible as a gesture to his deceased grandfather, and even spent the better part of one afternoon searching everywhere for the full-size Goofy so he could get his autograph and take a photo with him. Sometimes at night, before he fell asleep, Will could see his grandfather standing there in the space between the foot of the bed and the dark closet.

The truth of the nickname was not revealed to Will until he was thirteen, on a trip to Holland with Oma. She'd taken him for two weeks, to see the dunes and along the boardwalk, where they served the tiny pannekoeken he loved to eat by the dozen for breakfast and the kroketten he had for dinner. These he re-membered that his mother tried to make for his father before he'd disappeared—though they were softer and blonder in color than the rich, crispy ones Will had first in Holland.

He and Oma were walking around a little farther into town one afternoon—going to see the Peace Palace. He remembered going there with his father, years earlier. He and Oma had stopped at a McDonald's and got a Happy Meal and Will had been enjoy-ing the familiar taste of home (the Dutch burgers he'd ordered elsewhere were all hard as rocks and stuffed with herbs)—here the French fries were served with spicy kerriesaus (curry sauce), but at least all the illustrations on his placemat were of all the famil-iar McDonald's characters: the red-haired Ronald; and the purple blob Grimace, who there was Grimas; and then the Hamburglar, or Hamburgerboefje. Oma pointed at it with her long finger and said, "That's what your opa used to call you. Boefje."

"Wasn't it Goofy?" Will said.

"Boefje," she said. "Pronounced *Boof-ja*."

Will looked down at the cheeky burglar. "What does that mean?"

"The translation, I think, is 'villain.'"

"*Villain?*"

"Yes, but a *cute* villain. Like a term of endearment. Like the show, with the little boys who are always up to trouble," and she made a little cowlick with her finger.

"*The Little Rascals?*" Will guessed.

"Yes! Like that. It's like saying 'little rascal.'"

Will was stunned. What about all the Goofy things he'd bought—including the fanny pack he was using on that trip, to contain all the little Dutch coins. It had all been wrong. Opa hadn't been calling Will a cheerful, lop-eared dog, but a little ras-cal. It had been more mischievous, more playful. Will didn't un-derstand why. He'd never been the sort to cause trouble. Wasn't a thief. Wasn't disobedient, ever. Hence the alignment with the tall, affable dog-person who said things like, "Aww, shucks," and "Golly!" He'd thought Opa had been highlighting the goodness of his nature by calling him that. But no—the whole time his opa had been trying to say something else. That a good kid *was* a troublemaker, a rascal, a knave! Burgling burgers! More Calvin, more Dennis the Menace. Will hadn't known that his grandfather had lanced sugar beets from the back of Nazi trucks or journeyed miles in tire-shoes to bring wheat to his family.

Similarly, Will then had no idea that the little stone fortifications out in the dunes, which he loved pretending were parts of a medieval castle, were actually the remnants of the Atlantikwall, preserved in memory of those hard years during the occupation. What must it have been like for his oma to see her grandson on top of those old fortifications, leaping around innocently waging war with invisible dragons? Innocently dancing on the graves of her worst fears and traumas. This was the world of gray areas, he remembered, where joy was possible, too.

OPERATION MANNA

~

At the hospital, the doctors stitched Will up and scanned him over and over in different machines. MRIs and X-rays and CAT scans, too. They agreed that Will should stay overnight while they monitored some residual swelling in his skull.

"Blood on the brain," they told him.

But it was resolving.

And as it did, Mieke sat with him and told him the last parts of her story, all of it—every detail she could remember. The whole truth, at last out. Passed on to the next generation.

IF IT HAD lasted another week, Mieke told her grandson, they'd have starved. Her, Rob, their mothers, Broodje and Truus, the men in the attic, even Mrs. Smit and the Müellers, with their extra rations. But then one day it was over. Mieke woke up to the sound of a grinding mechanical noise outside and ran to the window to see a line of tanks moving in. She had to look twice to be sure, but it was real. They were Canadian tanks. She'd screamed and shouted. Ran up to the attic to tell her father, no longer worried about keeping her movements a secret. Outside, she could hear the cheers rising just like on Crazy Tuesday. The men and women in the streets were shells of themselves now; on the outside, this was true. But it was like the lights inside of them had been relit. Mieke and Rob rushed to the field where the tanks were coming in, joined in moments by hundreds of children, pouring out from every corner. The soldiers waved and shouted in English. Some were throwing bananas and the little chocolate bars they had in their meal kits, and Mieke caught one and split the precious thing with Rob. A bite of it was all she wanted, then. For the rest of her life, she would not pass chocolate bars without thinking of the way that first one had dissolved into her mouth, richly, sweetly.

The soldiers threw out leaflets with instructions to go to the airfield in Ypenburg, where they'd soon be dropping baskets of food from the airplanes. Operation Manna, they called it, but this she learned later. From all over, men and women were already beginning to come out of their homes with baskets and pillowcases to gather the food up. Mieke saw someone carrying a pile of fine porcelain plates toward the field, expecting some great feast to fall from the sky: roast beef and Brussels sprouts and apple pies.

Mieke had gone out to the field with Rob, so excited they could barely speak. Her legs wobbling under her with each step. But buoyed up by the hundreds of other children there, all around them, people she had not seen in such a long time. People she'd feared had already been lost. Mr. Koot, from the gas station, in his oily coveralls. And Dr. Mees, who had put on a clean white shirt. Mrs. Seyss in her apron. Mr. Veening. All standing there in the field, erupting with joy as the planes approached from the horizon line. A swarm of great silver birds, flying dangerously low—only a hundred and twenty meters from the ground, their bellies opening to release white packages, which fell directly to the ground. Then from higher up, other planes released more and more, these bursting with white parachutes, until the whole sky was blocked out by a thousand ghosts, falling down. People caught the boxes in mid-air. They leaped up, they fell to the ground in deliriousness. They hugged, they sang, they cried. *O zo! O zo!* Orange will triumph. So there. So there. And Rob kneeled down so that Mieke could climb onto his shoulders to reach the falling parcels half a second sooner.

And when the first one came into her reach, a breeze pushed in and for a moment it lifted her. She was weightless for joy, weightless from hunger, lighter than air.

WHAT THEY GOT at first was saltine crackers. Every single box, that day, and every day for a week, was filled with saltine crackers. There was something that could happen, Mieke explained to Will—if you give rich food to a person who's been starved, their systems can't process them. It can kill them. So for a week, nothing but crackers. And then bread, with butter. Then finally fruits, vegetables. Meat. With each new element, their bodies resumed some new ounce of service, their minds some function. It was like coming out of a dream, she explained to her grandson. It was like waking up from a nightmare and not knowing if it was ever real.

On the afternoon of the first airdrop, there was a huge bonfire on the tram tracks behind their house, where her neighbors burned every single Nazi flag from every building. And from inside of the butcher shop, the Meijmans stepped out, at first to jeers and shouts—the tables turned now on all sympathizers. For a moment, Mieke expected the whole town would move from the bonfire to tear them apart. But then from behind the Meijmans in the shop door, two American airmen emerged—half-starved themselves, bent over with weakness. The same ones that she and Rob had seen parachuting from the plane before it went down. They'd been hiding out inside the butcher shop the entire time, the story eventually came out. The Meijmans had kept them alive. They'd been double agents from the start, gleaning German intelligence from the snacking soldiers and feeding it on to the resistance.

IT TOOK YEARS, Oma explained, before things returned to normal. That summer her parents sent her and Rob away for a few months to stay with a host family in the countryside, where they would have more food. When they returned in the fall, things had begun to change. They cleared out the land mines, pulled out the stock-ades, battered down the fortifications along the beaches. They re-paired the dikes and restored the flooded farmland enough to begin preparing for next year's harvest. Many of the men returned from the work camps, but the Jewish families had been murdered—just as DeVries had said. The Meiers did not come back.

There were stories of collaborators being sent away, some to Groente, which had been rebuilt after a destructive flood. Of their wives being dragged out to have their heads shaved in the town square, then forced to stand out with a sign around their necks saying *Ik ben een landverrader.* But Mrs. Smit avoided such a fate— Oma said she never knew if her parents had anything to do with it or not. She and Werner lived there together for a few months and then moved off to start over somewhere new.

School resumed, and her new teacher was finally able to help her with her reading. Show her how to keep the letters from danc-ing away from her. And the Red Cross sent food to the schools— milk in cartons, she remembers, and *oranges,* which she'd never tasted before in her life. She'd bitten into the first one like it was an apple. It took months, but she and the other children got their weight back, their color back.

"And they always put in a stick of gum," she complained to Will. "I never understood that. Why would you have something you can chew but not eat?"

THERE WERE THINGS that would never be the same. So much had been lost. So many had died. So much had been destroyed and could not be rebuilt. Each day Mieke came home, she looked up at the bullet holes in the wall of her building, and she remembered. It had not all been a bad dream. It had really happened.

They waited for news about Professor Naaktgeboren. Mieke's father's contacts said they thought he'd been taken and sent to

Groente, but so far there were no records of him being there. Rob by then had stopped believing that he saw his father's shape in the wood carvings on the cedar chest. Mieke didn't bring it up— didn't see the point in reminding him. After all, hadn't she, in the end, seen her own share of things that should not be? Hadn't she believed in enough strangeness by now?

Bit by bit, normal life returned. Windowpanes were reset. Trees replanted. Curbs rebuilt. Tram tracks repaired and even brought into full operation by the end of the year. The coal shipments came back, and the electricity soon began to flow. And after another few years, Mieke said, it was almost as if it had never happened.

Sintje remarried, an importer named Drukker, and they took Rob and Truus with them to Indonesia. At eleven, Mieke could not begin to explain the pain of that separation. As long as she could remember, he had been there. Right next to her. Now he was gone. She waited for him to come back without realizing that was what she was doing. She waited and waited, into her teenage years. They sent photographs, wrote letters. And in them they never spoke about the Hunger Winter or the war at all. It was too painful. The things they'd seen and done—how could they ever revisit it? No one else talked about it, either. Life was good, and there was no point in returning to those brutal times. Who wanted to think about Jacoba, the girl in the minefield? If she closed her eyes and saw that purple coat or the head of Mrs. de Witt's dog in the gutter, she'd say nothing of it. No one spoke about these things, as if through silence they could erase them.

WILL HAD WONDERED if Mieke's father, free from the attic, had rebuilt his bakery. Why weren't they all still living over in Holland, selling bread? No, his grandmother explained, half-choked with regret. Her father had come out of the attic a changed man in many ways. No longer the nimble-fingered, strong-armed baker he'd been in her youth. With no interest now in going back and rebuilding or starting over. Like the others, he did not speak of those days, but she could see that he also had never left them.

Her father soon signed up, as many of their neighbors did, for a civil service post. He volunteered as a policeman and then, after a few months, became a guard at the penitentiary institution in Scheveningen. The old prison had been taken over by the Germans there and named Polizeigefängnis, known by most as simply the Oranjehotel, or the Orange Hotel. It had been a way station where the local Nazis had kept the Jews before their ultimate removal to the concentration camps. Now once more it was a place to keep petty criminals and minor lawbreakers, of whom there were plenty in the hard months just following the war. People had lost their money, their homes, their families, their minds. But Mieke's father had no desire to see his countrymen imprisoned and he grew to hate the work. He took to spending much of his free time sitting in a special cell there, 601, which had been preserved as a historical artifact, in just the way it had been during the war: the plaster and paint marked with the scratchings of its former inhabitants; a small wooden bed with two corner shelves; a plain wooden desk and a stool beneath; only 3.7 meters by 1.9. Doodencel, they called it. The Death Cell.

Her father would go and sit in there for hours and hours, alone.

And then an opportunity came up in Groente.

"Camp Vegetable?" Will asked.

"Yes," she said. "They needed a new director of the prison there. My father took the position, and we moved to 's-Hertogenbosch."

"That's where your father wanted to be?"

"Yes," she said solemnly. "He wanted to see them punished for what they'd done. But he was not a monster. He believed in justice; he ran the prison well. For some reason he needed to stay in that place that had taken his brother's soul and silenced him. But . . . I hated it. Hated living there. Hated that he worked there. Hated all of it. Someone had to do it, but why should he be the one? I just wanted him to be who he was before, to laugh and twist his mustache and bake bread for painters and ride around on his bicycle with me on the handlebars—but that part of our lives had ended. My father became someone I did not know anymore. Someone I did not want to know."

THERE WAS ONE thing to come of it all. The carved wooden tile that she'd given to Will with the image from the postcard of the spot where the Archduke Ferdinand had been shot. It had been made, she explained at last, by not just any prisoner, but by the German captain who had previously run Groente. The former kapo, Nachtnebel. He'd been captured by the Allied forces while fleeing to Belgium. He'd been returned to Groente to be held until he could be brought to trial for his crimes. And during that time, Mieke explained, her father had kept a close eye on him as the captain met with officials, gave testimony. He was apparently quite forthcoming, not shy to divulge the details of his operations, the locations of burial areas, the names of his former officers and lieutenants—he seemed to have no particular loyalties or to care about any of it. Mieke's father described him as mild-mannered, well-spoken, imaginative. Always looking for things on which he might sketch this or that. Barbed wire, the little woodland animals he spotted out in the frozen plains beyond it. The most bother he ever caused was asking sometimes if there could possibly be music? Her father had heard tell of the warped little concerts Nachtnebel had orchestrated during his time in charge, and so he denied him that pleasure. Instead, the man would just stand there by the fence looking up at the fortifications around 's-Hertogenbosch, lost in his dreams. It did not take long to try him for his crimes, and he was executed by hanging in June of the next year.

The wooden carving Mieke's father had found in Nachtnebel's cell, sitting out on the table where he'd been able to see it from his bed. Who carved a locked door to nowhere? Mieke couldn't say why he kept it. He told her that he wished, sometimes, he'd asked the man about his *broer*. There was no record of him there, but her father felt certain this was where he'd been taken. If only he had had the courage to reveal himself as some avenging angel. But what could possibly avenge it? The calm way Nachtnebel went about his final days, just the same as before, seemed only to underscore the fact in her father's mind. There could be no amount of justice dealt out, nothing capable of setting the scales right. The tightening of one noose around one neck would only ever be a million too few. The only balm, then, was time. Each day, each week, each month, each year of continued survival. Of never forgetting, but also of no longer remembering. The promise of times to come.

AND THEN ONE morning, around Mieke's sixteenth birthday, she woke up one day and couldn't get out of bed. She was exhausted, even having slept through the whole night. Her parents brought her to a doctor finally, who took some blood and confirmed his suspicions.

"Acute anemia," he pronounced. "Lack of iron in your blood. We are finding this all over now. Girls your age exactly."

It didn't need to be explained. Something had been badly broken back then in her body, as she'd lain there starving to death, gone months without proper nutrition. And even though she'd been fine for eight years, now it was coming back, as she grew into adulthood and womanhood. All around the Hague it was happening just as the doctor said. Girls her age in particular, bedridden, unable to stand up for long times. The only cure was to go in for iron shots every week, which were painful and had to go into the buttocks. It took nearly a year of these to completely recover, and all these years later, she told her grandson, she was still hearing it from her doctors. "Eat more red meat," they'd tell her. "A little low on the iron count." Sometimes they even think it could be a sign of cancer, and she needed to tell them, *No, it's a long story. I don't have cancer. But when I was eight years old the Nazis almost starved us all to death.*

"They said that to me just yesterday. When I first came in,"

Will responded. "Severe anemia." And it had come up when he was in the hospital during medical school as well.

"You got that from me," Oma said. "Your father had it, too."

"Has it, too," Will corrected her.

"Yes."

OMA CONTINUED TO explain what had happened after the war. More and more, Will knew parts of the story already. His opa came back from Indonesia at seventeen, already studying to become an engineer. She had not seen him except in photographs in six years, and barely recognized him at first. Like her, he'd gotten tall. He had a thick mustache and his face had broadened, the smooth apple cheeks of his childhood hardening to a rough oaken jaw. But his hands—his hands were unchanged. Nimble as ever at every finger's joint, swift and light at every tip. He held his pencil the same way as ever, somehow an extension of his wrist, pressing and pushing it in the same strokes on the pages. Only now instead of fairy-tale monsters he drew schematics for machines, designs for factories.

When they married a year later, he was able to get them visas to come to America, thanks to his new stepfather's business connections. Going through immigration their last name was shortened from Naaktgeboren. They became officially the Geborns. In Chicago, Rob got a job working for Colgate-Palmolive. Oma started work as a secretary at a law firm, improving her English as she went. She watched *Gone with the Wind* dozens of times and read the book cover to cover, and soon enough she had a baby.

She had the telegram, which her own mother saved, on the old green Western Union paper:

Maywood, Ill. VERZEND UW TELEGRAMMEN VIA
HOLLANDRADIO PTT
    BOY 6.3 POUND ROBERT WILLEM MOTHER AND SON
DOING FINE BORN MONDAY 13 BOB ++++

Truus became an actress, just like her mother had wanted to be, and in the 1960s starred in four Dutch films. She worked with Van der Linden and Ditvoorst, and even received a Berlinale Silver Bear for her short film *Stille Sneeuw, Geheime Sneeuw*, an adaptation of a story by Aiken, and later won a Palme d'Or for her work on *Tachtigers*, a film about the Movement of Eighty and the Dutch poets who wrote before the First World War. Then she'd died, sadly, of an overdose, sometime in the late 1970s. Mieke had read a poem at her funeral, wondering the whole weekend, and ever since, if there was anything anyone could have done differently to help her. When she thought of Truus, she still thought of a red-faced child, wailing out against anything and everything. It didn't seem so unreasonable to Mieke anymore.

MIEKE'S BROTHER, BROODJE, back to being simply Robert, never grew past five feet tall. Something about the memory of that day when the planes had come with the food at last—it had stayed with him his whole life. He became obsessed with airplanes. Studied them, drew them, painted them, and finally learned to build them. He went to work for KLM for many years, repairing planes, and eventually did come to America, where he settled in Tampa and taught training courses for United Airlines, preparing future generations of repairmen.

He married, had children, and they, grandchildren.

They'd fought in new wars, traveled to new countries.

It all went on and on.

MIEKE EXPLORED THE world. Colgate-Palmolive sent her and Rob far and wide, to retrofit their factories throughout Europe and later, in Indonesia. Rob's innovation was simple, but effective and lucrative for the company. They had, for many decades, made the bottles, jars, tubes, and various other containers for their products in various factories, but bought the caps for those containers from a competitor. It was Rob who figured out how to reorganize some of the factory equipment that was already fashioning the containers and make it produce caps as well. It transformed the business, streamlined the process, and resulted in his advancement in the organization to an executive level. But then, leukemia. He'd fought it for six years, through three rounds of chemotherapy, which is why he'd had no hair for most of Will's childhood. His father had given bone marrow—incredibly painful, back then. He'd done this three times. And it had bought them time. Ten years. Enough that Will was able to know him and become his *boefje*.

HER MOTHER, CORA, had lived to be one hundred and three years old. The last time Will had gone to Holland had been for her hundredth birthday. Born into a world of oil lanterns and horse-drawn carriages, she'd died in a world of cellular phones and jet planes, having survived two world wars in the process. She'd seen men walk on the moon. At the time of her death, she was completely blind. Her country was celebrating twenty years in the European Union with its neighbors: France, Germany, Italy. After their time in Groente, she went back to Den Haag and lived most of her life within four blocks of the old apartment on Laan van Meerdervoort.

MIEKE AND SINTJE had not spoken often after she left Holland. She had grown distant after Truus's death, and Drukker had gone after a heart attack a few years after. The loss of Rob proved too much.

Later Mieke learned that when Sintje heard about Rob's passing, she stopped eating. Stopped drinking. She did not stand. She did not move or speak. She died two weeks later, and at the inquest afterwards the doctors declared her cause of death to be a broken heart.

Will remembered learning in medical school that this was not just poetry or metaphor.

Death by broken heart. Also known as stress-induced cardiomyopathy, sometimes called takotsubo cardiomyopathy.

He'd texted Teru again, who was by then settling in out in Osaka for her training program. He asked what the word meant—*takotsubo*.

She'd had to ask her grandmother, but the word came back:

Tako tsubo was the name for a trap once used to catch octopuses in the little fishing village where her grandmother had grown up. It was a kind of clay pot, enlarged on one side, and it resembled, apparently, a human heart that had ballooned out on the left side—which is just what had happened to Will's great-grandmother.

Going fishing? she asked.

Will sent back a smiley face. But what he wanted to write was this:

You can love someone so much that when they die, your own heart collapses.

THE MAN WITHOUT A SOUL

~

We have promised a final tale, and we eels are creatures of our word. How to begin? Ah yes. With this: In the times when the rivers and streams of the Low Countries often flooded with seawater, there was a woodcutter named Robrecht who was unpleasant, disliked, miserable, dour, sullen. Fortunately for the others in his village, he mostly kept to himself, living in a cottage out near the forest's edge with only his daughter, Kora, a girl about ten years old and uncommonly sweet, particularly given her company in life. Robrecht had arrived in the village when she was only a baby. Everyone said that her mother had died in the recent plague that had claimed many souls across the Low Countries. And since the illness had also taken the town's previous woodcutter, they accepted the pair even when Robrecht showed absolutely no gratitude or charity in return.

Displeased with everyone and everything, the woodcutter quarreled with each neighbor, gouged his customers, spoiled the land around his cottage with neglect, and spat constantly on the ground whenever he came into town for business. Like some kind of animal, he growled and hollered and paced in agitation whenever dealing with anyone for any reason. Many assumed he was a drunk, but no one had ever witnessed him take a drop of liquor. Others feared for the safety of dear little Kora, but there never seemed to be a scratch on her and she was perfectly happy as far as anyone could tell. Her father provided amply for her, and she in turn kept their home barely above squalor, which was all she was capable of at her age.

Who knows what might have become of the situation had it gone on—perhaps Kora would have married someone in town and left home—but tragically the girl fell ill on her fifteenth birthday.

After three days of fever and sweating, Robrecht called for the town's doctor.

Dr. Valsen attended to the girl there in the cottage using every instrument in his black leather bag before pronouncing to Robrecht with regret that Kora was unlikely to recover. In a day or two at most, she would succumb to her illness. All Valsen could do was make her more comfortable in the meantime.

Valsen expected that Robrecht would erupt into his usual rage and swearing, but the man instead absorbed the news solemnly. It seemed to Valsen that he was in some sort of trance, not there in the room at all.

"This must be difficult, after losing her mother the same way," Valsen said softly.

But Robrecht said, "Her mother is not lost. She lives west of here in a village called Dorp."

Valsen did not know of the town, but no matter. This was wonderful news. If it was possible to find Kora's mother, Valsen might be able to help the girl through a transfusion of blood—a new technique had been developed in England—but it had to come from the mother.

Robrecht left right away, traveling on Valsen's horse, out through the forests he knew well from his daily cutting, but as Robrecht tried to recall the paths and routes he'd once known back to Dorp, he found that he could not. Fifteen years had passed, true, but how was it that he had no recollection of the old village at all? All he knew was that it was where he and Kora had lived before. That it was near a river where his father had once fished for eels. But he could not recall a single building in the town or even the face of his own wife, the mother of his daughter.

Traveling as swiftly as he could, Robrecht went west along the riverbank. But when he arrived at the place where the village ought to be, he found instead a gigantic lake, placid and gray, inhabited only by the kingfishers and crakes along the reedy shore.

Hesitantly Robrecht followed the boundary of the water farther west, thinking that the village must be still beyond it, and as he went, he began to run across odd bits of detritus lodged among the rocks and in the shallows. Bits of blue and white tile, the sort that came from Delft. Children's dolls made of wax with cracked china faces, their clothes having long rotted away. The legs of tables, a crooked chandelier distended in muck. In one place, a great mountain of books, warped and swollen from sun and water. Then a barrel organ on great red wheels, split in half by a fallen poplar. In time, Robrecht began to see the roofs of houses peeking up from the waterline some distance away, and unmistakably, the tilted sails of a windmill sticking up from the other side of the lake. As soon as he saw it, he recalled the windmill, which had been the tallest structure in the little village of Dorp. Where he'd been born and lived and married and had children.

Children. Four others. Sons and daughters. They had drowned here, it came to him, along with his wife. He had not been able to reach them in time, had saved only the baby, kept its swaddled form up above the rushing waters as he'd stayed afloat on his carving bench.

In those days he'd been a woodcarver, he recalled. From poplar, he'd fashioned the wooden clogs worn by the farmers out in their fields, and little ornamental ones that children left out for Sinterklaas to fill with treats. He'd carved dolls and furniture and boats and canes for the oldest of them. He had been a happy man, one who loved his work and his neighbors and his family.

Now he sensed that he ought to feel waves of grief, sadness returning to him as he stood there looking at the collapsed windmill and the lake that held the bodies of everyone he'd once known. But no such grief arrived. Even when it occurred to him that now Valsen could never save his daughter, even at this sure failure, Robrecht felt nothing.

As the man shambled numbly on, he came slowly to the spot where his house once would have been, wondering if anything might remain. All he could find, however, was a single wooden shoe, washed into some thorny bramble. Picking it loose, Robrecht saw immediately that one of us, an eel, was curled up there inside of it. Carefully he pulled our slimy friend free and let him go into the waters before turning back to the shoe.

Robrecht knew immediately that it was one of his—carved in his style, and with a design at the front that he was oddly drawn toward. Yes, he had been carving this design into the toe, there in his shop, while the baby slept, as the waters had begun to rush toward them.

The carved design was a simple scene, of a man behind a plow in a sunny field. As Robrecht looked at it, he felt almost as if the little man inside was moving, shifting around behind the machinery. He watched the figure for some time, marveling at it, even before he realized that the man in the wood was him. As he did so, the little figure seemed at last to notice him and waved in his direction. Robrecht wondered what he must look like to it, some giant, some god on the horizon, who had made it in his own image. Then he considered he must have gone raving mad.

There was nothing left to do. Keeping the shoe, Robrecht lumbered back to Valsen's horse and rode back the way he'd come. Still he felt nothing.

In another half a day's time he returned to his home and found, to his surprise, that Kora was alive and well, tending to their weedy garden as happily as ever.

"A remarkable recovery!" Valsen proclaimed to Robrecht. "If I were the sort of man to believe in miracles—"

Robrecht had half a mind to strangle the doctor for worrying him so much and for sending him all that way back to Dorp for nothing. But as his daughter happily hugged him and welcomed him home, it occurred to Robrecht that he still felt nothing.

He could hug her back. He could wipe imaginary tears from his eyes—that was all. He could feel no joy, no relief, nothing.

Then he took out the wooden shoe from his bag and held it in his hands. The little figure moved about behind the plow, peering up at him as if waiting to be released.

And if he did, the man thought—if he took his soul back, then fifteen years of pain would come with it. The loss of so much, the memory of his wife and his sons and his other daughter. He'd have to bear having nearly lost Kora, knowing that he might lose her anytime—he was not certain he could withstand it all at once.

Still then he touched his hands to the carving on the shoe, accepting it back gladly.

We have tried! Still we try to warn you.

What good are souls, after all?

Troublesome things.

Still we, the eels, will watch on from our narrow hiding places. Whispering. An absence, touching everything.

In time immemorial, in time inescapable, we will soothe you until you sleep.

—V.S.

SLIPS AND FALLS

~

On a starless night, Will met Dr. Mizrahi at the corner of Eighty-Fourth Street in Manhattan. She had a plum-colored scarf that wound around her head. They walked together from there, half a block, toward the door to the offices. When he'd taken his leave of absence, she'd barely been showing, but now her belly was so large she could not button her coat. It was not so cold now, almost to the end of April. Will was glad—she and her husband, a day trader for Goldman Sachs, had three kids already but had been wanting a fourth for a while. He didn't know how she did it. Where would they put another one, in their little brownstone in Bed-Stuy? But these were not his problems. He had enough of his own. Still, he was glad to help her get up to the office, though she insisted she didn't need it. But she was doing him a favor, after all. It seemed the least he could do.

Soon they arrived at the door to their office building. The doorman was watching soccer on a little TV behind his desk. Will saw orange jerseys and wondered if it was the Netherlands team. Dr. Mizrahi waved her ID card at the man, and he buzzed them both past the barrier toward the elevators. Silently they rode up to the ninth floor and got off. It took only a few minutes to get into the office and shut the door behind them.

246 ~ KRISTOPHER JANSMA

"Sorry we couldn't squeeze this in during normal hours," she said. "I feel like we're almost through the backlog from when you took off."

"You're the one who told me to go," Will reminded her.

"Damn right." She grunted a little and gestured to her rounded stomach. "In about ten weeks, you'll be returning the favor, believe me."

Mizrahi hit the lights on in Exam Room 3 and told Will to take a seat.

"You hear from Teru today?" she asked.

"She calls every other day or so," Will said.

"You must miss her."

"Tons."

"She'll be back."

Will nodded and began to unbutton his shirt so he could pull it free. Mizrahi watched him closely and smiled as he nimbly twitched each button free with just two fingers.

"Isn't that amazing?" she said. "Six weeks ago, you couldn't pick up a pencil."

His brain had literally rewired itself, he knew. Made new pathways, trained new muscle combinations, new reflexes. Incredible what you could adapt to with just a small amount of time.

Will stuck his entombed hand onto the table while Mizrahi began to untangle the cast saw from the other items in a lower cabinet. He looked around. This was the exact room where it had happened. The dent in the doorframe was still there. He supposed they'd fix it eventually.

EARLIER THAT AFTERNOON Will had made the phone call. To Robbie's Handmade Furnishings in North Carolina. When someone picked up, he asked if he could speak to Robbie personally about a special order. The guy said that he was in the back, in the middle of a project, but he'd see if he could break for a minute.

Muffled background noise. Shop sounds. A door opening, a binder shifting, a saw or sander somewhere, buzzing away.

Then a click, a fumble, a pickup.

"Yeah? Robbie speaking," came the voice on the other end, a little impatient.

Will closed his eyes, tried to imagine the little man he'd seen inside the wooden block, which he held in one hand like a lucky charm.

"Hi," he began. "I'm hoping you can help me out. I'm thinking about ordering a crib. Is that something you guys can handle?"

The man's tone shifted considerably. "Yeah, man, we can sure do that. But I got a bunch of orders right now, so the best I can say is six or seven months. When's the baby due? Congratulations, by the way."

"That's fine," Will said. "I'm in no rush."

"We thinking oak? Cherry?"

"What do you like?"

"Personally, I like the darker woods. Maple. I have some great walnut here."

"Let's go with walnut, then."

"Ah, you won't be sorry. Now, before I forget, let me get the name, for the headboard."

"We haven't picked one out yet. But if it's a girl, I like Yui after her grandmother."

"Is that Japanese?"

"That's right."

"Always wanted to go out there. See the bears up there on Mount Kurai. Near Takayama."

Will's heart pounded. His father knew stuff about Japanese bears?

"My wife's family's from outside of Osaka."

"Incredible. You ever get out there?"

"Not for a while now. She's spending time there by herself right now. Unfortunately."

There was a sigh and he said, "Sorry to hear that. I got divorced myself. Some years back."

Will shivered a little. He hadn't imagined they'd get here this fast.

"Hard on the kids," Will said finally.

"Well. Harder on them if you stay and keep on making everybody miserable, am I right?"

"I guess that's right."

"Nice of you to get the crib, though. Thoughtful."

And did Will detect an ounce of regret there, in that single word? Was he imagining it?

His father cleared his throat. "I can send you some design sketches, if you're on email?"

Will gave him the general address for the practice.

"All right, well. Let me get your name for the order and we'll start this up."

"Sure," Will said, taking a deep breath. "The last name is Geborn."

And his father laughed on the other end. "What the hell! That's the same last name as me. What are the odds of that?"

Will didn't know what to say. He just breathed. And then:

"Uhm. Well. Actually. You see—my first name's Will."

There was a very long silence. Then Will's father just said, "Ah, fuck—"

And the line went dead.

AFTER THE CAST was off, Will and Mizrahi chatted a little as he helped to clean up. Cautiously he moved his fingers back and forth, rolled his wrist, tested its current limits.

"Has your grandmother gotten the house fixed up since the storm?" she asked.

Will nodded and said, "Mostly," explaining how Giancarlo was helping her make the repairs. "She had some bad damage to her first floor, but it's looking a lot better now. She's lucky she wasn't hurt. Her friend—one of her neighbors died."

He wanted to say more. That he'd lifted her body from the water. That he'd rescued her fish. He thought about that moment all the time still. He wasn't over it—he wasn't sure he'd ever be over it. But it was not going to get the best of him. Not this time.

"I had no idea it was that bad," she said. "Up here it wasn't much."

"With the winds coming in off the bay," Will said, "we had drifts over three feet."

She shook her head. "When I was little, before we moved to Israel, we lived near Warsaw, and it was like this every winter there."

"In March?"

"On into April even."

Will nodded. "My grandmother's friend—the one who died. She was really worried about climate change, my grandmother was saying at the funeral. She kept saying this was the beginning of the end of the world."

"Well as *my* grandmother used to say, 'No, the end of the world happened half a century ago. All this is still just the beginning of the next world.'"

There wasn't much left to clean up, and Will was getting his shirt back on again, with considerably more difficulty than before, now that he was attempting to use both hands. He tried to do it with just one again and realized that wasn't working anymore, either.

Mizrahi was still talking. "You know, back when I was living in Tel Aviv—this one summer there were missile attacks from Iraq every day for a week. We'd get very little warning, only a few minutes, to seek shelter. So we'd all run off into the closest bunker and wait. Each time it was horrendous. The stress—waiting, waiting, waiting. Thinking you were about to be blown to pieces. You *were* about to be blown to pieces! Or not. Always. But the first time we heard the siren and went to run into the bunker, I heard this voice. It sounded just like my grandfather's voice. He'd died years before, in Poland. But I *heard* him, clear as anything. Saying to always put my right foot into the room first. That if I did that I would not get hit by the missiles."

"Why not?" Will asked.

"No explanation. Nothing logical to it at all. But I wasn't going to ignore it . . . just in case, right? Every time, I'd make sure I went into the bunker right foot first, and I'd tell all my friends and all my family: *right foot first, right foot first*."

"And?"

"And we survived. The whole month, all those missiles they fired, only two people died."

"Did those two go in left foot first?"

She laughed. "I have no idea."

"But you felt like the 'right foot first' thing saved you?"

"Yes, I did. It's silly, but I did. And still, this is what, thirty years later? I still always, always go into *every* room right foot first. Why risk it?"

Will said he'd never taken her for someone so superstitious.

She shrugged. "What's real in certain times is not the same as what is real at other times."

He lifted his phone and saw he had gotten a message from Teru. A picture of a beautiful field with thin white clouds above it, so low they seemed to be caressing a hilltop. If it hadn't been for the three ghostly pink cherry blossom trees in the background, it might have been anywhere.

He texted her to say he'd call her in a few minutes and then went to help walk Mizrahi back downstairs and past the doorman. It was not the Dutch team, Will saw—oh well. He got her a cab and thanked her one last time.

"See you Monday," she said.

"See you Monday," he agreed.

ALONE, WALKING DOWN the bright and lonely avenue, Will dialed Teru's number and waited. She picked up as he was walking toward the East River Greenway.

"Hello," she said as he looked out at the dark, silver river.

"Konnichiwa," Will said brightly. "What's it like out there?"

"So many *people* here," Teru said, half shouting over what did sound like quite a crowd of some kind. "Even out in the countryside. How's your grandmother?"

"Good," Will said. "She's good."

"I miss you," Teru confessed.

"Yeah," Will said. "I miss you, too. What's this picture of?"

"This is where my grandfather was," she said. "August seventh, 1945. The day the bomb dropped on Hiroshima. He was out here walking."

"Could he see it?"

"He says he did. But people here say no, it was too far."

"How far is it?"

Will gazed out past the skyline of Roosevelt Island and Queens beyond. Why did it feel best when he was pointing in her direction? He supposed Japan was just about as near to him going west as going east, and yet only this felt correct to him.

"Two hundred miles. Like if you were in New York City and someone nuked Boston."

"But he says he saw it."

"Yeah."

"What's it like there now?"

"Incredible. Will, I wish I could show you. Standing there, it was, like, perfect. Like something out of a fairy tale. I feel like I finally came home, except it's to this place I'd never been before. Isn't that crazy?"

"Super crazy," he agreed.

"Will, they asked me to stay for a few more weeks. It might be another month."

He closed his eyes. "You sound really happy there."

"I am," she said, and paused. "I wish you could be here, too."

Will closed his eyes and tried to imagine it. He bent his mind around the curve of the planet, across an ocean, two continents, past Holland, past Düsseldorf, on and on and on. Toward her.

"I'll come whenever you're ready," he said. "I'll stay as long as you want."

And he heard it then but was not afraid. A little voice saying just:

Right foot first. Right foot first.

MAYBE HIS FATHER had lost his mind because of what happened during a war that ended when his own mother had been only eight. Maybe it's still in Will's genes now, and maybe it will be in the genes of their daughter someday. And if so, then they'll have Hiroshima in there, too, and who knows what else? At least Will can't help but feel a deep hope inside himself. Even now that he knows what happened, none of that spells out in any surety what will happen next.

Had his grandfather really deposited his soul into the carvings on a chest of wood for safekeeping, as his body went to hell on earth? *What's real in certain times is not the same as what is real at other times*, Will reminds himself.

He flies out to Osaka twice over the next month and stays a few days each time. Each time he sees Teru again it feels almost like she is a stranger at first, some other person he's never met before. Then, within even just a minute, he has the strangest experience, as if he is falling in love with her all over again, only it isn't the same *her* as before, only of course it is.

He's told her at last, all of it. About med school and his father. About what his grandmother has been telling him about the Hunger Winter. And as he retells her tales again to Teru, a strange thing happens. In his mind now he is there, seeing it all, feeling cold and hungry. He tells the stories as if he half remembers it happening to him now.

While Mizrahi is home with her baby, Will keeps to his promise, making up his absences to her so she can be with her new daughter, Ruth.

He works overtime, until the latest hours, and thinks about Teru and when she'll come home for good. He thinks about what it was like, seeing her there, how much happier she is, how much warmer she always is in his arms than he remembered.

Coming home, he jokes to her that he is bringing an oni with him in his luggage. A little hobgoblin, a little imp, to cause mischief and keep him on his toes.

And sometimes he wonders if it isn't true, or if he's made it true. He can't explain it, but more and more there are things missing from around the apartment. The plates rattle in the cabinets. He's slipped and fallen into things.

Over email, Will and his father begin to exchange a few ideas for the crib. It's not much, but it's a start.

Teru has told him how she's seen a therapist there in Osaka, Dr. Nakamura, and how they are untangling her intergenerational trauma and how it explains a lot of what she's been through in her own life. This all makes sense; he would never deny her an explanation. But he wonders. Can there be any person, anywhere, walking the earth free of these things? Whose mothers and fathers and grandmothers and grandfathers never experienced hunger, pain, betrayal, fear? His doubt lifts a weight from his shoulders. All the traumas he'll pass forward aren't his alone. Weren't his to begin with. By now he's found a few new ones to add along the way. But that's the price of admission to this world and to this life.

And what else comes along? Something more honorable—that stubbornness to stay alive, which once kept a child alive through the coldest of winters.

He speaks in his mind sometimes now to his daughter-in-uncertainty.

How do you show someone who they are? he asks her. Dignity is essential. You're born naked, but already you are so many little pieces, expertly assembled. Fairy dust and sourdough. The eye of a dead dog, the slime of an eel. Whatever isn't already swirling inside your ribosomes will eke in through a hundred thousand tales told to you. However it comes—it comes.

This is who you are, he tells her. *You are made of this.*

IN TIMES TO COME

~

It is morning, and Mieke wakes up in the bed next to Giancarlo and he is happily snoring. She remembers, the night before, how he'd been talking for a while before he fell asleep—about history. He'd said that if he could do everything over and go back in time to be a young man, he'd do better in school and go to a big university to study history. She'd said that he still could. She had gone to college after Rob's death and gotten her degree in communications, and that was after spending half her life two grades behind because of the war, and what she now knew was dyslexia. She hadn't let it hold her back. Had instead made it her reason for going ahead of where she might have. But he'd fallen asleep as she was telling him this. She'd told him before.

She watches his head moving there on the pillow, his eyes still closed, lips parted in a drowsy smile, dreaming. They have a whole day planned, Mieke thinks, as she gets her clothes on. He wanted to take her hunting—he's made arrangements to take her out to his friend's blind up at the lake, to shoot ducks. She doesn't really want to shoot a duck, but she's never done it before. Even at her age, there can be new things, can't there?

Like going with Giancarlo to the shooting range across town

yesterday, to practice. Who said she couldn't? It didn't make her a nut. It didn't make her a violent person. Shoshana wouldn't have approved, of course, but Mieke knows she wouldn't ever own a gun. Wouldn't use one on a person, even if they were trying to kill her. But she'd enjoyed it, she had to admit that much. Lining up, holding the pistol in her hands. Squeezing the trigger and feeling the explosion. She'd wondered if some rage would rise in her, left-over from the old days. But no, she had never wanted to kill any-one then, either. Not even Captain Schneider, who'd come to their apartment all those times. He had to be dead by now. They all had to be dead by now.

Mieke puts on some coffee and turns past the rows of fish tanks she's acquired in the past few months, moves to the record player in the living room and places one of the black discs onto the spindle. She keeps the volume low so it won't wake Giancarlo. The trembling notes follow her to the kitchen table as she sits in her red silk robe. *Memories of the Alhambra*. She's seen it many times by now—the real place. A magnificent fortress in the cliffs of Spain. She's been there and walked inside its halls in the company of so many, many ghosts.

She drinks her coffee and goes over the final paragraphs of the last page of *Verhalen uit de Lage Landen*, which by now is fat with Post-it notes and dog-eared corners. She feels bad to have written all over the margins; she forgets sometimes that she won't ever need to return it to Shoshana. Up the block, there is a construction crew now, working day and night, dismantling the old home. Soon there will be another plastic house there, with stones for a yard, but Mieke promises herself she'll still walk by twice a day and tell her old friend how things have been going. Today she's excited to let her know that the job is finished. The book is translated fully now. Will has said he can type it up and get it bound, for poster-ity's sake. Mieke wishes her uncle could know that these pages have outlived him, have made their way to his great-grandchild, and who knows how much farther now. She stares down at her looping dark handwriting, hoping Will can decipher it properly.

She is tired, and the script seems to swim around there, between the ruled lines, and Mieke decides she will go back to bed after all. The record has stopped playing.

Coming back to the bedroom and lying down beside Giancarlo, she closes her eyes. Since the war she's never liked to sleep without someone next to her.

You'd be a great historian, she thinks to her companion. Someone needs to explain history—not dates and facts, but whys and hows. Why it repeats itself, how it goes on.

Her son, down in North Carolina, tells her in his letters that he's been born again. She humors him, accepts his need to stay where he is, in a second life. She wishes, for Will's sake, it wasn't that way, but it is. Born again. It makes her laugh. No, you get to be born only once, and the rest is just history repeating until you die, and that's just the once, too.

Shoshana once claimed that while being culturally Jewish, she thought of herself as *spiritually* more of a Buddhist. Mieke doesn't know about this. But, benefit of the doubt, maybe Shoshana has been reincarnated as some other thing now. A marmoset or something. Or perhaps an Asura with three heads and six arms. Mieke wishes it could be true. She doesn't know. Doesn't know what's possible and what isn't.

Mieke remembers the fairy lights she saw when she was dying. The sound of the ocean. These comfort her, make her think that there could be more, even after. She's never believed it, truly. And yet she's never not believed it, either. Life's full of surprises. Why not death, too? Every day she waits for it to come. She feels a lump in her neck or her heart clenches up, and she thinks—now or nearly now—it is starting to happen. And then it passes. The doctors say everything is fine, although she should regulate her diet and get more exercise. Each day her life goes on she wonders if there is something she's still supposed to do. How she is like the eel in the story, living down in the well for a century, waiting for the rock to slide away.

The air from the fan moves through the gray curls on

Giancarlo's chest. She closes her eyes and waits, listening to the comforting sounds of his snoring.

Mieke dreams of the beach now, most nights, except that she is not there. This, she knows as she dreams it—this is in times to come. She sees the hands of her great-granddaughters in the wet sand. Two of them. They scoop up handfuls and let it drip down to form bulbous towers. Finding tiny shells still hinged in the middle like angel's wings, purple, small as pinkie nails, and decorating the borders with these and bits of sea glass. Green shards of tossed-out beer bottles worn smooth in the rolling waters. One finds some piece of a soft, bleached skeleton, and she and her sister study it together, working out what creature it came from. They designate one tower of their sandcastle as a museum of curiosities and place it there with the blobby clear body of a little jellyfish, handled cautiously with bits of driftwood just in case it can still sting them.

This is the shoreline near Kijkduin in Den Haag. Mieke would know it from even just the feel of the sand's grain and from the stiffness of the sea air, and when the girls look up, she can see the dunes behind them, the stony remains of the old bunkers still lost there between the Technicolor beach umbrellas. Generously, the waves bring wet treasures right up to their toes: crimson crab claws and pearly stones and webs of deep green seaweed. Foamy fingers reach half-unpolished toenails and leave trails of bubbling in the sand as they go. Salt creeps up sweetly on their delicate anklebones, washes them, waits for them, returns to them. Endlessly, timelessly, harmlessly. A larger wave rushes in and fills the crater they've pawed out in the sand, creating a briny lake. As the water stills, the girls notice something moving inside of it. One of them reaches down, cups her hands, and brings the bowl of it close to her face.

There they are, sliding among her fingers. Six or seven glass eels. Perfectly clear, long and flat, like ribbons, with just the faintest dark pencil line inside, running from the tip of the tail to the head, where two buggy specks of black peer up at them.

Eyes, no bigger than two flecks of shaken pepper. *Elvers*, they're called, newborn eels, which have emerged from the distant calm of the Sargasso Sea and beaten a long path to the shallows around the continent. The girls stare in wonder, these bare filaments of life stored with secrets. Ancient and everlasting. They curl around in hooked shapes, a mound of question marks, so slight that their absence cannot even be felt, so near to invisible that once free, they will not be found again.

ACKNOWLEDGMENTS

~

To my entire family, this book is for you. Especially I need to thank Mieke Jansma, my oma. Had the war lasted one week longer, she and her brother Rob would have joined the 22,000 Dutch persons who starved to death during the Hunger Winter. Thank you to my father and mother, and to my wife, Leah Miller, and our wonderful children for their love and patience. Thank you to the staff at the Verzetsmuseum in Amsterdam and to Dr. Ingrid de Zwarte, whose research into the Hunger Winter was invaluable. Thank you to everyone at the Vrijheidsmuseum in Groesbeek, especially Rense Havinga and Gerrit Kok. I am particularly indebted to the beautiful diaries of Etty Hillesum, murdered at Auschwitz in 1943, and to *At the Edge of the Abyss*, a memoir by David Koker of his time in the concentration camp at Vught before his murder at Dachau in 1945. I'm similarly grateful for the stories shared in *The Dutch in Wartime: Survivors Remember*, volume 8, and to *Het Verre Westen* and *Het Wilde Westen* by J. M. Knaud. Thank you to William Elliot Griffis for his beautiful collection of *Dutch Fairy Tales for Young Folks* and to Patrik Svensson for *The Book of Eels*. Thank you to Dr. Gerlof Verwey for the permission to use your grandfather's poem to open this novel. Thank you to

Cam Terwilliger and Stijn van Rossem and Klaas van der Hoek of the Allard Pierson at the University of Amsterdam. Thank you to Dr. Proznitz and Dr. Cusak. Thank you to the Yaddo Corporation and to Mimi's Café in Mount Kisco. To Vicki Tromanhauser, Cy Mulready, and all my colleagues at SUNY New Paltz: your assistance was invaluable at every step of the way. Thank you to Helen Atsma and to the entire team at Ecco, and to Doug Stewart, my Agent 0. Thank you to Alice McDermott, Tim Horvath, David Burr Gerrard, Yang Liu, Matt Bell, Neil Bardhan, Emily Ethridge, the Chappaqua Public Library, and the Columbia University Library.